DREAMING OF YOU

ALEXA RIVERS

To C.M.
For a lifetime of friendship.

1

---

*C*larissa Mitchell lit the bergamot-scented candle beside her bed and settled amongst the covers. She grabbed the bowl of honey soy chicken her assistant had cooked from the bedside cabinet and reached for a glass of wine with her other hand. After taking a sip, she placed it back on the cabinet and switched on her laptop, which sat on the far end of the bed. The screen was tilted at such an angle that she could easily see it while leaning back on a mound of pillows and eating her dinner.

She was glad—not for the first time—that the podcast's livestream connection was one-way, so she could stare at Mark Talbot's gorgeous face while stuffing her own with food, and he was none the wiser. As both the owner and head designer of a bridal boutique, she didn't have the luxury of time, so she couldn't give her full attention to the weekly podcast for small business owners. She had to multitask. Hence, dinner and learning simultaneously.

Her screen flickered and came to life, the image of Mark flashing across it. She sighed around a mouthful of chicken. With unruly brown hair, twinkling eyes the color of milk

1

chocolate, and a ready smile, she was sure he'd broken hearts all over New Zealand. Fortunately, hers would never be among them because she had no desire to feel the effect of those eyes in person. She was perfectly happy admiring him from a safe distance, thank you very much. That said, she did try to catch the livestream each week rather than listening to the later-released podcast. She'd never get enough of seeing his smile and knowing that, at this particular point in time, they were sharing similar thoughts and space, even if it was virtual.

"Hello, everyone," he said with a lopsided grin that caused heat to pool low in her belly. "Welcome to episode two hundred and seventy-four of 'Your Main Hustle.' You're here with me, Mark, and our topic today is the legal aspects of email marketing."

That particular combination of words shouldn't have made her hot, but it did. She had no control as far as her fantasies about him were concerned. He could, and did, frequently speak in legal jargon, which really got her going. She suspected Freud would have a field day with her, especially considering she never gave men the time of day in person, unless it was work related.

He started talking, and Clarissa paid close attention. The sessions typically lasted for forty minutes, with the last ten dedicated to answering questions his listeners had sent in the previous week. When the question segment began, Clarissa clutched her wine and waited with bated breath to see whether he'd get to hers. Sometimes he only had time for one or two, and lately he seemed to prefer answering hers by email. She liked to think it was because he enjoyed interacting with her, but she had no evidence to support that theory.

She had to admit, she looked forward to receiving emails from him and tried to come up with a question each week so she could initiate contact. But no email could conjure up the same level of excitement she experienced when he raised his eyes to the camera, as he did just then, and said, "This one is from Clarissa Mitchell, one of the podcast's regular listeners."

She shivered. Holy moly, she loved his voice. And that velvety brown gaze… Even in the form of pixels on a screen, it could melt her.

"Clarissa asks, 'Would you advise a single opt-in or double opt-in to marketing emails from a legal standpoint?'" He smiled, and bunnies somersaulted in her stomach. "The answer, Clarissa,"—ooh, he said her name again—"is that a double opt-in is always preferable from a legal standpoint, even if it isn't necessarily a legal requirement in all countries. Using a double opt-in is a great way to cover your backside." Said backside tingled at his mention of it. "Of course, I need to remind you that I don't know your exact circumstances and that this doesn't constitute fully informed legal advice."

He always made that disclaimer—yet another thing she liked about him. He was a professional down to his toes. And, yeah, she might like to pretend he was flirting with her sometimes, but he was never anything less than appropriate. He was also cheerful and too handsome for his own good.

As he moved on to another question, she refilled her wine glass. She jotted notes when he was discussing the legal requirement to have unsubscribe options in every email and an address for service if recipients wanted to make contact. Finally, he drew to a close. She reluctantly exited the livestream, brushed her teeth, changed into a silk teddy—she loved the feel of silk against her skin—and imagined Mark Talbot speaking only to her as she drifted off to sleep, all alone in her queen-size bed in the one-person apartment above her boutique.

~

"You'll be a groomsman, of course, and your sisters will be bridesmaids. I won't have a maid of honor because I refuse to choose between Megan and Mikayla."

"You'd never hear the end of it," Mark Talbot agreed, smiling at his mother, Rose, who sat opposite him, at a table in their favorite downtown cafe. "But I don't expect Joe to make me one of his groomsmen. Surely he'd rather have his brother or one of his tennis buddies. But," he added, hoping to erase her frown, "maybe I could give you away?"

"Oh, Mark!" Her hand flew up to her mouth, and her eyes shone. "That's so sweet of you to offer. It hadn't even occurred to me that anyone would want to give me away. Are you sure I'm not too old for that?"

"Psh." He swatted her worry aside. "You're never too old, and it would be my honor."

He knew immediately he'd said the right thing, because she beamed at him and nodded to herself. "Wonderful. And, yes, you're right, Joe probably would like Craig to stand up with him. Are you sure you don't mind?"

"Of course not, Mum. Your wedding is all about you, so don't worry about me or Meg or Mik. We'll be happy if you're happy." Though the twins would no doubt be thrilled by the opportunity to dress up. They'd inherited their mum's interest in fashion.

She leaned toward him. "I truly want you all to enjoy yourselves."

"We will," he promised her. "But it's your day."

She ducked her head, her cheeks pink. He could tell he'd both pleased and embarrassed her.

"What have you got there?" he asked, gesturing at the stack of magazines beside her elbow.

"Oh, these?" She laughed, the sound light and cheerful. "I've been scoping out wedding dresses." She selected a magazine from a pile and showed him the dog-eared pages.

"I've marked my favorites, so I can find something similar or by the same designer."

Mark held out a hand. "May I?"

She passed it to him, and he flipped through the pages, pausing at the ones she'd marked. He scanned the photographs and the names of the designers that produced each of the dresses, noting that she seemed to prefer ones with sleeves and slender forms rather than puffy skirts or extravagant lacework. He was about to look at the fifth one when his subconscious sounded an alarm and his gaze skittered back to the designer's name on dress number four. *Clarissa Mitchell.*

"Hey," he said, as much to himself as to her. "I know her."

He turned the page around, and Rose shuffled closer, reading over his shoulder. "That dress is in my top three." She traced the line of the bodice with her finger. "Isn't it elegant? And I love the color."

"Pale pink?"

"Champagne is what it's called." As if he should have known. "I like that it's clearly not white—I don't want to be wearing white at my age—but it's not far off, and it's very flattering."

"Anything would be flattering on you, Mother."

"You're such a suck-up, darling."

"But you love me."

She pinched his cheek. "Rascal. So, did you say you know Clarissa Mitchell? How did you meet? She's one of the rising stars in the wedding industry, or so I've heard."

He chuckled at her enthusiasm. "I wouldn't know about that, and I suppose it might have been going a bit far to say I *know* her. She's one of my podcast's regular listeners, and we correspond by email sometimes. She seems like an intelligent woman. She certainly asks some good questions, anyway." Questions that occasionally stumped him to the extent he had to hit the books or use Google to find the answer—not that he'd ever admit such a thing.

Rose clapped her hands. "This is a sign!" she declared. "What are the chances I'd find a magazine that just happened to have a dress by a designer you know, and which just happens to be one of my favorites? It's meant to be." She settled back into her chair and crossed her arms over her chest in satisfaction. "I simply must have a dress by Clarissa Mitchell. That's all there is to it."

Mark groaned and buried his face in his palms. "Don't you go getting all 'cosmic force' and 'grand design' on me. It's a coincidence, pure and simple."

"No such thing," she said, setting her chin in such a way that he knew she'd made her mind up. Come hell or high water, she'd get what she wanted. "Now, why don't you be a dear and email your friend to arrange an appointment?"

He tried again to make her see reason. "The article says her boutique is in Dunedin. You'd have to fly to the South Island for an appointment."

"Something I can easily afford to do, as can you."

"But you'd find something you like just as much here in Auckland."

She shook her head. "It wouldn't have the same meaning."

He sighed. "Okay." Never let it be said that he didn't indulge his mother—especially when he'd been arguing only minutes earlier that her wedding was all about her and she should have what she wanted. Reneging now would be the height of hypocrisy. "I'll email Clarissa later today."

"Much appreciated."

For the remainder of lunch, they discussed more mundane topics, like his work, her upcoming jaunt to the Pacific Islands, and the latest stupid thing his sister Megan's boyfriend had done, in an ongoing saga of stupid things. They finished with coffee, then separated outside the cafe,

Mark heading toward the Lockwood Holdings offices while his mother made the short walk to her private law firm. He took the elevator up to the top floor of the glass-and-chrome skyscraper, where Lockwood Holdings was based, and used his key card to let himself in, nodding to the receptionist as he passed.

In his office, he stripped off his navy blazer, adjusted his tie, and started his laptop. He opened the email account he used for the podcast and found the latest email from Clarissa. He knew exactly where it was, because he paid more attention to her emails than many of the others he received. Truth be told, she was refreshing—concise and to the point, which was very much not Mark's standard MO. She never engaged in pleasantries or included meaningless small talk. Perhaps others would find that off-putting, but considering the number of women who fawned over him because of the way he looked—not that he minded their fawning, mind you—her businesslike approach was a nice change. He never needed to worry that she might read more into their interactions than he intended. He tapped out a brief email.

Hi Clarissa,

My mother is newly engaged. She found out we know each other and has her heart set on wearing one of your dresses. We're looking at a wedding date about a year from now. Can you fit her in for an appointment sometime in the next month?
Regards,
Mark

HE READ OVER IT TWICE. The email seemed too short and unemotional to convey how much this wedding meant to him, how important it was that his mother have the fairy-tale day she deserved. But really, what else was there to say? He hit Send.

2

---

*C*larissa stared, unblinking, at her computer screen. She minimized her emails, opened them again, and it was still there. She blinked, then rubbed her eyes. Nope, the email from Mark Talbot hadn't gone anywhere.

She massaged little circles over her heart, which was pounding wildly, and the short message blurred before her eyes. She held her hand up and focused on her trembling fingers until her vision sharpened.

With horror, it dawned on her that this was actually happening. By some awful quirk of fate, her fantasy crush was encroaching on her real life. Her place of work. Her *haven*. She backed away from the computer and tripped over a roll of yarn, half falling and half sinking to the floor. She raised a hand and clamped it tightly over her mouth so she didn't make a sound.

Oh, God. What a monumental idiot she'd been. How could she have allowed herself to fantasize over someone? How could she have been so *irresponsible*?

Yeah, she'd figured it was safe to have a crush on him since he lived at the other end of the country and there was no reason for them to ever meet face to face, but it seemed

9

she'd been mistaken. She should never have let her guard down. Should never have let herself think about him as anything other than someone to learn from. But her crush had seemed like such a normal, healthy thing, and she couldn't remember the last time she'd had an innocent attraction to a man, so she'd indulged. Now everything was going to hell.

She stood and dusted herself off. It would be okay. She was a professional, he was a professional, and there was no reason for any awkwardness between them as long as she kept her mind strictly on business. She couldn't think about the way she liked to fall asleep to the sound of his voice, or the things she imagined him doing to her when she snuck her vibrator out of her underwear drawer late at night. She'd be fine.

Totally fine.

Then why was her heart marching in time to the William Tell overture while her stomach felt like it was swan diving off the Sky Tower?

"Boss lady, you okay?"

She flinched and looked up into the concerned eyes of her assistant, Leo, who'd entered her office while she'd been staring into the distance like she had a screw loose.

"Fine," she said, spinning away and going to the mirror to examine herself. She tucked a loose strand of hair into the tight bun atop her head.

"Are you sure? Because you sound like you did when Felicity was kicked off *Designer Wedding*," he said, referring to their favorite reality show. "And we both know you were anything but okay."

"I'm fine," she snapped. He backed up a step. She rubbed her temples and searched for patience. He was her friend, and he was trying to help. It wasn't his fault her stupid decisions were coming back to bite her ass, and *not* in a good way.

She pondered that. Could one be bitten on the ass in a good way? It wasn't like she would know. "Sorry, Leo. I just…." She tried to think of how to explain away her predicament.

"Wait, is that an email from Lawyer McHottie?" he asked, coming around to read her laptop.

She reached over, but he grabbed the lid, preventing her from slamming it shut. "No," she lied.

"It *is*," he said with a shit-eating grin.

Why had she ever confessed her crush to him? He was a pest. A menace.

"And his mum's getting married. How lovely of her to think of us. We'd love to have her, wouldn't we, Rissa? Especially because she'll go and tell all of her upper-crust friends how wonderful we are, right?" He tweaked the end of his gold bow tie, gazing up at her from behind thick black lashes. "What a perfect *business opportunity*, boss."

She sighed. This was his way of reminding her to think of the boutique and not of herself, and damn it, he was right. Her sales were booming in the South Island, with other boutiques clamoring to get their hands on her designs, but they could use more publicity up north, and word of mouth was not to be underestimated as a marketing tool.

"Okay, okay," she relented. "I see your point. I'll reply soon."

He leveled two fingers at her, then aimed them back at himself to indicate that he was watching her. "Do it before the end of the day. I want photographic evidence. You can't let your crush on him get in the way."

"You do know *I'm* the boss," she grumbled.

His expression softened. "You're a genius with silk and lace, Clarissa Mitchell, but sometimes I think you'd be a happy addition to the Teenage Mutant Ninja Turtles. Just think how many excuses you'd save if you had a shell to hide in, and what a waste that would be when you're one of the smartest, most beautiful women out there."

She rolled her eyes. "Stop buttering me up. I'll give you a pay rise when I can afford one."

He shook his head and pressed his lips together in that way he did when they both knew she was being intentionally obtuse. The fact was, Leo was outgoing and boldly pursued anyone who caught his fancy, whereas Clarissa preferred to keep to herself, and nothing would change that. It was a behavior she'd adopted to protect herself, though it had been too little too late.

Her thumb went to the touchstone ring on her right hand and smoothed over the opaque blue surface. "I'll be out soon," she said, effectively dismissing him. He nodded and left.

She returned to the computer screen and opened the window to reply. If she couldn't ignore Mark's email, then the best option was to get back to him as soon as possible so it was out of the way. Besides, she had to look on the bright side. There was a good chance his mother would come down for her appointment without him. How many women brought their son to shop for wedding dresses with them? She'd yet to meet any.

Please don't let this man be the exception.

As it turned out, Mark Talbot was the exception.

There he stood, in the center of her boutique, which seemed to shrink until he dominated the space, looking even more gorgeous than she'd expected. It simply wasn't fair.

With a groan of dread, Clarissa stopped spying on him in the security feed connected to her computer and checked the clock—1:00 p.m. He and his mother were punctual to the minute. She glanced back at the feed, taking a moment to study Rose. The elegant older lady wore her hair in a white pixie cut that emphasized her high cheekbones, and she had a slim, girlish figure. She floated from one end of the racks on the shop floor to the other, moving with an innate grace Clarissa envied.

Leo stuck his immaculately groomed blond head around the door. "Hey, boss, is it safe to enter?"

"You can come in."

He did so and immediately feigned a swoon. "Oh, my lord. I'll give you one thing, you've got good taste. Teacher McHotPants is the most scrumptious morsel of manliness ever to walk through the front door." He fanned himself with a piece of paper from a stack that rested on an overfull book-shelf. "I think I'm having a hot flush. That man is sending out some serious heat waves."

Her lips tugged up at his antics. He had a knack for making her laugh even when she was tense—one of the reasons she'd hired him. Left to herself, she could get far too serious.

"Do you want to deal with him, then?" she offered, only half joking.

He crossed his arms over his maroon blazer. "Lawyer McHottie and his equally genetically blessed mother flew all the way down here to see *you*. They couldn't give a flying *feijoa* about me, so get your marvelous self out there and wow them."

Clarissa nodded, then checked her hands for pencil smudges and, finding none, wiped her palms on her skirt. She patted her hair and touched up her lipstick in the mirror. Call her vain, but if she had to meet the subject of her fantasies, she was going to do it looking her best. Satisfied, she headed out, walking more slowly than usual because her heels had an extra two inches on them.

"Hi there," she said when she rounded the corner and offered her standard workplace smile. "I'm Clarissa." She addressed Rose, who was her client after all, and did her best to ignore the almost overwhelming compulsion to ogle the woman's son. "It's lovely to meet you."

Rose took her hand with a warm smile and squeezed it. "Clarissa, this place is simply wonderful." She had a low, melodious voice. "I'm so glad I insisted we come here. Never mind the distance, I *need* one of your dresses for my wedding."

"That's very kind of you." Even when she was on edge, praise for her work always improved her mood. "I'd love to design your dress." It was true. Regardless of her concern over the whole Mark situation, designing a dress for his mother would be a pleasure, she could already tell.

"Clarissa." Speak of the devil.

Oh, man. His voice was even more potent in person than it was in cyberspace. Rich, deep, sexy—she shivered, then realized she hadn't responded and he was watching her with the corners of his lips tilted up, as if he wanted to smile but wasn't quite sure whether that was the appropriate reaction.

Same here, handsome.

"Oh, h-hi," she stammered, discreetly wiping her palms again before offering one to him. When he took it, a delicious sizzle shot up her arm. He held on for longer than necessary, prompting her gaze to venture up to his, where it was captured. She could sink into those cocoa-brown eyes forever if she weren't careful. Instead, she tried to focus on the sensation of his hand. His fingers were long and tapered. Pianist fingers. Strange how she felt like she ought to have known that.

"You're different than I expected," he said, releasing her hand but not her gaze.

She rocked back onto her skyscraper heels, subconsciously putting distance between them. "You expected something?"

His brows drew together in a bemused frown, and she

cringed. That had come out all wrong. Unfortunately, her tongue didn't want to cooperate.

"Never mind," he said, waving a hand. "It doesn't matter."

Except it did. She'd very much like to know what he'd meant by his comment. But she didn't ask, because she needed to keep this on a professional level and not think about how pretty his eyes were or how much she'd like to run her fingers through his tousled hair and see if it was as soft as it looked. Her fingers twitched, and she glued them to her sides.

"Remind me how you two know each other," Rose asked, having watched their exchange with interest.

"I listen to Mark's podcast," Clarissa told her. "Religiously." Then she blushed and ducked her head, wondering if she should have admitted that in front of him. "It's very helpful."

"I'm glad he's putting that big brain of his to good use," Rose said. "Do you mind if I go back to browsing your racks?"

"No, please, go right ahead. If you'd like to give me your size, I can make some suggestions. Would you prefer an off-rack dress or a custom design?"

"She wants a custom design," Mark said at the same time that Rose declared she had no preference.

They glanced at each other, and Rose laughed. "Don't scowl so, darling; it does you no favors." To Clarissa, she said, "If I find the dress of my dreams on your rack, then I'll take that. If not, then I'd love for you to design one for me. How's that work?"

Clarissa smiled. "Perfect. You go have a look, and I'll be over here if you need anything." She kept her attention firmly on her client but sensed Mark sidle over to her, close enough that she could smell his cologne. Yum. What *was* that?

"I want Mum to have everything she desires for her wedding day," he said, voice pitched low. Clarissa strained to hear him but refused to move any closer. She was a nervous wreck around this man as it was. If she'd thought crushing on him over a livestream was safe, having him here and realizing he was exactly as alluring in person was the definition of unsafe.

"Whatever makes her happy, okay?" he continued. "She deserves it, and money is no object."

She fought the urge to fan herself. How sexy was a guy who looked out for his mum? "I'll do everything in my power to make sure she has the dress of her dreams," she promised. "I believe every bride deserves that."

It was her standard line but the truth, nonetheless. The grooms, on the other hand... well, she didn't always have such a high opinion of them.

Rose exclaimed in delight, and Clarissa hurried over to see what she'd found. She held an A-line gown with delicate lace sleeves and the kind of bodice that would cling lovingly to a woman's curves. Bead-work dotted the skirt, and she traced the edge of a rosette with her fingertip.

"How beautiful," she said, beaming. "Can I try it on?" She turned to Mark. "Do you think it's too much?"

He looked aghast at the thought. "Of course not."

Clarissa draped the dress over her arm. "You should wear exactly what you want. You have the figure for it and the confidence to pull it off. Would you like to try on any others while you're at it?"

Leo came forward with two more gowns. One was a sleek sheath dress and the other had a puffy skirt and tiny shoulder straps. "How about one of these, doll?"

Rose giggled and shook her head when she caught sight of the poufy dress. "Oh, you're a flirt. I could never wear Cinderella's ball gown. That's designed for a far younger woman. This one though"—she caressed the length of the sheath dress—"is stunning."

"We'll take that too," Clarissa said to Leo. "Remember," she called over her shoulder as she led them to the changing

16

room out back, "that you don't need to choose a dress from the rack. Just use them to work out what you like, and I can design something unique, especially for you. But also remember that the more dresses you try on, the more I'll be able to see which styles suit you."

She stopped, and Rose flung an arm around her. Clarissa stiffened so imperceptibly that the other woman didn't notice, but to Clarissa, her slip blared as loudly as a fire siren.

"I'm so pleased we came here," Rose said. "I just know you're going to make sure I look my best on the big day."

"I will." She drew the curtain back. "You strip off and slip into the dress, then call me and I'll do it up so we can have a proper look. Mark can be the viewing board."

MARK COULDN'T STOP STARING at Clarissa Mitchell. She wasn't at all what he'd expected—a no-nonsense woman on the dark side of forty who always treated people with respect but maintained a cool distance. No, Clarissa was a knockout. A total babe who couldn't have been more than thirty, with white-blonde hair, eyes the color of a glacier, and curves to rival any Instagram model he'd ever seen. She walked with a sway that was unconsciously sensual, and he just knew that if her hair was loose, it would rest on the curve of her butt.

Suddenly, it was his life's mission to free her hair and see it caress that curve. To twine his hand through it and discover whether it was as silky as it looked.

Whoa, boy.

He took a deep breath and calmed the hell down. Okay, so she was a surprise—a clever, curvaceous surprise. He could roll with that. He tried to align his new perception of her with the one he'd held for months, but the two refused to mesh.

"She's in good hands, I promise," Clarissa said, apparently mistaking his silence for concern. "I'll take care of her."

"I know." He met her eyes, which were level with his, courtesy of her stiletto heels. "We've known each other for months. You take your business seriously, and I know customer satisfaction means a lot to you."

She nodded. "It does. In the wedding industry, word of mouth is one of the most effective marketing tools we have." She hesitated, then added, "Even if it wasn't, I care about my brides." She offered him a little smile. "I want them to be happy."

"Clarissa," Rose called, "I'm ready for you."

She bustled toward the curtained-off changing room, giving Mark a prime view of her shapely derriere. Beads of sweat broke out on his forehead as he willed his body to behave itself. They were in public, for crying out loud.

A moment later, the curtain on the changing room was drawn back and he gaped at his mother. *Jesus H. Christ.* She wore the dress she'd taken from the rack and it fit like it had been made for her.

"Stunning," he said, one-hundred-percent truthfully. She was a striking woman. Fortunately, her husband-to-be knew how lucky he was.

"It is, isn't it?" she replied, with less enthusiasm than he'd anticipated. Twisting, she studied her reflection in a massive mirror that dominated the wall of the changing room and sighed. "It's too heavy. I want to be able to dance the night away, but I can't do that in this dress."

"Mm." Clarissa's finger tapped her bottom lip, which formed a plush cushion for her bowed upper lip. "You're right. Why don't you tell me more about your wedding while we get this off you? If I know what you've got planned, it will help me ensure we set you up with the perfect dress."

She pulled the curtain closed, and the women vanished from view. Mark paced around the room, pausing to touch a sparkly tiara and run his hand along the length of a satin veil. Clearly, men were rare visitors to the boutique. The decor couldn't be more feminine. Classic and elegant, much like its owner.

The salesman he'd spoken to earlier approached, wearing a mischievous smile. Mark liked him instantly.

The man plucked at the fussy bow tie around his neck, looked him up and down like an edible treat, and said, "Hey, hot stuff."

Mark's mouth stretched wider. "Hey, yourself."

"So." Arms akimbo, his new companion cocked an eyebrow. "Clarify something for me."

"Sure. Go ahead."

The man cleared his throat. "Are you single? Because I could be imagining it, but I feel some vibes between you and the boss, and I think you should know, Madam President doesn't have a significant someone in her life. It's been that way for as long as I've known her, but not for lack of interest." He glanced at the changing room, then spoke behind a hand. "Well, perhaps *her* lack of interest. She's picky with men. Like, *insanely* picky. If Brad Pitt walked in here and asked for her number, I don't think she'd hand it out, but I'm definitely getting the sense she's into you." He poked Mark in the ribs. "This is me being a good wingman and giving you the nod of approval, okay?"

Mark was unclear exactly what was going on, but he nodded. "Thanks for the heads-up—sorry, what's your name?"

"Leo," the man said.

"Leo." They shook hands. "Nice to meet you."

Clarissa emerged from between the curtains. Leo crossed to her and they spoke in low voices. Mark tried to eavesdrop but couldn't make out the details, so he settled for watching her mouth move. He'd never seen lips more perfectly designed for erotic acts. He'd bet his Hugo Boss watch that they were as soft as they looked, and probably tasted of berries—a little tart and a lot sweet.

Her finger tapped the corner of her mouth again, presumably a subconscious habit. His pulse picked up. He wanted to still her finger. To tell her to take it easy on her soft mouth. She said something else to Leo, and they separated and headed in different directions. A few moments later, she returned, weighed down by another two dresses.

"Can I help?" he asked, touching her shoulder as she glided past.

"I'm fine, thank you," she said, sidestepping him. "I'm stronger than I look."

Leo, close on her heels, rolled his eyes as if to say, "Is that all you've got?"

Moments later, Rose came out in another dress, this one made of some floaty fabric that looked more dance-floor friendly. He nodded, but she shook her head.

Next was a knee-length dress that would really shake up some of their conventional friends and family, but he wasn't surprised when she rejected it. At her heart, she was a romantic, and she wanted her traditional gown. They tried a few more dresses before Clarissa called an end to the session and Leo went to put them away.

"That was fun," Rose said, slumping on a pink chaise. "But I'm feeling rather wiped out."

"You were fantastic," Leo said. "The boss has her thinking face on, which means it was all worthwhile."

Sure enough, Clarissa snapped her fingers, a smile curving her lips and transforming her from merely beautiful to absolutely breathtaking. "I've got it!"

Leo hastened back to her side and handed her a sheet of paper and a pencil. Leaning against the wall, she sketched a few fluid lines.

"Keep in mind, this is very rough," she said, pointing out features with the pencil. "I'm picturing a single-shoulder gown, with floral beading over the bodice and a cinched waist on the right side. It will hug your figure down to the hips, then fall into a tulle skirt that flairs out ever so slightly. It will only reach your ankles, and the tulle will be light, so you can dance until your feet ache, but it will look like it has volume. The best of both worlds. You have such a lovely figure, I'd really like to highlight it with the cinched waist design. Your new husband will never know what hit him."

For a long moment, Rose said nothing, and Mark grew concerned. She wasn't prone to silence. But then she sniffled and raised the back of her hand to brush her eyes.

"That's perfect." Her voice was watery. "Thank you so much, darling. I knew coming here would be the right thing to do."

"You're very welcome," Clarissa replied warmly. "And thank *you* for making the trip down here. That's pretty amazing."

"We're down for the night," Mark said, seizing the opportunity to extend their visit with her. "Why don't you come out for dinner with us?" They all stared at him, and he shrugged, oddly self-conscious. "I mean, we don't know the best places to eat, and we've talked so many times online, I'd like to get to know you better in person." In fact, he felt a clawing desperation to spend more time with her and learn everything there was to know about Clarissa Mitchell.

"Thank you, that's so sweet of you to offer, but I couldn't possibly." He tried to catch her eye, but her attention was firmly on the floor. Was it his imagination or had her cheeks flushed a pretty pink to match her outfit? "I don't want to intrude on your private dinner."

"Dear girl, you wouldn't be intruding at all." Rose took up his cause with verve. Praise the lord for meddling mothers. "Come out with us. Let me treat you to dinner and a glass of wine."

"That's very kind, but really, I couldn't." She hadn't raised her eyes from the floor. Mark studied it himself, wondering what had her so fascinated.

"Don't be silly," Rose said. "Of course you can. I insist. I want to hear all about how you got into the wedding industry. You must have some wonderful stories to tell. Do say you'll join us."

Clarissa's shoulders dropped an inch, and she looked up and nodded. "I suppose I could."

Mark's hormones threw a celebratory party. "Tell us where to make a reservation, and we'll pick you up at seven." He wanted to lock it in while his mother's influence was fresh and before Clarissa changed her mind. She named a restaurant, and he made a mental note of it; then she and his mum wandered over to the counter. He couldn't stop grinning. She wasn't even out of his sight yet, and already he couldn't wait for this evening.

Leo sidled over and jostled him with an elbow. "Knew you had it in you."

He didn't. It was all down to Rose. But who was he to argue with the results?

3

"*N*o. Absolutely not. That won't do."

Clarissa jumped, startled, because she hadn't heard Leo come up the stairs and let himself into her apartment. He stripped off his blazer and folded it over the back of a chair.

"That outfit is not worthy of a date with McHottie."

She studied her dark jeans and pink jacket in the mirror. "It's not a date."

"Nah-uh," he said, waggling a finger. "I'm not letting you sabotage yourself. I can see inside your head, Rissa. That tasty hunk of man candy was putting out all the right signals, but you're scared. You prefer the electronic version of him who never asks you any questions and who you can turn off at the end of the night. You don't want him to be a real person. But you can't put the cat back in the bag, so dig out the chiffon dress that matches your eyes, strap on some heels, and wow him."

Clarissa sighed and shifted from foot to foot. "It's too cold for a dress."

"Pfft. It's spring, and you'll be inside." He crossed his arms and leaned on the doorframe. "Come on, what's the harm?

Dress like the classy woman you are; go along to dinner and have fun. If you have a miserable time, get a taxi back and you'll never have to see him again. What do you have to lose?"

A comfortable evening at home by herself. Her dignity. Her peace of mind. She didn't voice either of these options because he'd have another argument prepared, and he was right. She didn't want to put herself out there. She was trying to hide. But Leo didn't realize how important it was for her to have this crush on Mark, which felt pure and normal, and not to have it polluted by reality. Reality was the worst.

"Fine," she agreed. "I'll wear the dress, but you're not allowed to make a fuss of it when this doesn't go anywhere."

"Deal," he said, coming forward to shake her hand. She knew he'd renege, but she changed anyway, ignoring him when he suggested she opt for a matching underwear set. No one would be seeing her lingerie.

"Much better," he told her when she was done. He kissed her cheek. "Have a nice night, Riss."

"You too." She patted his arm and went back to applying mascara as he left. Her doorbell rang as she put the final touches on her lipstick, and she grabbed her coat and shrugged into it before locking her apartment and leaving the boutique via the front door, where Mark was waiting.

"Hi," she said shyly. In the dim streetlight, he seemed even more handsome. Or perhaps that was because she had his complete attention. He greeted her with a smile, and his eyes never left her face, as though he were trying to memorize every contour of it. Her cheeks heated. "Where's Rose?"

"Waiting in the car," he replied, gesturing to a black hatchback with a rental company logo on the side. "You look beautiful."

"So do you," she replied automatically, then gasped, realizing what she'd said. "I mean, good. You look good." Oh God, she was messing this up. She wanted to bury her face inside her jacket to conceal her humiliation. Instead, she straightened her spine. "That's a nice suit, Mark. Very tidy and well-tailored."

"Uh, thank you."

Well-tailored? She might as well dig a grave for any romantic prospects right now.

Not that she wanted him to be romantically interested in her. She wasn't about to change her rules when it came to dating just because she'd had a cyber crush on him for far too long. The rules existed for a reason. Regardless of that, she'd quite like it if he were at least *attracted* to her. After all, she'd spent months daydreaming about him.

That's when you thought you'd never meet him. He was safe.

Mark Talbot wasn't a safe fantasy any longer. He was very real and present, the heat from his body almost tangible. A hint of his deliciously spicy cologne permeated the air between them. She'd imagined how he might smell. Now she knew, and she could never unknow.

"Shall we?" he asked.

She followed him to the car and opened the back door, but Rose was already in the rear seat.

"You go up front, dear," she said, her eyes crinkling at the edges. "I have some messages I need to respond to before dinner, so I won't be great company."

Clarissa slid into the passenger seat, taking care to position herself as far from Mark as possible, afraid that if she didn't, she'd end up plastered to his side, intoxicated by his scent. She directed them to the restaurant, and they parked a block away and walked to the entrance. They were shown to a table beside a window, which had four seats. She sat on one side, assuming Rose and Mark would sit opposite, but Mark pulled out the chair beside her.

Suddenly, the table felt much too crowded.

Clarissa's throat was tight. "Thanks again for inviting me out," she squeaked. "It's very kind of you."

"It's our pleasure," Rose said.

A waiter took their drink order. Clarissa requested the house white wine. She'd need fortification to get through tonight, but not too much in case she made a bigger fool of herself than she already had.

"So, Clarissa," Rose said when the waiter had gone. "How did you get into weddings? I want to hear the whole story."

Clarissa rubbed her blue touchstone ring, her hands in her lap. She hated being the focus of attention. Yes, she worked in a field where being in the public eye was crucial, but she preferred to take a back seat and let her designs speak for her.

"I've always been interested in clothing and fashion," she said, leaving out the part where she hadn't had the opportunity to indulge her passion until university, because of her conservative parents. Their earlier control over her life had backfired. Rather than being put off, her fascination with stylish, forbidden clothing had grown. "I earned a diploma in fashion design, and the only place that offered me a job was *The House of Bliss*, which is not what it sounds like, I swear. That's what my boutique used to be called before I gave it a much-needed name change."

Mark chuckled, and pleasure suffused her. She'd made him laugh. *Her.*

She peered over at him beneath her lashes and ventured a smile. Since she'd gone through puberty, she'd heard hundreds of flattering—occasionally creepy—remarks about the way she looked, but none of them had made her feel half as good as the sound of his laughter. Having a man enjoy her wit, rather than her appearance, was something new.

She *liked* it.

"I imagine you had a few misunderstandings," he said.

"More than a few. But I straightened them out." Sometimes with words, once or twice with a well-placed slap.

"And then you worked your way up from employee to owner in, what, a few years?"

She cocked her head. Was he fishing for her age?

"Four years," she said. "But it wasn't really a matter of working my way up the chain. I was happy to be a designer employed by someone else, but my boss wanted to retire, and I loved the boutique too much to lose it."

~

MARK WAS ENTHRALLED. When Clarissa felt passionate about something, her pale eyes glittered and the pitch of her voice became high and breathy.

"So, what did you do?" he asked, wanting to hear her story and keep her talking so she'd forget the awkwardness between them earlier.

"It wasn't so much what I did. Let's just say I had a guardian angel watching over me—this woman from the town where I grew up. She reached out to me. Told me she had some money left over from her late husband and wanted to invest in a partnership."

"What perfect timing," his mum exclaimed.

"A little too perfect," Clarissa mumbled, and he didn't think she even noticed she'd done so. He was intrigued. There was a level of subtext he felt he was missing. He wanted to ask but was afraid she'd clam up if he pried. She continued more clearly, "Yes, that was the turning point for me. Eliza loaned me enough money to buy the boutique, and I paid her back with interest."

"Already? Wow, that's efficient." And impressive. While he'd been mistaken about certain aspects of Clarissa Mitchell, he'd been right on point when he'd thought of her as a clever, determined businesswoman.

"Eliza isn't the sort of person you want to owe money.

Don't get me wrong, she really came through for me, but she can be a pushy little busybody at times."

"She saw a good investment, and she went for it," Mark said. "You've got to admire that."

The flush on her cheeks deepened charmingly. "You think I'm a good investment?"

If she were a different person, he'd think she was fishing for a compliment, but she seemed genuinely surprised and delighted by his comment. "Well, you made her money, didn't you?"

"I suppose I did."

"The very definition of a good investment."

She smiled. "Thank you, that means a lot coming from you."

The waiter interrupted with their drinks and took their orders. Clarissa requested salmon with caramelized scallop xo sauce, a choice he heartily approved of. One of Mark's passions was good wine and fine dining, and he admired a woman with good taste.

When the waiter left, he noticed that Rose was glancing back and forth between him and Clarissa with a speculative gleam in her eye. Normally, he'd be embarrassed that she'd picked up on his interest in a woman so easily, but considering she was the primary reason they were here and that they had such little time before they had to return to Auckland, he was willing to roll with any motherly support she might decide to throw behind him.

"Clarissa," Rose said, sipping her wine and studying the younger woman over the glass. "How long have you been listening to Mark's podcast?"

Clarissa's eyes widened, and she looked like a kid caught with their hand in the cookie jar. He wondered why.

"A few months."

"She's one of my most dedicated listeners," he said,

keeping his gaze on her while she squirmed in her seat. "Asks a lot of questions. Really engages with me."

"Some of my questions are probably silly," she muttered.

"Not at all. They're insightful, intelligent, and useful for the other listeners."

She was beet red now, and he wondered if she ever received compliments. A woman who looked like her, how could she not? But she wasn't behaving like a person who was accustomed to kind words.

"How did you find out about it?" Rose asked.

Clarissa took another mouthful of wine, and it left her bowed upper lip glistening in a way that made him want to lick it. "Word of mouth. Mark has quite a wide reach."

The conversation flowed more easily after that. Rose asked for stories about the dresses Clarissa had designed, the fashion shows she'd been to, and the celebrities she'd met. Once she got talking about work, her confidence increased in bounds. As she regaled Rose with a story about meeting an Italian *duchessa* in Milan and being conscripted to design outfits for her daughter's bridal party, she was witty and animated, using sweeping hand gestures and flourishes to embellish her tale.

Mark rested his chin in his hands and didn't take his eyes off her, even when dinner arrived. He couldn't stop wondering how he'd corresponded with her for months and been totally in the dark as to how vibrant and intense she was. How completely and utterly fascinating. He was stunned by how much he didn't want to say goodbye to her at the end of the evening. He felt a pang of loss at the mere thought.

"Enough about me," she said eventually. "I want to know what made you start the podcast, Mark."

He glanced at his mother, and her expression softened. "I got the idea when a friend of mine was first setting up his business. It reminded me how hard it had been for Mum, navigating the legal and tax requirements when she started her firm, and I wanted to do what I could to make it easier for other people in the same position."

"What a selfless motive."

If he could photograph her face as it was this second, full of admiration, he'd never tire of looking at it, but he wasn't sure he was 100 percent worthy of her praise.

"Not totally selfless." He shrugged. "It was also an effective way to get my name out there as a junior lawyer."

"Not that you needed it," Rose said.

Clarissa's brows inched up. "What do you mean?"

"That friend I mentioned?" Mark said. "He employed me soon after I started the podcast, but I kept it up anyway because…" He trailed off, not really sure of the exact reason, just that it had seemed necessary.

"Because you're a good person," she concluded.

"I don't know about that." Though he tried, he wasn't perfect. Far from it. But if she wanted to make him out to be a saint, that was fine by him.

4

*T*he drive back to Clarissa's apartment passed quietly, but it was a different type of silence from the one that had reigned as they'd been on their way to the restaurant. It was natural. Comfortable. She was full of good food and wine, sleepy and content from hours of conversation that had gotten progressively easier until she felt like she'd known Mark and Rose for years.

Her eyelids drooped heavily, and her breathing was slow and even. She'd be asleep as soon as she hit the bed. When the car stopped, she stretched and opened the door. Mark came around to help her out, and she took his hand, though she knew she shouldn't, and let him walk her around to the rear entrance.

"Thank you for dinner," she said. "I had a lovely time."

"So did I."

His tousled hair threw his face into shadow, but the shadows were kind to him, caressing his features and making them seem mysterious and compelling rather than ominous, as might be the case with another man. Or perhaps that was just her skewed perception. Whatever the case, he was handsome, and her body instinctively wanted to sway closer. She maintained the space between them.

He hadn't released her hand, and now he raised it to kiss the back. Tingles sprang from the spot his lips touched and spread along her arm. She reclaimed her hand and tucked it into her coat pocket.

"Listen," he started, with an odd note in his voice that hadn't been there previously, "I know that dinner with my mum wasn't the best setting for romance, but I like you. I'm drawn to you more than I've been drawn to anyone in a while."

He stroked her cheekbone with the back of his fingers, then cupped the side of her face in his palm. She longed to close her eyes and lean into him, but this was all a dream— one perfect moment with her fantasy prince that couldn't be anything more. Not when she knew how these things came crashing down.

She wanted to be able to savor this moment in the dark with him, and if she opened herself to more, it would be ruined eventually. She needed to cherish this little snippet of time and keep it safe in her heart to warm her on long, lonely nights.

"Can I call you?" he continued in that whiskey-smooth voice. "Socially, I mean, as a man who's interested in a woman, rather than as a business acquaintance." As if he'd been ambiguous. "I want to know you better than that."

Tears of frustration flooded her eyes, but she blinked them back. She wished she could say yes. Wished she could be swept away by passion, but there was no place for that in her life. All of her passion was channeled into work, as it should be, because investing it in people inevitably resulted in disappointment. If she wanted to retain any kind of professional relationship with Mark and continue watching him once a week without fail, falling asleep to the memory of his voice, she couldn't allow any lines to be blurred.

"I'm sorry, but I think it's better if we keep things professional," she told him, and she could have sworn she heard her heart shriek in protest. "I like you too, but I'm not in the right place for a relationship at the moment, and even if I were, we live at opposite ends of the country."

She held her breath, praying he wouldn't explode like some men did when she rejected them, but he nodded—a little sadly, she thought—and said, "Well, I guess this is goodbye then."

"I'll still watch your livestream."

His lips twitched but didn't form a smile. "I'll be waiting eagerly for your next question. Good night, Clarissa."

He walked away, into the dark, and she tried not to be disappointed when he didn't look back. She'd done the right thing. She was sure of it.

Almost.

∾

MARK SIGHED at the list of emails awaiting his attention. Seven responses to his latest podcast, and none of them from Clarissa. That made two weeks in a row without hearing from her. Considering she'd had a question after every podcast in the preceding four months, the absence seemed significant.

She was avoiding him. But why?

Was it because she was afraid he couldn't take no for an answer? He didn't like that possibility. Perhaps she'd simply been busy, but that didn't ring true either. She'd made a point of saying she'd keep listening to him, so where was she?

"That's an awfully black expression."

Mark's head jerked up. His friend Eli stood opposite him, but he'd been so preoccupied he hadn't noticed. "Don't mind me," he said. "I was thinking about something."

"Some*thing*, or some*one*?" Eli asked, dragging over one of

33

the stools from the breakfast bar to sit on. They were in the new home Eli shared with his fiancée, located near the shore of a lake in the small town he'd recently relocated to. "Sterling said you'd been out of sorts. He wondered if it was over a woman."

Mark shook his head. "It's nothing." He wasn't about to bother Eli with his minor problems when the other man had enough on his mind. His wedding was in a matter of days, not to mention some of the boxes from his recent move hadn't been unpacked yet, and he hadn't seen his fiancée in far too long because she'd insisted on staying at her old cottage during the lead up to the wedding.

"If you say so." Eli looked skeptical but didn't push. He dragged a hand down his face. "Who knew there was so much to do to get married? If I'd known it would be this crazy, I'd have insisted on eloping."

"Sure, mate." Like that would ever happen. Not only did Eli tend toward being conservative, but his bride wanted a big wedding, and Eli—a wealthy CEO—would make sure she had whatever she wanted, or God help anyone who stood in the way.

Mark closed his emails and tried to distract himself from Clarissa and her conspicuous absence. "What needs to be done before the big day?"

Eli shook his head. "I have no idea. As far as I can tell, everything is on track, but every time I call Aria, she's doing a million and one different things, and I feel useless. She needs to slow down, all the stress can't be good for the baby."

"Does she seem stressed?" Mark asked. "Because from where I'm sitting, it looks like she's having a great time."

"She is," he conceded. "But that doesn't stop me worrying."

Since Mark had never had a relationship as serious as Eli's, he couldn't relate. But he did have two little sisters, so he understood wanting to protect someone.

34

"I'd worry about Sterling if I were you. He still hasn't been able to push through the purchase of that property in Haven Bay, and I think he's going to snap and do something stupid soon."

Eli sighed. "Why is he so hung up on that place?"

Mark hid a grin. "Uh, maybe because of how fabulously successful your endeavor here has been. You're his mentor. He wants to follow your lead and do you proud."

"He doesn't have anything to prove to me."

"You're telling the wrong person. He's the one who needs to hear it. He hasn't stopped trying to one-up himself since you promoted him."

"Which I did because I trusted him and wanted to show how much I appreciate and value him."

"And because you wanted to move to paradise with the woman you love."

"That too. The point is—"

A door clicked shut behind them, and they both fell silent.

"Realtors!" Sterling exclaimed as he stalked into the room, his vivid blue eyes furious. "They're a nightmare to deal with." He grabbed another stool and joined them, leaning on the edge of the seat and crossing his long legs at the ankles.

"You know, there are other people who can deal with realtors for you," Mark said. "Like me. If you look, you'll see it's actually in my job description." He wasn't sure why Sterling was insisting on handling this case himself, especially when he was getting wound up about it. It wasn't like having underlings do the leg work while he coordinated the acquisition from on top would reflect poorly on him.

"It's all right," Sterling muttered. "There's no need for you to get involved. I've got it under control."

And Mark was a shoo-in for President of the United States.

"Just let me know if you change your mind."

"I won't."

"What time are we meeting the other groomsmen at the bar?" Mark asked, keen to shift the conversation to a less controversial topic.

"In fifteen minutes," Eli said. "Speaking of, they're a little rough around the edges compared to what you're used to. The important thing is not to show fear."

Sterling didn't seem to know how to take this, but Mark laughed. "You played fisticuffs with one of them and survived. I'm not worried at all."

～

CLARISSA RAPPED on Aria's front door, a bottle of sparkling grape juice tucked under one arm and a cake of artisan chocolate in her hand. The door flew inward, and Aria launched herself into Clarissa's arms, bringing with her the sweet scent of strawberries. Clarissa stood still, unable to return the hug since her hands were full, and waited for Aria to notice her predicament. But her friend liked to hug and had a helpless victim in her grasp, so she clung like a limpet, her pregnant belly thrusting forward.

"Aria," she prompted. "I'm stuck."

Aria shot back, tripped over her own feet, narrowly avoided falling, and righted herself on the doorframe. "Oops, sorry. I'm just so excited you're here," she exclaimed. "The others are in the kitchen." She caught sight of the chocolate and squealed, reeling Clarissa in for another hug. "You're an angel. Thank you so much."

Clarissa laughed. "Anything for you."

She followed Aria into the kitchen, which was the heart of her home. Her friend loved to cook, and when people hung out in her kitchen, she treated them like family. The others glanced up as they entered. Avery sat behind the table, shuffling a deck of cards. Sophie was pouring wine into glasses, and Evie was perched on a chair, her knees drawn to her chest, giggling at something on her phone.

"No Teri?" Clarissa asked.

Aria shook her head. "Just us tonight. She's sleeping over at a friend's place."

Avery stopped shuffling cards. "Hey, Riss." The tension around her eyes had eased since Clarissa had last seen her, and they twinkled for the first time in years. It seemed she wouldn't need to slap Gareth Wayland, Avery's once-and-again boyfriend. The man had kept his word and made her happy.

"You look good," she said.

Avery sauntered over and gave her a quick hug. "I feel good."

"Being with Gareth agrees with you."

Avery waggled her eyebrows playfully. Clarissa rolled her eyes and laughed; then she embraced Sophie, who also looked totally comfortable in her own skin. In fact, Clarissa would go so far as to say she glowed. Evie, on the other hand, looked the same as ever—gorgeous, and unconcerned about anything.

Evie studied Clarissa over the top of her phone, scanning her work attire with a sigh. "Let loose for once, Riss. Change into something else. Go a little crazy."

"I came straight from work," Clarissa explained. She'd struggled to leave, even though she knew Leo could take care of things while she was away. But this was more leave than she'd had in ages, not counting work-related trips. "I'll change as soon as I know what the plan is."

Evie snorted. "I'll give you one guess."

Sophie swatted the back of Evie's head. "Don't be a spoil-sport, babe. The local places might be too 'small town' for you, but the rest of us still love them. Besides, we went up to Christchurch for the bachelorette party. This is just a low-key night out with friends. No need for anything fancy."

"Dux for tea, Davy's for drinks," Clarissa guessed when Sophie finished berating Evie.

Evie aimed a finger gun at her. "Got it in one, clever clogs."

Clarissa accepted a glass of red wine from Sophie and sipped. "Mm. Sweet."

"It's my new favorite," Sophie said.

Aria's lips smooshed together as she gazed at the wine longingly. "I can't wait until I have this baby. Did you know, I won't be able to drink wine again until after I finish breast-feeding?"

Evie nodded. "You can't risk expressing the alcohol or any alcohol derivatives in your breast milk." Everyone stared at her. She shrugged. "What? I spent a couple of seasons calving on a dairy farm, and I nannied for a while too." She helped herself to the white wine and addressed Aria. "Do we have to go to Davy's? Can't we spend the night at Dux?"

"Don't be selfish," Avery said bluntly. "Going to Davy's is a tradition. We love it, and the next week is all about Aria."

Aria looked uncomfortable, and Clarissa sympathized. Her friend wanted everyone to be happy.

"It'll be fun," Clarissa assured Evie. "Just a couple of hours. If it's not, you can do a few tequila shots and forget about it in the morning."

Evie downed her wine in one long swallow. "I suppose I can handle that."

Clarissa hugged her with one arm, put her drink down, and then went back out to her car to drag her bag inside. "Where can I change?" she asked her friends.

Aria led her to a bedroom. "This is Teri's room. The bathroom is across the hall if you need it." She checked the time on the digital clock atop the bedside table. "Our reservation at Dux is in an hour."

"Thanks, sweetie." Clarissa leaned over and kissed her cheek. "How are the nerves?"

Aria waved a hand up and down. "I'm not worried about marrying Eli. I love him to bits. I'm just worried I've forgotten something, or that I'll screw up my speech or forget my vows."

Clarissa rested her palms on Aria's shoulders. "Everyone adores you. Even if you fumble your vows and completely forget your speech, we're all here for you, and we'll still love you after. The worst-case scenario really isn't so bad."

The tension in her friend's shoulders eased. "God, you're good at this, Riss. I bet you'll be the calmest bride in history on your wedding day. I'm just a mess."

Clarissa rubbed her upper arms soothingly. "You're not a mess. You're pregnant, and you've planned a wedding in less than six months. Give yourself a break, honey. You're a miracle worker."

She ducked her head. "You're so good for my ego."

Clarissa laughed. "I'll be out shortly."

Aria stepped back, hands on hips. "Wear something you love," she ordered. "And do your makeup properly. No down-playing yourself for my benefit. You're not allowed to look anything other than your best for the next few days."

Clarissa nodded. It would seem that Aria was determined her friends enjoy the wedding at least as much, if not more, than she would, and since she was undoubtedly the sweetest of them all, they'd indulge her.

5

"*S*o let me get this straight," Mark said, hand outstretched above a glass of pinot as he gestured in turn at each man around the table at Davy's Bar. During his brief time in Itirangi, he'd learned that the bar was an institution. Run by an Irishman who'd emigrated in his teens, it attracted everyone under the age of fifty, locals and tourists alike. The maroon furnishings, though outdated, were comfortable, and the ambiance couldn't be beat.

"Since the start of the year, you," he pointed at Justin, the scruffy, hulking brother of Eli's bride-to-be, "have fallen madly in love with the cheerful florist who healed your wounded soul."

Justin scowled and chugged his beer but didn't disagree.

"You," he moved on to Eli, whose lips tugged up at the corners, which for him was the equivalent of a full-on grin, "moved to the middle of nowhere and met the love of your life. Now you've got a ring on her finger and a baby on the way."

Eli shrugged one shoulder and nodded.

"You," Mark said to Aria's other brother, Cooper, a muscular blond veteran-turned-photographer, "discovered you're crazy about your sister's best friend, after knowing her all your life—"

"She's a pocket rocket," Cooper interrupted. "But I was too stupid to see it for years."

"And you," Mark leveled his finger at Gareth, the stoic, broad-shouldered police sergeant, "convinced your ex-girl-friend to give your sorry ass another chance."

"It wasn't quite like that—" Gareth protested.

"Yeah, it was, Gaz," Cooper said, grinning.

Gareth crossed his arms and dropped his chin.

"And now," Mark waved his hand in an all-encompassing circle, "you're all deliriously happy?"

There was a rumble of agreement.

"That's about the sum of it," Eli confirmed.

Mark exchanged a glance with Sterling. "How do you feel about moving?" he asked. "Neither of us has had much luck with women in Auckland, and it sounds like Itirangi is the place to be."

Sterling sipped whiskey, pondering the men over the rim of his glass. "It's charming enough, but I'd never move to a place like this, even for a woman."

Justin stared at Sterling across the table, his expression bordering on hostile. The men were the opposites of each other. Justin, dark and unkempt. Sterling, golden and immaculate.

"Are you saying there's something wrong with Itirangi?" Justin demanded.

Sterling frowned. Mark knew he hadn't intended any insult, he simply struggled to understand that the way he worded things could be misconstrued at times.

"It's a lovely town," Sterling said, "but there are limited opportunities for someone in my line of work."

Mark considered pointing out that Sterling worked for Eli, who'd managed to acclimate to Itirangi reasonably well, ingratiating himself with many of the locals. The fact of the matter was, Eli ran the business, whereas Sterling managed it, and those were two different things entirely.

The bartender, Davy, sauntered over, carrying a tray with three beers, another whiskey, a wine, and a ginger ale. He handed them around, the ginger ale going to Gareth, who was the sober driver. Always on duty.

Unfortunately, Mark had first met Gareth when he'd been flirting with the women the sergeant was hung up on, and therefore hadn't made the best impression. He'd hoped the sergeant wouldn't recognize him, but he'd been out of luck. The man had taken one look at him and the lines around his mouth had firmed in dislike.

"Anything else for you, boys?" Davy asked, leaning against the edge of the booth, his ropey forearm near Mark's head.

"Just keep the beers coming," Cooper said, raising his bottle to chink it against Eli's. "On his tab."

Mark stopped Davy before he retreated. "Tell me, have you been felled by the Itirangi lovebug?"

Davy raised a ginger eyebrow. "What are you on about?"

"Ignore him," Gareth said, speaking over Mark's head. "He's an overdramatic jafa."

Mark rolled his eyes at the derogatory term for Aucklanders. Many South Islanders, especially those from the country, thought Aucklanders had more style than sense.

"Hoo, no, I can't leave until you've explained." Davy shuffled onto the seat beside Mark. "My superstitious Nan would roll over in her grave if I didn't find out about this lovebug."

"Who's watching the bar?" Justin asked, as annoyed as Gareth that their friend was humoring the out-of-towner.

Davy shrugged. "She'll be 'right. No one will steal anything. This is Itirangi." He had a point. Not that either of the scowling comrades would admit it. "So, go on. Start talking."

Mark looked around the table, catching each man's eye. "The lovebug that's spread like wildfire around this

42

delightful little town." He spoke in a stage whisper, and Davy leaned forward to hear more clearly. "All of the single men and women are falling down like dominoes, and we might be next."

Davy hooted and clapped, his large palms smacking together. He reached over and tousled Mark's hair. "I like you. You're good fun."

A whistle at the bar drew his attention, and he raised a hand to the plaid-wearing farmer waiting for a refill. Then he nodded to Eli. "You enjoy the last of your nights of freedom, my friend. Being leg-shackled to Aria will be an adventure and a half." He grinned at her brothers. "I say that with love in my heart."

As Davy strolled off, Mark watched Eli, wondering if his friend was suffering from any last-minute doubts, but he had the look of a man well-satisfied with his choices. Of course he did. Aria was a lovely woman—intelligent, sweet, and vivacious.

For a moment, sadness squeezed around his heart like a rubber band. He *envied* Eli. Mark had never been with a woman who loved him unconditionally, and he feared he never would. Not when he couldn't give her children, and especially not when he shared his father's DNA, which might make him a ticking time bomb. It wouldn't be fair to let anyone that close. He didn't want to die young and leave his family abandoned or, worse, pass on his shitty genes.

A jab in the ribs yanked him from his maudlin musings. Sterling tipped his whiskey glass toward Eli. "I propose a toast. To Eli and Aria, may they have a lifetime of happiness."

Mark swallowed the bitter taste of regret as he raised his glass, then washed it away with wine. He was happy for Eli. Honestly.

Gareth started discussing the recent Crusaders versus Hurricanes rugby game with Cooper and Justin, and Mark turned to Sterling. "Do you have any ideas about how to progress your Haven Bay negotiation?"

"Not yet," Sterling admitted. "Did I tell you I made an appointment to discuss the sale with her and she stood me up?"

"After you'd driven to Haven Bay?" Eli asked in disbelief.

"Yes," Sterling replied through gritted teeth. "The woman never turned up. But six old ladies did. They surrounded me. Badgered me. Assassinated my character." He lowered his voice. "Two of them thumped me with their handbags."

Mark guffawed, the image too good to resist. Eli didn't laugh. This was his business, and he had to treat it seriously. The crinkle of his eyes betrayed his amusement though.

"What did you do?" Mark asked.

Sterling became intrigued by something on the ground. "I told them they were being rude and that, at their age, they should know better. Then I excused myself and drove back." He cleared his throat. "They were little old ladies, it's not as if I could yell or throw my case at them."

Mark shook his head, awed by the women's nerve. "You let those little old ladies walk all over you."

Sterling clenched his fists and grumbled, "There was nothing I could do."

Eli patted him on the back. "Wily old biddies."

"I'll regroup and try again," he vowed. "They won't get the better of me next time."

"I'm sure they won't." Mark wondered if he could justify tagging along to have a front-row seat.

The door chimed, and he glanced up, then froze, thunderstruck. The breath whooshed from his chest. "Oh, *wow*."

CLARISSA SWEPT ASIDE the cream-colored curl that fell across her forehead as she held the bar door open for the others. On workdays, she straightened her hair into submission, but given the opportunity, she preferred to wear it loose. Closing the door softly behind Avery, she blinked as her eyes adjusted to the dimness.

Once they'd become accustomed to the indoor lighting, she beelined to the bar. At the far end of it, Davy chatted with a guy who'd been several years ahead of them at school. She couldn't recall his name. Davy glanced over and indicated he'd be with them in a moment. Aria leaned against the bar and rubbed her prominent belly. Sophie and Avery claimed a pair of barstools, and Sophie's feet hung a foot above the floor, making her look like a schoolgirl. Evie hovered behind them, uncharacteristically subdued.

Davy made his way over, and Clarissa smiled hesitantly. They'd been friends once, but they'd barely spoken since she'd slapped his best friend across the face at the end of senior year. In her defense, Gareth had hurt Avery—her personal savior. Gareth and Avery were back together now, but she wouldn't hesitate to do the same thing again if he hurt her bestie.

"How ya?" Davy asked, beaming at Aria.

"Great," she replied, stretching a kink out of her back, "but I'll be better when this little one is outside of me."

"I'll bet." He mixed a lemon, lime, and bitters for her without asking. "I got a suit picked out for your wedding."

"Please tell me it's not the peach one."

He dropped a wedge of lime into the drink and handed it to her. "I wouldn't do that to you, love. I'm borrowing a special one, just for you." He touched the side of his nose. "It'll be splendid."

She laughed. "I'm sure it will."

"Have you seen your soon-to-be husband?"

She spun around. "Is he here?"

"In the corner." Davy pointed to a booth. Both women followed his finger to see a group of men watching them.

45

Aria waved to her fiancé, so excitedly you'd think they hadn't seen each other for days, but Clarissa noticed a different man, one she'd never expected to see again.

Mark.

What was he doing here?

He stared right at her, lips parted, eyes alight with interest. He blinked, glanced at his glass of wine, and then looked back. His mouth quirked in a smile. Clarissa clutched her purse tightly to her chest and wondered if this was how a rabbit felt caught in the headlights of an oncoming truck. Her heart hammered, and a pulse beat at the bottom of her throat.

She was shocked to see him but also pleased. They'd only spent one evening together, not even a date, but she'd missed him. Or perhaps it was the fantasy of him that she'd missed. She'd watched the livestream of his podcast, sighed over the sound of his voice and the occasional glimpse of his smile, but it hadn't felt right to think of him as she drifted off to sleep or to send him a question and pretend she didn't know there was a flesh-and-blood man at the other end of the internet connection. She didn't want to encourage her crush now that he seemed tangible, so she'd kept her distance.

Yet here he was. And here she was.

Her feet took a step toward him of their own volition.

"Clarissa? What can I get you?" Davy's question broke the spell.

She spun around to face him. *Wine.* She had enough brain capacity to think about wine. "Sav, please."

"Sure thing." He grabbed a bottle. "How're the bright lights of Dunedin treating you?"

Her smile widened. It didn't seem as if he held a grudge. "They're pretty good," she said, "but it's always nice to come home."

And it was. Except for the part of her that feared she'd encounter Heath or her parents around every corner. As long as she traveled in a group, she was fine, but sometimes when she walked through town on her own, she found herself ducking her head and scurrying like a criminal or a mouse who expected a cat to pounce at any moment.

"It's nice to see you here." He placed a glass on the counter, filled it, and pushed it toward her, then rested on his forearms, which were dusted with freckles, as was the bridge of his nose. "Don't see you much anymore."

Guilt sat heavy in her gut. She should visit more often. It was easy to forget she had friends when she got caught up in the solitary cycle of her Dunedin life. "Work keeps me busy. It's hard to get away sometimes."

He nodded, his expression knowing. "You keep telling yourself that, Riss."

God, would no one give her a break? "You don't know the half of it," she snapped.

"Hey." He touched her hand gently. "I didn't mean anything by it, sweetheart. I miss seeing your pretty face, is all."

She nodded, accepting his unspoken apology, and tasted the wine. "Thanks."

She took a moment to study the other patrons in the bar, wondering if she should go and say hello to Mark before she joined her friends. That would be the polite thing to do, and it would cut off any potential awkwardness at the knees. But he was seated with Eli—they must know each other somehow—and if it was obvious she and Mark also knew each other, her friends would ask questions. The type that would embarrass the heck out of her. Anyway, if Mark wanted to speak to her, he'd have come over here already.

She watched two women playing pool as she dithered. One was a stunning girl in skinny jeans with brown skin and dark shining eyes; the other was a blonde in a knee-length skirt. Clarissa eyed the blonde. The way she held herself seemed familiar.

The blonde paced around the table and bent over to line up a shot. Clarissa's insides turned to ice as the chips fell into place.

Jen.

She hadn't seen the girl in years, but she'd recognize those features anywhere. They were nearly identical to the ones she saw in the mirror every morning. Her chest felt like it was going to explode, and she sucked in air, realizing she'd stopped breathing. Her head spun, and her palms tingled. Of all the awful, rotten luck. How was it possible that Jen was here, in the same bar as her, not even twenty yards away?

What was she doing in a bar?

If Jen had grown up as their parents wanted—as Clarissa had assumed she would—she'd never have set foot in Davy's. Her sister sank a ball and pumped her fist in victory. Clarissa clasped one hand over her stomach, which was roiling so wildly she was afraid she'd throw up.

Jen raised her head, and Clarissa knew the exact moment her sister spotted her. She froze, wearing the same expression Clarissa had a minute earlier. Clarissa set down her wine glass, surprised she had the presence of mind to do so without smashing it. The sudden movement jerked Jen into motion. Dropping her pool cue, she took several steps forward. Clarissa bit her fist, hard enough to taste blood.

Enough. She spun on her heel, raced to the exit, and darted out into the darkness beyond.

6

*S*he was mesmerizing.

Mark watched Clarissa Mitchell's blonde curls bounce as she stepped into the bar. She was with a group of women, two of whom he recognized as Eli's fiancée and Gareth's girlfriend. The women walked between tables to the bar, and he noticed a number of male heads turning in their direction. Hardly a surprise. Their arrival was the most interesting event at the bar in a good while.

He heard Eli murmur something about Aria but didn't pay any attention, fixated on Clarissa, with her pin-up girl curves and graceful movements. How was it possible she was here? That of all the country villages in New Zealand, she'd ended up in this one at the same time as him? Could he be imagining her? He rubbed his eyes and glanced at the wine as if it could be to blame. But he'd hardly had enough to cause hallucinations.

She must know Aria.

Obviously, dumbass.

At that moment, Aria and Clarissa both turned and looked his way. Clarissa's cobalt eyes locked on his, and her chest rose as she gasped. He could have sworn he heard it across the room. He didn't look away. Nor did she. He felt her intense gaze penetrate to the core of his being and knew that he should be disturbed that she had such an effect on him, but he wasn't. They might have only met once, but he felt like he knew her. They'd connected on a level that didn't make sense, but didn't have to. Then Davy said something and she spun away, severing their connection. Mark stared at the back of her head, willing her to turn to him, but she started chatting with the Irishman.

He touched Eli's arm. "Do you know Clarissa Mitchell?"

"She's one of Aria's friends," he said. "They grew up together."

"*Here?*" Of all the strange coincidences.

"Yes, here," Eli replied impatiently. "How do *you* know Clarissa? Because I'm not sure I like your expression."

Mark was affronted. "Excuse me? What's wrong with my expression?"

"It's a little too interested. The bridesmaids are off-limits. I don't want any awkwardness on the wedding day."

Mark rolled his eyes. "No awkwardness. Pinky swear. I know Clarissa from my podcast. She's designing a wedding dress for Mum." He'd seen the sketches she'd sent through, and they were impressive. She was a talented artist as well as an intriguing woman. He ducked his head and grinned at his drink like a loony. Running into her here was too significant to be random. He'd longed to see her again, and the universe had set it in motion. He had enough of his mother in him to recognize a sign from the cosmos when he saw one.

"I'm going to talk to her." As he shuffled off the bench seat, Clarissa jerked like she'd been electrocuted, put her wine down, and sprinted out the exit. He watched her go, then looked back to see what she'd run from. A blonde in her early twenties was staring after Clarissa as if she'd seen a ghost. She took two hesitant steps forward, then another woman gripped her arm to prevent her giving chase.

Strange.

Someone cleared their throat, and it was enough to jar Mark into action. He slid out of the booth and hurried after Clarissa. When he got outside, he looked left and right, spotting a person in a blue dress jogging away faster than anyone ought to be able to in high heels. She reached the end of the block, checked both ways, and crossed the road. He broke into a run, his legs eating up the distance between them since he had the advantage of height and decent footwear.

"Clarissa, wait," he called when he drew near. "Slow down!"

She glanced over her shoulder and stopped so abruptly he only narrowly avoided bowling into her. "Mark?" She panted and peered over his shoulder, then looked back at him. "Is anyone else following me?"

"No," he told her. "You're safe."

Her hands came up to her bare shoulders and rubbed them. The night breeze was chilly, and she'd left her sweater inside.

"Here." He shrugged out of his jacket and offered it to her. She stared at it, apparently failing to comprehend him. "Take it. You need to keep warm."

"Oh." The word puffed out from between her lips. "No, thanks. I'll be fine. I just need to get back to Aria's place. It's not far to walk. You can go back to Davy's."

Mark glanced around. The streets were nearly deserted, the temperature was rapidly falling, and she was a lone woman in pumps and a dress. Did she really think he'd leave her like this?

"Come on, I'll give you a ride."

"I'll be fine," she reiterated, but her voice was tight. He suspected she was fighting back tears and wanted to cry in peace. Except he couldn't allow that, not without knowing she was somewhere safe. "Like I said, it's not far. You don't need to go out of your way for me."

"Let me help you," he said softly. "Please. I swear I won't even get out of the car at the other end if that's what you'd prefer. I just want to know you made it there."

She tapped her bottom lip with her finger, her gaze skittering from him to their darkening surroundings, back toward the bar, not fastening on anything. He hated her uncertainty and the way her shallow breathing hinted at panic—particularly when he feared *he* was the reason for it. He tucked his hands into his pockets, hoping it would make him seem less imposing.

"How about this?" he asked, keeping his tone low and even. "You wear my jacket, and I'll walk you home. I'll even stay on the other side of the road if it makes you feel better. Do you think you could live with that?"

She nodded. "I suppose that would be all right."

He offered the jacket, and this time she took it and slipped it on over her dress. Though he wasn't a lot taller than her, the jacket dwarfed her, hanging loosely from her frame. She pulled it tight and buried her hands in the folds, presumably to keep them warm. Her shoulders hunched inward, and he ached to put an arm around her and pledge to protect her, but the trouble was, she seemed to think she needed protecting from *him*.

He paced away until several yards separated them. "How's this?"

"Good," she said. "Thanks."

They started walking, side by side, although the space between them would have been wide enough to fit another four people. After a block, he realized she didn't plan to talk, and he didn't intend to waste precious time with her in silence.

He glanced over at her, silhouetted by a streetlight, and said, "Fancy seeing you here."

She laughed, though it sounded strained. "What are the odds?"

"Anywhere else in the world? Almost nil. In New Zealand? Exponentially better, but still pretty slim, I'd have thought."

She sighed. "You must be wondering why I ran out of there like a crazy person."

"You don't have to explain yourself to me." He was just grateful for the opportunity to see her again, whatever the circumstances.

"I appreciate that." She spoke so quietly he almost missed it. "But it was nothing sinister. There's really no need for you to escort me back."

He pressed his lips together to suppress a smile. "If you keep talking that way, I might think you don't like me."

He'd only been joking, but she whirled around, her hand coming to her mouth. "No, that's not it at all. I just…." She scowled and looked away. "It's complicated."

"Isn't it always?" he murmured, wondering what it was about the blonde at the bar that had thrown her so off-balance.

Silence descended again, but it was more comfortable this time. They'd left the main street and were crossing through a residential neighborhood. He hadn't bothered to pay attention to directions because he could use the GPS on his phone to find his way back later.

"She was my sister," Clarissa said, after a while. "We're… estranged… I guess. I haven't seen or spoken to her in years. It was a shock. It shouldn't have been, considering Itirangi is her home, but it never occurred to me that I'd run into her. In my mind, she's still fourteen."

Mark processed that. If he'd estimated her sister's age right, they must have been estranged for nearly a decade. What could cause a rift like that between teenage sisters?

Something pretty traumatic. He was treading on thin ice here.

"I'm sorry, that sounds hard. I can't relate, but I understand what it's like when your siblings grow up unexpectedly. It seems like one minute my sisters had pigtails and ballerina dresses, and the next, they were graduating from high school and moving out on their own." A sensation he definitely hadn't liked. He adored Megan and Mikayla, but sometimes he struggled with the thought of them paving their own path when he still imagined them as his baby sisters.

"You have sisters?" she asked.

He nodded. "Two of them."

"What are they like?"

He thought for a moment. "Mik is a little dynamo. She's an executive assistant to a big-time businessman and completely runs his life. Meg is a bit more reserved, but once you get to know her, she's the sweetest person. She works at a bakery. The kind of place where you have to apprentice in France before they'll even consider you. She's a superstar."

"Wait," she said, holding up a hand. "Your names are Mark, Mik, and Meg?"

He couldn't be sure in the dark, but he thought she was smiling. "Mum has a thing for 'M' names. 'Mik' and 'Meg' are short for Mikayla and Megan."

"And Mark?"

"Isn't short for anything," he replied. "I'm just boring old Mark."

"I happen to think boring old Mark is pretty great."

Warmth oozed through him, slow and sweet, like honey. "Thanks. You're not so bad yourself." He fished for something else to say, wanting to hold onto the ease that had grown between them. "I've missed your questions over the past few weeks."

She stiffened, and he winced. Clearly this wasn't the life-line he'd been hoping for.

"I hope I didn't put you off," he continued, trying to unbungle the situation. "I promise I won't be inappropriate or flirt with you if you don't want me to. I'll be totally professional, cross my heart. I'd hate to lose you as a listener."

He also hated the thought of her out there, watching him online but afraid to reach out. He wanted to be a source of knowledge to anyone who needed it, but especially women like his mother, who tended to have more difficulty finding their footing as business owners.

"I've been listening," she said. "I can't not. Podcasts were never really my thing, but after Aria introduced me to yours, I've become addicted."

He frowned. "Aria recommended my podcast to you?"

"Yeah, she said it might help me work through some of the things I was having issues with."

And just like that, he understood.

None of this had been random. Not Clarissa finding his podcast or corresponding with him via email or even them meeting here in what would otherwise have been the mother of all coincidences. She'd found him *because* they were connected through their friends.

"I never realized that. You said you'd found me by word of mouth. I just assumed you meant on an internet forum, like most people."

She laughed, and this time it sounded genuine. "As if I'd have time to surf the web. I barely have time to get myself presentable in the morning."

"I'm sure you manage just fine." She could wear jeans and a ratty T-shirt and she'd be stunning.

They slowed to a stop outside a cottage surrounded by a wild garden.

"This is me," she said, slipping his jacket off and holding it out to him. As he took it, her perfume drifted toward him, and he longed to bury his face in the fabric and inhale deeply to see if it smelled like her. "Thanks for keeping me company."

"You're very welcome." He didn't want the night to end, but at least he knew he'd see her again soon. "You're one of Aria's bridesmaids?"

"Yes," she confirmed.

"I'm one of the groomsmen, so I'll see you at the rehearsal dinner. Or maybe sometime before."

Her eyes crinkled at the corners, and her lips tugged up ever so slightly. "I'll look forward to it. Bye, Mark."

"Good night, Clarissa."

She gave him a parting wave, then glided up the porch stairs and let herself in the front door. He waited until he heard it click shut before he left.

~

EVIE SANG at the top of her lungs in time with Beyoncé, crumping her way across the carpet. If she couldn't sing as well as she did, Clarissa would have cringed, but as it happened, she had a superb voice.

It was the day after she'd fled the bar, and she was with her friends. She'd had a lot of explaining to do, but everything was smoothed over now and they were letting loose and nurturing their creative sides.

"Got me hoping you'll page me right now," Aria chimed in from the kitchen, where she was preparing the wedding cake she'd insisted on baking herself.

Avery clapped her hands over her ears. Unlike Evie, Aria was tone-deaf, but what she lacked in talent, she made up for in enthusiasm. Evie completed a circuit of the room, dodging armchairs, coffee tables, and masses of paper, and dropped to the ground beside Sophie, who high-fived her.

"Good choice."

They were taking turns choosing love songs to listen to while they assembled decorations for the upcoming wedding. Evie, Sophie, Avery, and Clarissa were folding origami flowers in every color of the rainbow while Emily practiced floral arrangements and Teri handed her stems and tools as requested.

Teri groaned. "You guys are so *old*."

Evie grinned, not bothered by the teenager's scorn. "You wait your turn, Little Miss Muffet."

Teri knocked her forehead against the wall, and Emily giggled. The two had reached a truce after their first meeting, when Teri had tried to steal from Emily's gift shop.

Clarissa made a precise fold in a piece of sky blue paper and tucked the ends inside each other, completing a tidy six-petaled flower, which she set aside in the uncluttered area they'd designated for successes. The unsuccessful messes lay discarded in mounds around the room.

"How do you do that?" Sophie asked, holding up the mangled pink rose she'd folded and refolded several times. "Swear to God, I've only seen you mess up one flower since we started, and to be honest, it was still good enough that I would have called it a winner."

Clarissa shrugged, picked up a piece of gold paper, and started on another. "I spend a lot of time doing intricate work. I'm used to it."

Avery dropped a demented dahlia in disgust and started gathering up the crumpled failures into a black rubbish bag.

"Shouldn't you be good at this?" Emily asked her. "It's basically science. Fold this direction, then that, until you're done."

Avery shot the redhead a glare and grumbled, "This isn't science. It's art. I'm not artistic." Once the crumpled remains of her efforts were cleared away, she sat on the arm of the couch and proclaimed herself supervisor.

"Slacker," Evie teased, finishing a rose and eyeing it proudly.

Avery scowled at the perfect paper blossom in Evie's hand. Clarissa hid her smile in her shoulder. Avery liked to be the best at everything, and the fact that Evie, who took nothing seriously, was better at something than her... well, if the set of Avery's jaw was anything to go by, Clarissa hoped Evie slept with one eye open.

"How's it going in there, girls?" Aria called as the song ended and Emily got up to select a new one.

"Great fun," Evie called, just as Avery replied, "It'd be better if there was beer."

"We're having fun," Clarissa confirmed, "*and* it would be better if there was alcohol. How's the cake?"

"Delicious, of course."

Sophie hopped up and went through the connecting door to the kitchen. Clarissa focused on her folding and had completed another flower by the time Sophie returned with a cask of wine under her arm and carrying a platter with half a dozen wine glasses.

"Wine," Avery muttered, not at all a wine drinker. "Fantastic."

Sophie laid the platter on the coffee table and, with a flourish, pulled a bottle of beer from her back pocket and tossed it to Avery. Jason Mraz's "I'm Yours" played over the speakers, and Emily rejoined them, helping Sophie pour wines and hand them around. Even Teri got a small portion.

"Okay, maybe you guys aren't so bad," the girl admitted.

"Oh, my gosh." Aria peered around the corner, a cheeky smile on her face. "Did you hear that?" She directed the question at Evie. "*We're* not so bad."

Teri rolled her eyes and heaved a momentous sigh. "You know I love you, Ri."

"Yeah." Aria's smile softened around the edges, and her

eyes shone. For a moment, Clarissa worried she might weep, but she held herself together. "I love you too."

Avery made a gagging sound. "You're too cute. Cut it out."

Teri stared daggers at her. "I *don't* love you."

Clarissa repeated the methodical folding movements, enjoying her friends' banter in the background. Being around people was a nice change. She'd spent too many days in her own company, and being surrounded by people she liked and trusted relaxed her.

She could let her guard down. They didn't expect anything from her, other than for her to be herself. She hummed under her breath and exchanged smiles with Emily, who shifted several flowers and started wrapping twine around the stems.

"What are you grinning about?" Avery asked.

Clarissa shrugged. "I'm having a good time. This is nice. I haven't seen all of you girls together for ages."

Avery smirked, but she was enjoying herself too. She was an open book as far as Clarissa was concerned. They'd shared too many secrets for it to be any other way.

"As soon as Coop proposes to Sophie, we can do it all over again," Avery said.

Sophie laughed. "I think Gaz is more likely to propose to you first. Just to lock you down, make sure you can't up and leave him again."

Avery pursed her lips and tilted her head to the side, nodding. "Fair call."

"You know what I think?" Aria asked, still listening from the kitchen.

"What's that?" Clarissa said.

Aria bounced through the doorway, her hands occupied with a fondant lily. "I think Justin will beat Cooper and Gareth, and make an honest woman of Em." She sent a wicked smile to Emily, who blushed bright red to match her hair. "I'm not wrong, am I? He's mentioned it."

59

Clarissa felt for poor Emily, who clearly didn't like being at the center of speculation.

"He might have mentioned it," she mumbled, becoming a deeper shade of red, if such a thing were possible. "It probably won't happen for a while though." She shrugged self-consciously. "Don't get too excited yet."

"Eep!"

Startled, Clarissa turned toward Sophie, the source of the noise.

"We're going to be sisters," Sophie exclaimed. Jumping up, she hugged Emily, then Teri and Aria for good measure. Teri cringed away from the contact, and Aria held her lily carefully out of reach.

"I suppose we are." Emily beamed, her perfect teeth luminous against the red of her cheeks. "I always wanted a sister."

"So did I," Aria said warmly.

Despite all the loving vibes in the air, Clarissa went cold inside at the reminder of Jen. Goose bumps traveled up her arms. She hadn't spoken to Jen since the night everything had gone to hell. For three months, she'd seen her in the hall at school, or across the courtyard during lunch, but had been too scared to approach her and risk rejection. Jen must have known what Clarissa had done and what had happened because of it. If she'd wanted to talk, all she'd had to do was pause as they passed by each other, rather than brushing her aside as though they were strangers.

Jen had never outright shunned her, but her indifference had been just one more betrayal, and Clarissa had been scraped so raw that all she could focus on was making it through the year. Anger, hurt, and guilt had fueled her. She'd had tunnel vision, unable to focus on anything other than escaping Itirangi and outrunning the past. After all, Jen hadn't been the only person she'd feared running into in the school halls.

No, don't go there.

She looked around her friends and tried to summon the sense of comfort she'd had five minutes ago, but she was too busy wondering where Heath Shaw was. Her fingers shook, and for the first time, she fudged a fold.

She took a deep breath. In for four, hold for four, out for four.

She was strong; he couldn't hurt her now.

7

---

*M*ark bent over the pool table, lined up a shot, and knocked a banded ball into a pocket.

Eli, his teammate, murmured, "Nice shot."

He aimed at his next target, moved the cue, and missed, the white ball bouncing harmlessly off the edge of the table. He stood back so Gareth could have a turn. Gareth also sank one ball but missed the next.

Eli pocketed two balls, and Mark clapped him on the back. "What a master."

Then Davy, Gareth's partner, showed them all up by sinking four in a row before missing.

"Come on, that's hardly fair," Mark protested. "You probably spend all day practicing."

Davy winked. "Should have thought of that before you invited me to make up numbers."

Sparing a glare for Sterling, who'd taken a work call and was speaking madly into his phone—the reason Gareth had needed a new teammate—Mark took another turn and missed.

"How are you feeling about the big day?" he asked Eli while they waited. "No nerves or cold feet?"

62

"Better bloody not have cold feet," Davy said in a pleasant tone that belied his grim expression. "I'll truss you up like a stuck pig and tie you to the altar if it makes Aria happy."

Mark snorted with laughter. He thought Gareth might have cracked a grin too, but he could have imagined it. The man seemed incapable of anything other than glowering at him.

Eli wasn't bothered. "As far as I'm concerned, the wedding can't come fast enough. There's nothing I want more than to make Aria my wife." He nodded to Davy. "You told me she was a good woman the night we met, and you were right. I'd do anything for her."

Mark was happy for Eli, but seeing him show so much emotion was somewhat shocking. "That's great, mate," he said. "I'm glad you're happy."

To his surprise, Gareth said, "I know where you're coming from. Now that I've got Avery back, it's like I'm really living again, you know? I'd do anything to make sure I never lose her."

"You're both mad," Davy said. "I love those girls like they're my sisters, but I can't imagine tying myself to one of 'em forever." He took his turn, sank three balls, and asked Mark, "What do you reckon, buddy? One woman for the rest of your life?"

A month ago, the prospect would have made him sweat, but now he considered it seriously. "Actually, I like the sound of that. Look at these two." He gestured at Gareth and Eli. "Don't they seem pleased with life?" He didn't need to look at them to know Eli's jaw had dropped and even Sterling had started listening. "If that's what love can do for a man, it doesn't look half bad to me."

In fact, it looked damned inviting, like an alluring mirage, just out of reach. If only he didn't know what he did about his own mortality. If only he hadn't overheard his mother's phone call all those years ago, after the heart attack that killed his father. The heart attack that may have had a genetic component. He'd never mentioned what he'd heard to Rose. She'd had enough on her plate without him piling his own worries on top. Instead he'd made the decision to live his life in such a way that no other people would be saddled with his problems.

Eli turned to Sterling. "Did you hear what he said, or am I imagining things?"

Sterling grinned wickedly, and Mark could hear the cogs rotating in his brain. "I did hear it," he agreed, "and after last night, I think I know which woman it is that has him dreaming of wedded bliss."

Mark covered his face with his hands. "No, Sterling. Don't do this to me, man."

Eli's spine went ramrod straight. "*Clarissa?*"

"You... want... *Clarissa?*" Gareth asked in a strange, choked voice. Davy elbowed him in the side. Both men turned red like they were holding their breath.

Mark shrugged. "She's intelligent, sweet, and beautiful. What's not to like?"

Gareth muttered something, and Davy burst out laughing, his barrel chest heaving so hard his eyes watered.

Mark's hands went to his hips. "What's so funny?"

Between whooping gasps, Davy spluttered, "Rissa. Likes. To. Slap. Men. Gareth, especially."

Instantly, and wholly unexpectedly, Mark's hackles were up, and the blood pounded through his head so loudly he couldn't hear anything else. He rounded on Gareth. Never mind that the other man stood several inches taller than him and was a good deal broader.

"What did you do to make her feel like she had to slap you?" he demanded.

Gareth's face was still red, and he held his palms up like a gun was pointed at his chest. "Nothing," he insisted, the redness creeping down his neck.

"You must have done something," he persisted. "She wouldn't have slapped you for no reason. She's not like that."

Sterling stared at him. "I've never seen you like this over a woman."

Mark ignored him and raised a questioning eyebrow at Gareth, who sighed. "She saves the slap treatment for men who hurt her friends. I upset Avery, and Clarissa can be like a mother bear when Avery isn't happy."

The tension seeped from Mark's shoulders, and for the first time, he noticed everyone was staring at him with equal parts shock and wariness. The attention made him uncomfortable. He leaned over the table and thumped his cue into a ball.

"Hey!" Davy cried. "It wasn't your turn."

He shrugged. "Oops."

Eli and Davy started arguing over exactly whose turn it was. Mark exhaled, relieved they'd refocused on the game, then checked his phone, for some reason hoping to find a text from Clarissa. Ridiculous, considering she didn't have his number. Disappointed, he looked up in time to see Sterling's knowing smile.

"Is this all of us?" the celebrant asked, looking around the group. He counted them off. "Bride, groom, five bridesmaids, and one, two, three, four—"

A car roared down the drive, and seconds later, a young man raced around the corner of the building, his dark hair flopping over his face. He skidded to a halt in front of Teri and dropped a kiss on her nose.

"Sorry, babe, practice went late and I didn't notice."

She flushed pink to the roots of her hair. "We're just about to start," she hissed.

"Ah, five groomsmen," the celebrant said. "Good timing."

They were assembled on the deck of a private function

venue overlooking the lake. The view took Mark's breath away. Rippling blue water extended into the horizon, framed by brown-green hills on each side. The lawn, which sloped from the deck to the water's edge, was spotted with pink and purple lupins—tall, bright flowers that spoke of new beginnings. Cherry blossom trees formed a beautiful backdrop along the side of the deck.

The celebrant stood no more than five and a half feet tall, with a wreath of gray hair surrounding a shiny domed head. He had fine-boned features and clutched a folder to his chest.

"Thank you all for coming to this rehearsal," he continued. "I'm Bill, the celebrant for Elijah and Aria's wedding. I'm here to keep everything running smoothly and make sure you have the best ceremony you possibly can. To start out, why don't we have the men form a semicircle, with Elijah at the head of the aisle, and the rest of you fanned out to the side."

Mark shuffled around to where the celebrant directed him, between Eli and Sterling. Aria's two brothers were positioned to Sterling's right, with Teri's boyfriend at the end. The boy had come from rugby practice and dirt smudged his face, which he wiped with his uniform shirt. Sweat glistened on his tawny skin, and he kept sneaking glances at Teri.

Mark hid a grin behind his hand. Ah, young love.

"Ladies," Bill said, turning his attention to the women. "We're going to start around the corner, where you'll be dropped off on the big day. When you come around, I want you to pause, smile, count to three, then keep walking. Take your time; it's not a race. Hold your hands like this." He set the folder aside and clasped his hands together, letting them hang a little below his waist, as if he were holding an imaginary bouquet of flowers. "That way, everyone can see your lovely dresses. The first of you to come out—who's that?"

"Me," Teri said.

"Fantastic. Teri, is it?"

She nodded.

"Teri will stand opposite the young man over here," he gestured to her boyfriend, "and the next bridesmaid will stand opposite Justin, and so forth, until we form another semicircle around to the bride. Now, can you each stand where you'll end up, so you know where to walk to in a moment's time?"

They arranged themselves as he'd instructed. The girls had decided to order themselves from tallest to shortest, with the exception of Teri, who wanted to be paired with her boyfriend. First was Sophie, then Evie, Clarissa, and Avery, with Teri on the outer.

"Good, good," Bill murmured, stopping to adjust Avery. "Perfect. In a minute, I'll send you all around the corner to practice the walk out, but first, we need to test run the handover of the bride between Geoff and Elijah. Aria, will you please stand over here"—he motioned a few yards away —"and link arms with your father?" They did as ordered, Geoff's eyes sparkling like he might cry. His chest puffed up, and he looked proudly down at his daughter, who smiled back and kissed his cheek.

"Okay, you two." Bill stood in front of them, his palms pressed together. "Take it slow, practice walking in time, and then, when you get near the altar, Elijah will step forward and shake hands with Geoff, then Aria can give her dad a kiss if she likes and link arms with Elijah for the last few steps. Take it away."

Mark had to give credit where it was due. The three of them managed a reasonably graceful exchange, and Bill was satisfied. He led the women around the side of the house, and Mark watched Clarissa's back as she followed, chatting with Avery, whom he'd deduced was her closest friend. Her hips swayed from side to side as she walked, the tips of her blonde curls bouncing where they rested on her lower back. She was all sensual movement and curves. The heeled boots elevated her legs from shapely to drool-worthy, and the dark denim of her jeans conformed to the contours of her rounded butt.

He swallowed and tore his focus from the bridesmaid to the groom, who'd said something and now was looking at him expectantly.

Mark ducked his head. Caught out. "Uh, can you repeat the question?"

Eli glanced from Mark to the retreating women and back again. His eyes narrowed. "Were you mooning over the bridesmaids?"

"Only one of them."

He grunted. "At least you're honest."

Mark shifted his attention back to the corner where the women would emerge. Seconds later, Teri stepped around it, striding awkwardly as if counting the steps in her head. She paused and smiled, although it was really more of a grimace, and crossed the landscaped garden, gradually increasing her pace until she stood opposite her boyfriend. Sophie followed, moving with athletic grace, then Evie bounced behind her with barely concealed excitement.

Finally, Clarissa came into view. Mark's chest seized when she smiled widely, and he realized it was the first time he'd seen her do so. The smile livened her face. Pink lipstick brought out the rosiness of her cheeks, and he wanted to kiss her mouth, nibble it until the lipstick had vanished.

Need for her sucker punched him in the gut.

Her gaze traveled around the arc of groomsmen. When her guarded blue eyes met his, the pink of her cheeks deepened. Immediately, she turned away to face her friends. It wasn't fast enough, though. He recognized the way her cheeks had flushed on an instinctual level. Whether or not she wanted to be attracted to him, she was. She might be wary and afraid to admit it, but if he took things slowly with her and made sure she was comfortable every step of the way, he had a chance.

Her face tilted toward him, and her eyes darted in his direction. They met his, and she snapped her head around. His grin widened. She'd been sneaking glances at him too.

8

He's seen me.

Clarissa cursed herself. The last thing she needed was for a man like Mark—handsome, smart, and a million miles out of her league—to get the idea she held a torch for him. Not when she didn't have what it took to be in a relationship. Especially not when he looked at her like he thought there could be something special between them.

Yeah, she wished.

They finished rehearsing and headed inside, where dinner awaited them. She shrugged into a sweater to ward off the chill and breathed in the scent of steak and some kind of garlicky sauce. Her mouth watered in anticipation. In the main event room, a long table was set with fourteen places, and silver cutlery lay on navy napkins.

"Clarissa."

She shivered. That rich tone filled her ears late at night, and she wanted to close her eyes and relish it the way it deserved, but that would be on the wrong side of weird.

"It's good to see you again."

A hand touched her shoulder. She flinched, and the hand retracted. Mark stepped around to face her, his lips curving in a cautious smile. "Eli said you spent yesterday making the wedding decorations."

"We did." She smiled and twirled a curl with her finger, but stopped the moment she realized she was acting like a flirty teenager. As a matter of fact, the last time she'd intentionally flirted with anyone, she *had* been a teenager. "It was really nice. I haven't relaxed with the girls in so long."

He laughed. The brackets that formed around his mouth and crinkles at the corners of his eyes indicated he laughed and smiled frequently—another reason she wasn't a good fit for him. "You consider that relaxing?" he asked.

She ducked her head sheepishly. She sometimes forgot that other people didn't live at the same hectic pace she did. "My idea of relaxing is anything that doesn't involve dealing with customers, designing dresses, doing finances, or marketing."

The brackets around his mouth deepened. "That's a broad range, then."

"Exactly." She kept her gaze focused on the table as Eli and Aria claimed two seats near its center. Mark took the seat to Eli's left, and Clarissa was so flustered she didn't think to look for the other women, she just sank into the seat beside Mark. A blond man was on her other side, and Eli's sister and her boyfriend sat opposite.

"Hi," she said to the blond man, because talking to him was easier than making sense of her feelings for Mark. "I'm Clarissa."

The blond shook her hand, his fingers cold against hers. "Sterling."

Up close, she could see Sterling's eyes were a cool blue to rival her own, and his cheekbones and jawline could cut diamond. He was handsome, in an icy way. She wondered how to open a conversation with him. She could hold her own when working with customers, but she rarely engaged in social outings, so her small talk skills were limited.

"Clarissa," Teri called from across the table and fluffed her hair, which she wore in a bob. "This is my boyfriend, Wiremu."

"Nice to meet you, ma'am," Wiremu said, bobbing his head.

She winced. *Ma'am?* Surely she shouldn't be a ma'am for another ten years yet. She bit her tongue to stop herself from issuing a sharp retort. No doubt he meant well. She wracked her brain for a conversation starter. "You play rugby?"

Wiremu's eyes lit. "Sure do. I play for the Mud Dogs," he said proudly. "Blindside flanker on the A-team."

"That's wonderful." Clarissa wasn't a sports fanatic, but she kept up reasonably well. Following rugby was a basic requirement of New Zealand citizenship. "The season must be almost finished, is it?"

He nodded. "We're in the final tomorrow. Then it's all over, rover."

"Good luck." A thought occurred to her. "Will you have time for the game before the wedding?"

He and Teri exchanged tense glances. It seemed she'd struck a nerve.

"The game is late morning, so I'll have time to play and shower before the ceremony," he muttered, more to Teri than Clarissa.

Teri shrugged one slender shoulder. "If you're not there on time, you know what will happen."

He grinned and received a scowl in return. "You'll gut me and feed my innards to the *taniwha* in the lake."

"And not lose a wink of sleep over it."

Clarissa raised a hand to cover her smile. Hard to believe she'd been that innocent once.

"Do you live in Itirangi, Clarissa?" Sterling asked, drawing her attention away from the young couple.

"No." She poured herself a glass of water, then one for him as well.

He took it. "Thanks."

"No problem." She looked around at Mark and was disappointed to find him deep in conversation with Eli. She turned back. "I grew up here," she explained, "but I live in Dunedin now. I run a bridal business."

A spark brightened his eyes to a sapphire hue that matched the smooth touchstone on the middle finger of her left hand. She ran her finger over its surface unconsciously.

"You're a businesswoman?" he asked.

"A businesswoman *and* a designer," she clarified. "I run a boutique that sells wedding dresses and accessories. Some of those I import or buy from other New Zealand designers, and some I design myself. I also make custom designs on request. I run the business, but I'm also the business's key asset, if that makes sense."

He leaned toward her, apparently fascinated. "How do you find the time? Running a business is all-consuming, let alone making the product as well. Do you have a partner?" He hesitated, then added, "Business or otherwise?"

She shook her head. "I have an assistant who manages the customers for me. He's a lifesaver. No partner, though. I get by because my apartment is in the same building as the boutique, so I never have to leave except to get groceries and exercise."

He nodded, as if dedicating herself solely to work was perfectly reasonable. His response was a pleasant change from most people, who thought she was crazy for condensing her life down to such a degree.

"I admire your dedication," he said, his touchstone gaze sincere. His appreciation warmed her. "It's a lot of work to build up a business. Are you having much success?"

Most people shied away from asking about her finances, but she appreciated his directness. "I do well for myself. Business is good. I don't have a waiting list because I prefer to only take on work I'm capable of doing without creating a backlog, but I could easily have one if I decided to change that policy."

"Do you think you ever will?"

She considered. "It's possible. Perhaps if I'm able to hire more help to be sure I could make everything happen. At the moment, I always deliver on my promises. The bride gets what she wants, on the exact day I promised she'd get it. That's my business model, and I won't do anything to compromise it."

Sterling stared at her like she'd announced she was an Indian maharajah. Not a muscle in his face moved.

"What is it?" she asked self-consciously, smoothing her thumb over the ring again.

"You're a very impressive woman." He cleared his throat. "I'm in awe."

"Thank you." The strength of his regard made her uncomfortable, but she was also flattered. Often men in the business world dismissed her as being a frivolous female who only made a profit because of the whims of other frivolous females rather than from any intelligence of her own. They saw her as someone to be condescended to in the name of gender equality, but not someone to be respected as an equal.

"It's clear what Mark sees in you."

She tucked a curl behind her ear, unsure how to respond. Instead, she dodged the comment, asking, "What is it you do, Sterling?"

"I'm the chief operating officer at Eli's company." Passion colored his voice. "I keep things running in the head office and do whatever needs to be done to make the company shine."

"I can tell you love it."

"I do," he agreed. "Business is my first love, and Eli took a big risk when he appointed me. I owe him everything."

"I'm certain you've done a superb job." She really was.

Sterling gave every impression of being a perfectionist. From the way he spoke to the way he dressed—in a pale blue suit and tie—to his filed fingernails and tidy hair. He'd demand success from himself and his staff. He couldn't be an easy boss.

Clarissa heard a sexy chuckle and resisted the urge to turn toward Mark. It was like he was a heat source, drawing her to him. She closed her eyes.

"Hey, are you okay?" Sterling asked.

"Yes, totally," she exclaimed, embarrassed to have been caught in a weak moment.

"Are you sure?" He didn't seem convinced.

She nodded. "I am. Just a little overtired from the last few days." As well as being emotionally overwrought from seeing her estranged sister and spending time around a man who made her want to be a different woman. But she couldn't tell him that, so she sipped her water and asked him another question about work.

With one ear, Mark listened to Clarissa and Sterling, who were engaged in an intense conversation, shutting out everyone around them. He was glad they'd found some common ground. When Eli started talking to him, he'd worried they'd sit side by side in silence, since Sterling wasn't exactly chatty and Clarissa seemed equally reserved.

He speared a piece of steak, shoved it into his mouth, and chewed as he strained to hear what they were discussing, but their heads were bent close together and they spoke in undertones, so the words may as well have been gibberish. He shouldn't be surprised they were getting along well. They had a lot in common, and they'd figured it out quickly.

"Mark?"

He smiled inanely across the table at Aria's mother, who'd

said something while his mind had been elsewhere, and was looking at him expectantly. Eli answered, saving him. Mark looked from Eli to Mrs. Simons and frowned, a question arising in his mind.

He waited for a lull, then asked, "When are your parents coming, Eli?"

Eli stiffened. "They're not."

Mark's jaw dropped. "Are you serious? But it's your wedding!" A couple of people looked over at them curiously. He lowered his voice and continued, "Why aren't they coming?"

A muscle in Eli's jaw ticked, and a vein throbbed at his temple. "Because they have reservations about Aria, and I made it clear, in no uncertain terms, that they should only come if they could give us their heartfelt blessing. Maybe we'll get there down the track, but we're not there yet."

Mark's shock turned to outrage. "How could they not approve of Aria? She's sweeter than spun sugar."

Eli nodded. "You're preaching to the converted. But let's not make a big deal of this. She's already upset about it."

Mark rocked back in his chair, its front two legs raising off the floor. "I don't blame her," he muttered. "That's rough."

"Better not to have them here if they can't behave. I don't want anything ruining the day for her."

"It's cute how she has you wrapped around her little finger."

Eli shrugged, unconcerned. "Can you blame me?"

"For loving a beautiful woman with a heart of gold? Not at all." In fact, call him crazy, but Mark envied his friend more with every passing day. He swiveled his chair toward Sterling and leaned in. Sterling raised a haughty eyebrow, but it was Clarissa's shy smile that really hit home. His chest compressed almost painfully.

"What are you two kids talking about?" he asked.

"Where we went to university," Clarissa said. "What we

studied, things like that." She turned to Sterling. "So you studied business at Auckland University?"

"That's right," he confirmed. "I won a scholarship, but I still had to work part-time to pay my way through."

Unlike Mark, who'd had a free ride courtesy of his mum. He suppressed the twinge of guilt that always accompanied discussions where his level of privilege was abundantly clear.

"I worked while I was studying too," she said. "At the Monkey Bar, one of the student pubs in Dunedin. Then, in my last year, I got a job as an assistant at the boutique I own now."

"How long have you owned it?" Sterling asked.

"A few years."

"You must have been young." Admiration was evident in the tone of his voice.

She nodded. "But I was ready."

"You studied business *and* design?"

"Yes."

Clarissa had won another admirer. Sterling was looking at her like she were a heretofore unidentified species. A new discovery he couldn't wait to investigate further.

Mark hid a smile behind his hand. "Interesting combination," he remarked.

She tilted her head to the side. "It's served me well."

"We can see that," Sterling said.

Mark felt proud of her. Why was that? Sure, she listened to his podcast, but she was single-handedly responsible for her own success. He had nothing to do with it. Nevertheless, he wanted to high five her under the table. It wasn't often that Sterling Knight was impressed by anyone.

"Mark," Eli said, stealing his attention.

Reluctantly, he turned, only to hear Clarissa's tinkling laughter. He wished he could have seen her expression, but he tried not to be annoyed at his friend for distracting him.

Eli looked bemused. "Did you eat something sour?"

"Nope," he choked, feeling like a jerk for being so obvious. *Get a grip.*

"Are you okay?" Eli asked cautiously.

"Just dandy." Mark forced a smile that came out as a grimace. "What was it you wanted?

9

*C*larissa hugged Aria goodbye and kissed her cheek. "Thanks," she said. "I had a lovely evening."

"The men didn't bore you?" Aria asked, concern written on her brow. "Or drive you nuts?"

She shook her head. "Sterling is great company. Very interesting to talk to."

Aria nodded. "I suppose you would think that. You both enjoy business. What about Mark? Did he behave himself? He can be a bit cheeky at times."

"Really?" Clarissa's brows shot up. "He's only ever been sweet with me."

"Huh." Aria blinked. "What d'you know? Good for him."

This was the opening Clarissa had been hoping for. "When you told me about his podcast, I didn't realize you knew him."

"Oh." Aria seemed surprised again. "Did I not mention that? Sorry, pregnancy brain. Sometimes things escape me. Do you listen to it?"

"Yes, every week. He knows his stuff."

"He's sharp," Aria said. "And a nice guy. Just a little overzealous at times."

Clarissa had seen no evidence of that, except perhaps for when he'd made it clear how much Rose's wedding meant to him, but that had been totally understandable, and more than a little sexy. So, too, had been the way he'd asked if he could call her that night. He'd taken her rejection in stride and been nothing but the perfect gentleman since. There were few men she could say that about.

"He's knowledgeable, and he has a way about him. He's never condescending. I like him."

"Oh my God." Aria's eyes narrowed, then widened, as if she'd had an epiphany. "You *like* him."

Clarissa shushed her and glanced around to make sure no one had overheard. "Shh, we're not in high school anymore. No one talks like that."

Aria giggled and didn't pay her any heed. "You and Mark. Wow."

"Nothing has happened," Clarissa hissed.

"But you'd like it to."

She didn't refute the statement. If she were going to be involved with a man, she would like it to be Mark. He was the only one who'd captured her interest since Heath Shaw, but she wasn't in a good place to be having a relationship, and no matter how much she liked him, she wasn't sure if she could trust him—not with the truth about everything.

"Riss…." Aria's smile slowly transformed into concern. "Be careful. Mark's a fun guy, but from what Eli has told me, he can be a bit of a flirt."

Clarissa shook her head. "I don't buy it. That's not the kind of man he is with me."

Do you really know what kind of man he is? A little voice in the back of her mind whispered. *You thought you knew what kind of guy Heath was. You thought you knew better than everyone else, and look where that got you.*

"Okay, just make sure you know what you're getting yourself into. I worry about you, all alone in Dunedin. You deserve someone in your life who makes you happy, but don't jump into something blind."

Clarissa swallowed her irritation. She knew how to look after herself; she'd been doing it for long enough. Besides, she wasn't about to throw herself at a man. Any man. But Aria meant well. She was a mother hen, that was all.

"I'll be careful." She smiled to lighten the mood. "I'll see you first thing tomorrow. Make sure you get your beauty sleep."

"If there's one thing I'm not going to do, it's sleep," Aria replied, rubbing her swollen belly. "This baby makes it really hard to get comfortable, but the makeup artist can layer the foundation on so thick no one will be able to tell."

"That's the spirit."

"Are you sure you're happy at the hotel?" It was the millionth time she'd asked.

"Yes, it suits me well." She didn't mind moving out for the last night before the wedding. She was used to hotel rooms, and she didn't want to add to Aria's stress level when what her friend really needed was a quiet night to herself. "Besides, it's Eli's hotel. I'm sure it'll be great."

"Not as great as staying with a friend," Aria muttered.

Clarissa ignored her. "I'll see you tomorrow?"

"Bright and early. Ugh, I'm so nervous."

"Everything will be perfect." She tugged on a light coat to ward off the nippy spring air, shoved the restaurant exit open, and started toward her car. She'd barely made it five steps when a shadow separated from the building and rushed toward her.

Instinctively, she ducked and spun away. Then she ran, her two-inch heels wobbling dangerously beneath her as she scrambled toward her car.

"Clary, wait!" someone called. A female. One who knew her old nickname.

Clarissa hesitated. "Who is it?" Her voice wavered, but she tried not to show fear.

"Stop running," the woman puffed, picking her way across the parking lot, coming into the light cast by an overhead lamp that reflected off her gold-blonde hair. "It's just me. Jen."

Just Jen.

There was no "just" about Jen.

Clarissa squeezed her eyes shut and heard a pathetic whimper. Had that been her?

It will be okay, she told herself. *Everything will be okay. You're a strong woman. Your family can't hurt you anymore.*

She forced her eyes open and reinforced her spine with steel. She glared at Jen the way she did a particularly determined suitor who wouldn't take "no" for an answer. It was usually enough to deter all but the densest of men, and her sister halted a few yards away. When the outside lights illuminated Jen's delicate features, Clarissa was tempted to bolt even though she posed no physical threat.

The sisters hadn't spoken in nearly ten years. After their parents cast her out like a stray dog, Jen had wanted nothing to do with her. Why was she here now?

"I have nothing to say to you," Clarissa hissed, backing away.

Jen crossed the space between them and grabbed her by the elbow, preventing her from escaping. "Wait," she repeated. "Just give me a minute of your time."

Jerking her elbow free, Clarissa stalked over to her car and got in. Jen was hot on her heels and tried to tug the door open, but she'd locked it. Safe in the car, Clarissa sighed. Tempted as she was to drive away and pretend this had never happened, she had a heart, and Jen looked ready to cry. Her sister knocked on the window, then pressed a palm to it.

"Please don't go," she said, loud enough to be heard through the glass. "Not like this. Not after all this time."

Cursing her own weakness, Clarissa opened the window. "How did you find me?"

She didn't like the thought that she'd been spied upon. It gave her the chills.

"Davy knew when and where the rehearsal was happening. He told me."

Bloody men. Clarissa gritted her teeth. They couldn't be trusted.

"Don't be angry at him," Jen said, reading her mind. "I practically had to torture it from him."

She doubted it. The friendly bartender was always up for a gossip. "What do you want?"

"A minute of your time. To talk to you. That's all. *Please*."

Clarissa shivered. She was freezing, and her fingers and toes were tingly and numb. She wound the window back up, opened the door and stepped out. Much as she'd have liked to blast the heater and stay in the warmth of her car, she didn't want to invite Jen inside. Doing so would make it that much more difficult to get away from her.

"Fine. You've got a minute. Talk."

Now that she had Clarissa's attention, Jen dithered, her mouth opening and closing soundlessly. Clarissa crossed her arms over her chest and stared at her sister. Jen had aged well. She'd been a gangly fourteen-year-old when Clarissa had last spoken to her, but she must be twenty-three now, give or take. She'd filled out, and her skin had cleared up, but there were stress brackets around her mouth and dark circles under her eyes.

For the first time since she'd been accosted, Clarissa felt a twinge of sympathy. Living with the weight of their parents' expectations couldn't be easy. Especially when Clarissa had borne the brunt of it up until she hadn't been around any longer.

She tapped her foot, and Jen wrung her hands, less sure of herself than she'd been charging across the parking lot thirty seconds ago. She'd always been better at actions than words.

"I know you hate me," she blurted, taking Clarissa by surprise. "I don't blame you. Sometimes, I hate me too. But I miss you. So fucking much."

At the swear word, Clarissa's arms dropped to her side, where they hung, heavy. The Jennifer Mitchell she'd known would never have sworn.

Jen caught her look and said, "Yeah, Mum and Dad would cut my tongue out, right? I don't give a shit. I don't live with them anymore, and they don't control me."

Clarissa nodded slowly. Jen was a grown woman. Of course she didn't live with their parents, but that didn't mean she was free of their influence. Emotional abuse and manipulation could be so insidious that you didn't even notice it was happening until suddenly everything turned upside down and inside out and you didn't know which way was up anymore, or whether your inner compass pointed due north.

Jen let out a long, rattling breath. "You don't believe me." Her lower lip quivered. "I can't blame you for that either."

Clarissa fished for something to say. *Anything.* But her chest was so tight she didn't think she could squeeze words from it without passing out.

"Clary, talk to me."

It was the nickname that prompted her to respond. She hadn't been called "Clary" since she was seventeen.

"Don't call me that," she snapped. "You can call me Clarissa or Rissa, but not Clary. Clary was a weak girl, and that's not who I am anymore."

Jen looked stricken. "I'm sorry. I didn't know."

Clarissa sucked in a breath. Of course she didn't. How could she? Clarissa was being cold and unreasonable, but she couldn't help it. Jen's betrayal had hurt so much more than her parents' because they'd been friends. She'd never even given Clarissa a chance to explain.

"That's okay," she said slowly. "But I've got to go now." In truth, she did need to check into the hotel before reception closed for the night, but she felt a pang when a tear rolled down her baby sister's cheek.

Jen shoved a piece of paper into her hand. "I understand. This is my number. Please call me. I don't care how long it takes."

Clarissa nodded. Her ears had fogged over, and it sounded like she was speaking through water when she said, "I'll think about it."

Jen's lips curved up, ever so slightly, into a hopeful smile. "*Thank you.*"

The gratitude in her voice made Clarissa uncomfortable. She lifted one shoulder nonchalantly, as if to say it meant nothing. A lie, and they both knew it.

"Goodbye," Jen whispered. "We'll talk later."

"See you." Clarissa didn't add "later." She didn't want to make a promise she wasn't sure she could keep. She climbed back inside the car, shut the door, and watched Jen in her rearview mirror until she disappeared out of sight.

MARK AND STERLING sat in Sterling's room on the ground floor of their company's hotel, atop a hill overlooking Lake Itirangi. A set of French doors at the end of the room opened onto a manicured lawn shared by all of the guests. The curtains were open, and they occupied armchairs, looking out into the growing darkness. Mark clasped a low-carbohydrate beer, fresh from the chiller, and Sterling drank from a similar bottle with a slice of lemon wedged inside the top.

"This place turned out pretty well, didn't it?" Mark remarked, for the sake of conversation. Sterling could withdraw into his mind and happily remain there for hours if no one else took the initiative.

"It did," Sterling agreed. "And it brings in good money."

Trust him to think about the bottom line. Mark simply enjoyed the beauty of the location. He'd rarely stayed anywhere so peaceful. Truth be told, he rarely left Auckland. Perhaps he should change that. From what he'd seen of the South Island over the last few months, it was wild and gorgeous.

He glanced over at Sterling. His friend seemed reflective, perhaps more so than usual. "Did you enjoy your company at dinner?" he asked, wanting to gauge Sterling's opinion of Clarissa.

"Very much." A smile touched his stern lips. "Clarissa and I had an excellent conversation about different business and management styles. She's an extremely intelligent woman. Has some brilliant theories."

"She is," Mark agreed. "She's beautiful too."

"Yes, she's conventionally pretty, but I'm more interested in her brain. It's not often I find someone whose passion for work rivals mine." He glanced at Mark. "Does that ease your mind?"

Mark laughed. "Am I that transparent?"

Sterling rolled his eyes and didn't deign to answer. Mark considered his friend's choice of words. *Passion*. He'd certainly like to see Clarissa's passionate side. Would she channel that same passion for business and design into the other aspects of her life? He pictured her pink lips, ready to be kissed. Imagined how it would feel to embrace her and have her rest her head on his chest, over his pounding heart. God, he *longed* for that. How was it possible to be so crazy about a woman he'd only met a handful of times?

"Mark, are you okay?"

He twitched in surprise. He'd zoned out. "Yes, of course. Why wouldn't I be?"

Sterling studied him suspiciously. "You went for a good couple of minutes without talking. I'm concerned."

Mark grumbled and shook the cobwebs from his brain. "I'm fine. Sometimes I need a moment to think, the same as anyone else. You're right, Clarissa is an intriguing woman, and I'm interested in her."

Sterling nodded. "She'd make a good life partner."

Mark stared out the glass doors into the dark. Sterling was 100 percent right, despite his unromantic way of thinking. The man who ended up waking beside Clarissa every morning would be a lucky one indeed.

"I've never seen you hesitant around a woman," Sterling said. "I have to say, I like it. The unflappable Mark Talbot, uncertain about how to proceed."

"What would you do?" Mark asked, not expecting him to have an answer since, as far as he knew, Sterling rarely—if ever—dated.

But his friend surprised him, saying, "If I found a woman like her, and if I thought I had a chance, I'd do everything in my power to spend more time with her and make sure she knew exactly how I felt. That's not the kind of thing you want to have any ambiguity over."

"You're right," Mark said, stunned to find he was buoyed by the pep talk. "I shouldn't waste my time mulling it over." With renewed energy, he leapt from his chair and shrugged into a sweater. "I know she's staying here, and I'm going to go find her."

"Wait," Sterling called after him. "It's getting dark out."

But Mark didn't listen. He had other things on his mind.

10

The lake shimmered in the moonlight, the reflections changing in intensity as clouds drifted across the lake. A breeze ruffled Clarissa's hair, curving it around the side of her face. She tucked a lock of it into her jacket to keep it out of her eyes, adjusted her scarf, and inhaled deeply, relishing the perfume of spring blooms that was carried on the wind. Her eyes fluttered shut, and she inhaled again, savoring the scent.

You don't get this in the city.

Being in Itirangi stirred a host of unpleasant memories—sharp fear, shame, the memory of angry words exchanged, and finally, a loneliness like she'd never known before—but despite that, the town was beautiful. Even with her history, she believed it to be the most beautiful place in the world. And, yeah, she'd experienced her lowest moments here, but she'd also learned the strength of her friendships and the mettle of her spirit.

She sniffed the air again. It smelled like home.

A heaviness settled over her heart. Home or not, she couldn't stay here long. Too many ghosts roamed the streets. Her hands trembled, and the dim light cast by her e-reader wobbled. She crossed her legs and propped the e-reader on her knee, so she didn't run the risk of dropping it.

"Penny for your thoughts."

She squeaked. Her heart leaped to her mouth, and she jerked in response to the voice, then thanked the stars she'd had the forethought to put her e-reader in a secure spot.

"You scared the living daylights out of me," she said to Mark, who'd emerged from the shadowed lawn to her right. Technically, the spot where she was sitting, just outside her room, was a communal area, open to all guests on the ground floor, but she hadn't seen anyone since she came outside and hadn't expected to.

"Sorry, that wasn't my intention."

"What are you doing out here?" Her lips wanted to form a smile at the sight of him, with his tousled hair and faded sweater that may have been red once but now could be more accurately described as dusky pink. She liked that he wasn't afraid to wear it anyway.

He shrugged one pink-clad shoulder. "To tell the truth, I was hoping to run into you."

"Oh." She was grateful for the darkness, which hid the blush she was certain stained her cheeks. What was she supposed to do with a statement like that? Most men, in her experience, would have invented a reason for being in the area, then tried to press their company upon her. She wet her lips. "Why did you want to see me?"

His head dipped forward, his dark hair falling over his forehead and casting his eyes into shadow. "Because I like spending time with you."

Again, his honesty disarmed her. She studied the lower half of his face, all that she could see from this angle. Was it her company he liked, or did he hope she'd fall into bed with him? No matter how much she'd fantasized about him over the last few months, that would never happen.

"I'm actually quite tired. It's been a long few days. I'm enjoying spending some quality time with a good book."

He glanced at her e-reader. "I can relate. It's been full-on. Do you mind if I join you?"

"As long as you don't mind that I'll be reading," she said, waiting for him to realize there was no hope of getting her naked, but also crossing her fingers that he wouldn't prove himself to be a one-track-mind kind of guy.

He disappeared into the darkness, and her stomach sank, but then she heard a scraping sound, and he returned, dragging a chair. "Don't worry, I won't disturb you. I'll be quiet as a mouse."

She snuffled and hid her smile behind her hand. Something in the vicinity of her chest fluttered. However much Mark might try to fade into the background, she didn't think it was possible to *not* be aware of him on a molecular level. He had one of those presences that demanded attention.

"Was that a laugh I just heard?" he asked, a dimple popping in his left cheek as his mouth hitched up. The hollow in her chest filled with fizzy warmth because of that dimple. One man shouldn't be so endearing. It wasn't fair to the female gender.

"Just picturing you as a mouse," she said. "Now that's an image I can't get out of my head."

He looked alarmed but didn't say anything more, just withdrew his phone from his pocket, messed around with it for a few seconds, then slouched back into the chair and studied its screen.

Curiosity got the better of her. "What are you doing?"

He turned the screen toward her so she could make out the small text displayed across it. "Reading. Isn't that what we're doing here?"

She leaned closer, trying to make out the text. "What's the book?"

"*Romancing the Duke* by Tessa Dare. It's absolutely enchanting."

Her jaw opened and closed like a goldfish, and her eyes probably bulged enough to resemble one too. Finally, she got command of herself. "Is that a historical romance?"

If her voice sounded strained, she could hardly be blamed. She'd never met a man who read anything other than crime thrillers, science fiction, literary fiction, or non-fiction. This was yet another way he was unlike any of the other men she'd known. His handsome outer shell hid a romantic soul.

"It is," he said, almost gleefully, as though delighted by her shock. A little too delighted. She frowned, reevaluating. Was he excited about his book, or was he playing her? Was this how he picked up women—by pretending to be a romantic? That didn't seem like the Mark she was getting to know, but if she'd learned one thing in her life, it was that she had bad judgment when it came to the opposite sex.

"Most of the books I read are romances," he continued. "They're escapism of the purest kind." For a moment, his eyes turned serious, but the darkness lifted as quickly as it appeared, and she wondered whether she'd imagined it. He pointed to his phone. "Shall we?" Then he promptly started reading, leaving her no option but to do the same. She waited for him to interrupt the silence, or to say or do anything that might be construed as flirting, but he seemed to be absorbed by his story.

For a long while, they read without speaking. It was strange. This was what Clarissa had asked for, but she hadn't expected him to abide by her terms. Being with a man like this, peaceful and quiet, was something she hadn't experienced before. She found herself wanting to set her e-reader aside and converse with him, but doing so would be hypocritical when she'd insisted on reading in the first place.

After an indeterminate amount of time had passed, he rose and pocketed his phone. "Good night, Clarissa."

"You're going?" she asked, oddly disappointed.

He nodded.

"Okay, I'll see you tomorrow." She paused, weighing her words, still unsure of his intentions or what his angle was. "I enjoyed reading with you."

His smile softened. "I did too. Thank you for allowing me to stay."

"I'm glad I did. Have a good sleep and make sure Eli is at the altar."

"I will," he replied. "You just make sure he has a bride walking down the aisle."

They waved, and she watched his retreating back, not sure how or when Mark Talbot had managed to turn her world on its ear, nor having the faintest clue how she felt about it.

MARK STOOD at the end of the aisle, waiting for his woman to come around the corner. Well, not his woman per se, but the one he intended to have, if she were amendable. He shoved his hands into his tuxedo pockets and wondered how she'd look. They hadn't been allowed to see the women's outfits before the wedding and he didn't know what to expect.

The groomsmen had, however, been color-coordinated to match them. Mark's tie was deep green, which meant that Sophie, the bridesmaid he'd been paired with, must be wearing green. Adjusting his stance, Mark spread his legs wider for comfort. They could be waiting for a while. Hopefully, Aria would be a punctual bride. He rolled his shoulders back and smiled at the guests.

Over two hundred of them.

Aria's family, Eli's extended family and friends from

Auckland—his parents notably absent, and half the township seemed to have turned up. Justin's girlfriend, Emily, sat in the front row beside her in-laws. On her other side, a fragile-looking woman with a stern expression and droopy cheeks reclined in a wheelchair.

There were too many guests to fit on the deck, so several loitered on the grass, and half a dozen small children frolicked amongst the flowers in the garden. Mark smiled, even as his heart ached. He'd never have a child of his own. Never be among the ranks of parents who kept a watchful eye on their sons and daughters as they played. He'd never have the opportunity to dress his own little boy in a miniature tuxedo and struggle to keep him from getting dirt and food stains all over it.

He'd known this since he was only a boy himself, but it never struck as close to home as when he was surrounded by happy families, confronted by the very thing he couldn't have but desperately wanted.

He tore his attention from the children. It would do him no good to dwell on them. Today was meant to be a happy day. A day to celebrate his friend's commitment to his partner.

Next to him, Eli shifted impatiently. "What if she doesn't come?"

Mark patted his shoulder. "She's crazy about you, and she's having your baby. She'll come." This was his first time being best man, but from what he could tell, his job was to keep the groom at the end of the aisle and make sure he didn't faint from nerves. Oh, and to look after the rings, which were burning a hole in his chest pocket. "In half an hour, she'll have another of your rings on her finger, and it will all be done. Won't that be nice?"

If only his mother could hear him now. How she'd roar with laughter. He was sadly unequipped for this scenario.

Justin leaned around Mark and called, "Perhaps she finally came to her senses and decided to make a run for it."

Eli stiffened.

"He's joking," Mark soothed, shooting a scathing glare at the bride's brother. "Aria loves you."

Eli rubbed his temples. Beads of sweat were forming under his hairline, though it wasn't particularly hot outside. Finally, the procession music started.

Teri rounded the corner, looking pretty in a baby blue dress with a floaty skirt that brushed her knees as she walked. She held a bouquet of forget-me-nots interspersed with delicate purple rosebuds. Mark heard her boyfriend's rapid intake of breath as he saw her, and the young buck straightened his shoulders and puffed out his chest. Rather than stop where she'd been told, Teri sped up to a trot as she neared them and kissed Eli on the cheek.

"I'm so happy for you guys," she whispered.

Eli kissed her forehead. "Thanks, Teri."

She hurried back to her spot before the celebrant—whose face had reddened dangerously–burst a blood vessel. Avery came next, crossing the distance between the drive and the deck in long strides that were made possible by a loose-fitting purple dress. Like Teri's, it ended at her knees, but unlike Teri, Avery's hair curled loosely over her milky-white shoulders. She held a bouquet of purple rosebuds and soft pink gerberas. Mark recognized them because Rose had poured over bouquets in bridal magazines in his living room on more than one occasion.

Finally, Clarissa came into view, and he released a long, slow breath. If an asteroid had plummeted to Earth, he couldn't have torn his eyes away. She wore a light pink dress that caressed her curves and fell in a curtain to her calf. The bodice displayed a gorgeous breadth of cleavage, which he longed to run his hands over, and a cluster of gerberas and daisies brushed the underside of her breasts. The dress flattered her pale complexion, bringing out the roses in her cheeks. Her blue eyes seemed almost luminous, and her hair had been artfully gathered on the side of her head with tendrils spilling over her shoulders.

He heard murmurs in the audience as others recognized how beautiful she was. He'd always known it. As if he'd summoned her attention with his thoughts, her intense eyes met his and held. On, and on, and on. He could drown in the depths of her gaze. Then she smiled, and his heart danced a jig.

The other guests turned away as the next bridesmaid emerged, but he couldn't. Not until Evie passed Clarissa, blocking his view. She wore a tight gold cocktail dress and carried a bouquet of daisies and green roses.

Last was Sophie, in a sleek green gown that fell to her ankles, her feet in silver sandals that had a three-inch heel. Her strawberry blonde hair was drawn back into a sleek arrangement on the rear of her head, and she clutched green and white roses to her lower belly.

The assembled crowd turned as one to watch the bride make her entrance, but Clarissa, he noticed, looked the other way. At Eli. The oddity of this prompted Mark to sneak a peek at his friend. Eli wore the most stupidly happy, genuine smile he'd ever seen. So wide it risked splitting his cheeks. His eyes shone with wetness, and he blinked back tears as his bride ambled toward him.

In that moment, Mark knew. Eli was really, truly happy. He felt the kind of love for Aria that filled a man up and spilled over into the world around him, coloring everything red and gold. His expression prompted within Mark a desperate desire to experience that same overwhelming emotion for himself.

He turned away to watch Aria's grand entrance. A ray of sunshine glinted off a jewel in her hair and reflected light in his eyes. He lifted a hand to shield himself. Then, as Geoff looped arms with his daughter and escorted her the final steps to her future husband's side, an invisible hook seemed to lift Mark's worries from his shoulders, leaving him nothing but hopeful. He smoothed a hand down the front of his jacket and straightened his shoulders, the lightness in his chest making him feel as if he could float away into the blue sky amongst the fluffy clouds that hovered overhead.

Surely if Eli, one of the least emotionally available people he knew, could find his happily ever after, there was a chance for Mark as well, regardless of his concerns about his troublesome genes.

Unbidden, he sought out Clarissa, only to find her already looking at him. Hesitantly, he smiled, not his usual broad grin designed to charm everyone, but a small, personal smile, meant only for her. Her lips curved in return, and the breath caught in his chest. God, she was so beautiful it hurt to look at her, but at the same time, he wanted to drink her in and memorize every tiny detail.

The celebrant began an introductory speech, and they had to break eye contact. When the celebrant had finished, he invited Teri to recite a poem. Her lips trembled as she stood before them, and she adjusted her hair several times but delivered the words in an even voice, stealing glances at her boyfriend for reassurance.

When the poem was over, she kissed Aria on the cheek, and Mark heard her murmur to her brother, "Beat you to it."

Cheeky girl.

Then it was time for the vows. Eli went first. He took Aria's hand.

"Aria, I never knew a love like this was possible until I met you. After today, I'll be proud to call you my wife."

Aria's eyes sparkled, and she bit her lip. Mark crossed his fingers that she'd reign it in, or he might cry too.

"From the first time we met," Eli continued, "I knew you were different. You drove me crazy—you still do—but in the best possible way. I've been happier in the past months with you than in all the years before. You help me be a better person. A stronger person."

Mark sniffed. For stoic Eli, this was positively gushing.

Eli cupped her cheek in his palm, and they shared a tender moment, as if unaware that anyone else existed. "I promise you that I will always be faithful, and that I'll do my best to be worthy of you. I promise to take care of you, the way you take care of everyone else, and that you'll never be alone again. You mean everything to me."

Aria whispered something in response, then touched a finger to her lower eyelid, delicately wiping a tear away. She cleared her throat. "Elijah, I'm so glad I met you. It might not have been love at first sight." A woman in the audience coughed at this, and her friend thumped her on the back, but Aria continued, unabashed. "It was certainly lust at first sight."

Evie giggled. Mark winked at her. To his astonishment, she winked back, her top eyelid shimmering gold. In another life, he might've followed up on that saucy wink, but today all he wanted was to watch Clarissa and bide his time.

"After a while," Aria said, "I started to see what a special guy you were." At this, Justin chuckled. She ignored him. "You're sweet and thoughtful. You want the best for every-one. And I can't believe you're actually mine."

"Forever," he interrupted.

She smiled and agreed, "Forever. I promise to be faithful and try every day to deserve you. I promise to tolerate your stubbornness and hug you when you get cranky. I promise to be yours. I love you."

The celebrant gestured to Mark, who handed over the rings, fumbling them in the process.

"Do you, Elijah Russel Lockwood, take Aria Eleanor Simons to be your lawfully wedded wife?"

Eli leaned toward the microphone. "I do."

Aria slid the wedding band onto his finger.

"Very good. Do you, Aria Eleanor Simons, take Elijah Russel Lockwood to be your lawfully wedded husband?"

Her lips moved but no sound came out.

"I beg your pardon?" the celebrant asked, his lips twitching with amusement.

"I said, 'I do,'" Aria replied, so loudly Mark winced. She clapped her hand over her mouth, eyes wide. "Oops."

Eli slid the ring onto Aria's finger, raising it to kiss the knuckle. She blushed ferociously.

The celebrant spread his arms wide. "I now pronounce you husband and wife. You may kiss the bride."

With that, Eli swept Aria into his arms and dipped her into a low embrace. The crowd roared its approval. Mark clapped. Cooper hooted. Evie nudged Sophie with her elbow and said something in her ear. Clarissa just watched like a proud mama. He wished he could go to her, sweep her off her feet, and kiss her senseless, as Eli had done with his bride. But this wasn't the place, and now wasn't the time. They'd get there soon enough.

In short order, the newlyweds and Aria's parents went to sign the wedding register. Evie claimed the microphone and sung an awe-inspiring rendition of Mariah Carey's "With You." Her rich voice hit the notes so perfectly he shivered, and he wasn't the only one. Two rows from the front, Davy had fixated on Evie like he'd never seen or heard anything more stunning. The raw wanting painted across his face made Mark feel like he'd invaded the man's privacy simply by looking.

Clarissa, who was also watching Evie, nodded her head along to the tune. He wondered whether she liked to sing and what sounds she would make if he kissed her, or if he sank into her wet heat.

Whoa, slow down, boy. He shook himself. *Not a good time to get excited.*

It was easy to get carried away at weddings, but he didn't want a temporary hookup with Clarissa. He wanted something more, and that meant being patient. The song finished, and he clapped enthusiastically.

Then, with the grandeur of a monarch presiding over a royal gathering, the celebrant called, "Ladies and gentlemen, I give you, Mr. and Mrs. Lockwood!"

The married couple joined arms and made their way down the aisle. Mark followed on Eli's heel, offering his arm to Sophie, who accepted it with a smile but glanced back over her shoulder at Cooper, who was escorting Clarissa. They reached the gravel, and Mark released Sophie. She teetered across the distance to Aria and threw her arms around her friend.

"You did it!"

Mark's chest grew tight with emotion. He was a sucker for weddings. Cooper passed him, without Clarissa on his arm, so Mark went in search of her.

---

*W*hen the strums of Ed Sheeran's song "Thinking Out Loud" began, Eli took Aria's hand and swept her into a waltz. Clarissa watched them with a smile. After a few beats, she saw Sophie and Mark whirl onto the floor. He moved like he owned the room. His charcoal tux and green tie suited him to perfection, and his unruly hair had been combed back from his face, leaving every wonderfully symmetrical feature exposed. Clarissa watched Sophie with a green-eyed devil perched on her shoulder.

A hand touched her elbow, and a large body moved next to her.

"Shall we show them how it's really done?" Cooper asked, his chest rumbling against her arm.

She nodded, feeling a little like Sophie looked: awkward and out of place, but she couldn't deny she was excited to dance. She'd taken lessons until senior year and, while she didn't do it often, had the urge to put those years of lessons to use. Her foot was tapping along to the beat. Despite that, she hesitated. She knew that Sophie could be insecure and didn't want to make her uncomfortable by dancing with her boyfriend.

"Stop that," Cooper admonished.

She glanced up in surprise. "What?"

"You look like you're trying to solve the world's problems in your head. It's just a dance."

"Okay." He was right, of course. She let him take her hand and steer her onto the floor. They started the simple steps of a waltz. One, two, three. One, two, three. For a large man, he moved gracefully. They rocked back and forth, and the rest of the bridal party joined them, one couple at a time.

"Have you enjoyed yourself today?" Cooper asked.

"Yes," she replied. "It's been lovely. I'm so glad everything worked out well for them."

"They deserve it," he agreed. "Although, if Eli ever hurts her—"

"I'll slap him," she said firmly. "Never fear."

He laughed, the sound sharp, like she'd taken him by surprise.

"Same goes for you," she continued, while she was on a roll. "If I hear Sophie is anything other than blissfully happy, I'll be paying you a visit."

He raised an eyebrow. "How much have you had to drink?"

"Not that much," she assured him. "I'll remember this conversation."

He chuckled. "I never knew you were so evil. I remember you being the quiet, pretty one."

Clarissa stepped closer to him to avoid being knocked into by a couple spinning out of control behind her. "Don't mistake quiet for shy or timid."

"Noted."

The song ended and another began. Cooper dropped Clarissa so fast it would have upset her if he hadn't instantly attached himself to Sophie, displacing Sterling, who'd been about to claim her hand. She smiled at the display of possessiveness, and her smile widened as Sterling looked around, disgruntled and confused. When he saw her watching, she held out a hand, indicating that he should join her. Relief washed over his angular features.

"Don't be offended," she called over the music when he drew near. "Those two can't be separated from each other for more than five minutes."

"I see." He clearly didn't see, appearing even more confounded than before. "Would you like to dance, Clarissa?"

"Yes, very much."

A light weight settled onto her hip as he laid a hand there, and his fingers were cool against the curve of her neck. He maintained a respectable six inches of space between their bodies. His steps were more wooden than Cooper's, but at least he knew where to put his feet to avoid treading on hers. They shuffled around the floor, between the other couples.

"How long are you staying in Itirangi?" she asked, studying his firm lips and high cheekbones, wondering why they didn't make her heart sing. He was undeniably handsome and had attracted appreciative looks from many of the female guests, but all she saw was a man she could talk business with. An interesting man, but not one to make her stomach flutter and her palms tingle.

"I'm flying home tomorrow evening," he said.

"Home being Auckland?"

They twirled together, slightly out of step.

"That's right. What about you?"

"I'll be driving back to Dunedin tomorrow afternoon, so I'm there to open the shop on Monday."

He cocked his head. "Don't you have someone else who can do that?"

"Yes, my assistant is more than capable, but I've already been away for a few days, and I need to get back." She bit her lip. "I'm kind of a control freak."

He didn't laugh. In fact, when she chanced a look at him, he was nodding. "Me too. The company can run itself without me, but it doesn't feel right being away."

"Exactly."

He smiled and appraised her from head to toe as they swayed. "You're a fascinating woman, Clarissa. And beautiful."

Uh-oh, was he about to hit on her?

"I should be attracted to you."

She spluttered.

"I meant no offense," he said hurriedly.

"None taken," she wheezed. "I was thinking the same thing about you a few moments ago."

"But there's no spark."

She made a face. "None at all. No hard feelings?"

They came to a standstill as the music ended. "Of course not. I hope we can be friends."

She smiled shyly and stuck out her hand. He shook it. *A male friend.* A man she could discuss business with. She'd never had one of those before. Mark was the closest she'd come to that, and it wasn't friendship she felt for him, much as she might like it to be.

"My turn." Mark's voice near her ear made her jump. Speak of the devil.

"Don't I get some say in that?" She sounded breathy. Excited. The darkening of his eyes told her that he hadn't missed it.

He held his hand out with the confidence of a man who already knew her answer. "Dance with me, Clarissa."

She worried her bottom lip, not wanting to fall into his arms like a silly girl, even if that's exactly how she felt. Heavens, but he looked decadent in a suit. Several curls flopped roguishly over his forehead, and his teeth were especially white when he smiled. Gone was the professionally distant man of the podcasts and livestreams, the man she was comfortable daydreaming over. This man, with his strong, lean shoulders and lithe movements, was all predator. Not a bear or a lion, but a sleek leopard, and like a gazelle entranced by his golden eyes, she laid her hand in his and let him whisk her away.

"Aria looks gorgeous tonight," he said as he pulled her into a cozier embrace than either Sterling or Cooper had. Their torsos brushed against each other as they moved to the rhythm of the music.

"She does," Clarissa agreed.

"Your dress does her justice."

She rolled her eyes. "You don't have to flatter me."

"You deserve the compliment." His tone was sincere. Eager, even. "I can't wait to see what you do for Mum."

She liked this, liked how earnest he was. And, heck, the fact they were pressed together and she could feel just how firm his torso was didn't hurt. She hadn't been this giddy in, oh, ten years, give or take. She almost felt like her old self.

Concern tapped at the corner of her mind, but she pushed it back. Tonight she didn't want to worry over the past or the future. She was tired of always worrying. Tonight, she wanted to enjoy herself and her pleasant company.

"It astounds me that you can conjure something so magical from your imagination," he continued.

She lowered her eyes, focusing on his chest, to mask her flush of pleasure. "Thank you. It's taken a lot of work to get to a point where the end product actually resembles what I could see in my mind. There were a lot of disasters along the way."

"I refuse to believe that. You and I probably have an entirely different opinion of what constitutes a disaster."

Taking one hand, he twirled her, and when she returned to his embrace, she found herself plastered to him, their lower bodies swaying rhythmically against each other, mimicking the actions of lovemaking—or at least how she assumed lovemaking would be.

She swallowed, her mouth suddenly dry. Her nerve endings were on fire, and what was worse, she didn't know if it was his doing or hers. Had she been the one to thrust her body forward? She could well have been, with how many dirty thoughts were rioting through her mind. All of them half-baked fantasies because she had nothing to base them on besides the romance novels she no longer read.

Their dance was the complete opposite of her earlier one with Sterling. Mark smashed her personal space to smithereens and spun her in circles, her skirt swishing around her knees. Where Sterling's grasp had been light, the heat from Mark's palm singed her as it rested on the small of her back. His other hand traced a path from her shoulder up to cup her cheek. Body heat emanated from his chest and enveloped her. His breath stirred her ear, and then his cheek grazed hers. She gasped, and his fingers dug into the softness of her hips.

"You smell amazing," he murmured, rubbing his cheek on hers lazily, like a big cat scenting her. "What is that?"

Oh God, was this actually happening? She was high on his presence. She wanted more, *needed* more. She felt warm inside, deliciously intoxicated by his pheromones. She could stay this way forever. And maybe he was high on her too. What else would explain the way he was sniffing her like she was a scented candle.

"Ylang ylang," she whispered, suddenly shy.

His breath hitched, then he groaned, almost inaudibly. "I love it."

Unfamiliar heat pooled between her thighs, and she pressed them together, seeking relief. "Um-hmm." *Eloquent, Rissa.* "I use it in my bath. It helps with stress."

He sighed. "That's a detail I could have done without."

She stiffened, even as her mind remained languid. "What

do you mean by that?"

He squeezed his eyes shut, his eyelashes casting shadows over his cheeks, and he swallowed. "Just that I'm trying to be a good guy, and now I'm picturing you in the bath. It doesn't help."

"Oh." Had she thought she'd been high on him before? That was nothing compared to the exhilaration that thrummed through her bloodstream when he admitted to having the kind of thoughts about her that she was having about him. Did he also want to know how she'd taste? How it would feel to have no barriers between their skin?

She drew from her stockpile of courage, summoned the bold girl she'd used to be, and said, "I don't mind."

Now it was his turn to stiffen. His eyes flew open and locked on hers. "You don't?"

She didn't blink. Didn't look away. At that moment, no one else in the room mattered. It didn't even matter that the song had changed and people were swapping partners and forming groups. She weighed her next words carefully. She hadn't let a man close enough to hurt her in a long, long time, but she liked Mark, and she wanted him. Perhaps, with time, she could trust him too.

"No," she whispered, stretching onto her toes until their lips were only millimeters apart. "I don't." She wet her lips and hesitated before adding, "I might even like it."

Air whistled out between his teeth. His chest heaved, and his eyes glittered with promise. She couldn't believe she'd had that effect on him, that *she* was the focus of this gorgeous man's undivided attention.

"I want to kiss you," he told her. "So badly. But this isn't the right place."

"It's a wedding. Where could be better?"

He shook his head. "Not while everyone is watching. You deserve more than that."

Someone jostled him from behind, and he bumped

forward into her. Suddenly, the noise she'd tuned out filtered back into her awareness. People, music, colored lights. She ducked her head, breaking eye contact. He was right, this wasn't the time or place, and she was ashamed she'd nearly forgotten that.

"Hey." He hooked a finger beneath her chin and gently raised it. "None of that. I hear a salsa track starting. I don't suppose you know how to salsa?"

She collected her scattered thoughts and focused on that one simple question. "I could dance circles around the other girls in my Latin dance class when I was younger."

His eyes lit with interest. "Oh, really?"

She nodded, relieved that their crash back to reality hadn't ruined whatever this connection growing between them was. "Really."

"I'd like to see that."

"You think you can keep up?"

He laughed. "You're full of surprises, Clarissa."

"Rissa," she corrected. "That's what my friends call me."

"*Rissa.*"

She liked the way her name sounded in his mouth.

"I didn't do dance lessons, but my mother made sure I know my way around a salsa." He stepped back and held out a hand. She set her palm against his and took the first few steps, trying to remember the next moves. Many of the dancers evacuated the floor, and she hesitated, unused to being the center of attention, but she held Mark's gaze and pretended he was the only person in the room.

After a faltering start, muscle memory kicked in and her arms and legs moved as though she'd practiced salsa every day for the past three years. He matched her perfectly, and tension crackled in the air between them. She panted with exertion as the tempo sped up, and his pupils dilated in response.

The music built to a crescendo. They twirled around each

other, and he spun her again and again, touching her each time she passed him, sending bolts of awareness rippling through her. Friction fanned the flames between them. Finally, the song came to an end.

Their gazes caught. Electricity pulsed. People clapped, but Clarissa didn't hear. All she saw were Mark's lips moving as he said, "Come with me."

He led her from the dance floor, between the tables, into the foyer, and opened the door to the coatroom, tugging her inside. She closed the door behind them, laughing from the thrill of the dance and from being dragged into a private room by the sexiest man at the wedding. Her laughter stopped abruptly when he drew her close to him, tucked a loose curl behind her ear, and rested the side of his hand against her cheek. She closed her eyes and turned her face into his palm.

"You're remarkable," he murmured. "If nothing has changed from when we first met and you want me to leave you alone, just say the word and I will, but if you feel this thing between us as much as I do, I'd really like to kiss you now."

This was the moment. Make or break. She knew what she should say, but she couldn't voice the words. She surrendered to her desire. Allowed herself to indulge for once in her life. She prayed it didn't end the same way as last time.

"Please kiss me."

Their lips met in an explosion of sensation. She buried her hands in his hair and tugged him closer, tasting the wine he'd drunk when his tongue brushed along her mouth. Tentatively, she met his strokes with her own. He deepened the kiss, clasping her tighter.

On and on it went, each kiss more drugging than the last, until she had to pull back, gasping for air. Her breasts rose and fell as she tried to catch her breath. He panted heavily, her lipstick smeared on his lips. Reaching over with her thumb, she wiped the lipstick off, a pulse thumping low in her core when he sucked her thumb into his mouth and softly bit the pad.

She stared, wondering how she had ever thought he was merely handsome. He was, without a doubt, the single most breathtaking man she'd ever seen. The first man to kiss her in over a decade, friendly pecks on the cheek notwithstanding. He released her thumb, and she pulled it free with a pop.

"Wow," he said, shaking his head. "Just *wow*. That was…. You are…."

"I know what you mean." She shuffled back until she was far enough away from him to think clearly. "What now?"

He frowned. "What do you mean?"

She fought the urge to laugh like a loony tune. She had no clue what came after a kiss like that. Did this mean they were dating? If so, how would that work when they lived in different cities?

Panic fluttered in her chest. Did he expect her to go back to his room with him now? Was that what usually happened when women kissed strange men in closets?

Or did all of this mean nothing? Was it a single moment of insanity to be enjoyed and nothing more?

"I don't know," she moaned, sounding as agonized as she felt.

"Hey," he said softly. "Hey, now. Relax, Rissa." He wrapped his arms around her, loosely enough that she could break free if she wanted, and rested his cheek on the top of her head. "What happens now is entirely up to you. But if you're open to suggestions, we could head back, dance a little more, and each get a good night's sleep in our own room. I like you, but I'm not in the business of rushing women into things they're not ready for. We can talk more in the morning."

She sagged against him, grateful for how he was handling this. "That sounds wonderful."

$\mathcal{M}$ ark entered the breakfast hall the morning following the wedding, already smiling. The sun was up, and he'd fallen asleep with the memory of Clarissa's taste on his lips. What could be better?

He waved to Eli, who was sprawled like a king on a love seat, his new wife tucked into his side. "Good morning, Mr. and Mrs. Lockwood."

"Hello." Aria beamed. "You're very chipper this morning."

"I'm always chipper." He glanced around the room, taking in the other guests, all of whom had been at the wedding because Eli had booked out the hotel's breakfast hall for the wedding breakfast. A flicker of white in the corner of his eye had him turning his head.

Clarissa.

She was fixing herself a plate of bacon and eggs, adding a Danish pastry on the side, looking fresh and lovely in a blue dress with a white cardigan, her hair loose around her face, not wearing any makeup. He could have sworn he heard angels sing at the sight of her. He was going loopy, and he wouldn't have it any other way.

He snagged a plate from the side table and wandered over

to her, pausing just behind her to clear his throat, not wanting to give her a fright. He'd noticed she could be a little jumpy.

"Hey, there." As far as lines went, it wasn't original, but he simply didn't have the brain capacity to come up with something better when it was all he could do not to plant a kiss on her, right here in front of everyone.

"Hi, Mark."

Okay, so neither of them were winning awards for originality, but the way her mouth softened and her eyes warmed as they landed on him more than made up for it. Her expression said, "I'm happy you're here." He hoped his expression appropriately reciprocated the sentiment.

"Save me a seat?" he asked, and she nodded. He piled food onto his plate and followed her. She sank into a chair beside Evie, who had bed hair and a pale complexion, and opposite Avery, who was engaged in conversation with Cooper. Mark claimed the empty seat to Clarissa's right and smiled at her.

"Beautiful morning, isn't it?" he said, digging into a mountain of scrambled egg.

"Anyone would think you're a romantic, with how damned cheerful you are," Evie muttered, drawing circles in her cereal with a spoon and looking worse for wear. "Think you could talk a little quieter?"

"Oh, sorry." He lowered his voice. "Rough night, huh?"

She shrugged one shoulder and buried her face in her hands.

"She drank too much," Avery said, breaking away from her conversation with Cooper but looking unsympathetic. Evie didn't lift her head, just raised the middle finger of one hand. Avery rolled her eyes and turned back to Cooper.

Mark leaned toward Clarissa. "I had a great time last night," he murmured.

She kept her focus on breakfast, but her face went pink.

"So did I," she said. "Although I could definitely have danced you under the table."

He laughed, pleased she was comfortable enough to tease him. "We'll have to have a rematch this time next month. Give me some time to practice my moves."

Evie dropped one hand and glanced over at them. "You two really need to work on your dirty talk. My neighbor's goldfish could do better than that." Clarissa's jaw dropped, and Evie yawned and covered her mouth. "Sorry, I'll butt out now. You guys just go about your business."

Mark and Clarissa exchanged glances. Clearly a private conversation wouldn't be possible here.

"Do you want to get a coffee and go for a walk after this?" he asked, holding his breath as he awaited a response. She'd said he could call her last night. Had she really meant it? Would she let him into her life this time around?

After what seemed an eternity, she said, "Yes, that would be perfect."

~

CLARISSA WAS SO FAR out of her depth, it was laughable. She'd dated exactly one man in her life, and that had been for a few brief weeks in high school. Back then, she hadn't done anything to earn Heath's attention. She'd been a pretty girl with a well-developed chest, and all the boys asked her out. She never said yes, because her parents would have freaked out if she'd brought a boy home.

But none of those boys had been on Heath's level. He was the captain of the first fifteen rugby team, broad-shouldered, popular, and handsome. Other girls at school would have sacrificed a limb to be in her position, and she'd been flattered to be singled out, so she'd said yes. Big mistake.

She rubbed the touchstone ring and stopped herself from venturing further down memory lane. The point was, now that she was faced with a man she was interested in, she didn't know how to act or what to say. Rejecting men wasn't something she enjoyed, but she knew how to do it. Encouraging them was another matter entirely.

How did one express to a man that she found him attractive or that there was a chance they were compatible without outright saying it? Because saying it was out of the question. Unless he said it first. She could probably manage to respond in kind.

So it was with a great deal of trepidation that she made a coffee in her travel mug and left the relative safety of the breakfast hall with Mark. She clasped the coffee in both hands and steered them away from the public outdoor areas, along the lawn toward the end of the building. One of the rooms that opened onto this lawn was hers, but she wasn't sure which.

"My plane leaves in a couple of hours," he said, with obvious reluctance. "I wish I could stay longer, but I've got to get back to work."

"Me too," she said, glad for the easy opening. She swallowed the lump in her throat. "You'll keep in touch?"

His eyes met hers, and they stopped walking. "If that's what you want."

"It is," she croaked. "But only if it's what you want too." She bit her lip. Listen to her. It was bad enough that she felt like a scattered schoolgirl, but now she sounded like one too.

"Clarissa." His lips tugged up, and his expression was amused. "Are you trying to ask if I want to see more of you?"

"Yes," she admitted, grateful he'd been able to interpret her silly stammering.

His smile grew, and he set his coffee cup on the lawn, balancing it carefully, then took hers and did the same. When their hands were free, he held both of hers in his. "I would very much like to call you. That hasn't changed from the night we met in Dunedin. And I wasn't kidding about that rematch. I want to see you again. In person. Soon. What do you think of that?"

Her lips twitched as she fought a grin. "I think I can live with that."

"Great." He released her and fetched their coffees. "It's settled."

Her heart hammered, and a breath eased out between her lips. Was it actually that easy? Or had it only been easy because this was Mark and he seemed to be able to read her mind?

They resumed strolling, and she smiled into the distance, gazing out over the turquoise lake and the green hills on the horizon.

Yes, she decided, it was all Mark. He was special, and while she may not know how any relationship between them would work when the Cook Straight and several hundreds of kilometers separated them, she did know that when he called, she'd pick up. For the first time, she felt hopeful for the future—not just in her professional life, but her personal life too.

"What's that massive smile for?" he asked.

She shook her head. "Nothing, I'm just happy."

"Me too." He transferred his cup to one hand and held the other out to take hers. The slide of his warm palm against hers was glorious. His fingers were long and lean but strong. "Can I kiss you again, Rissa?"

She didn't reply but stretched onto her tiptoes and pressed her lips to his. That was all the answer he needed.

Leo swept through the boutique door, bringing the delicious smell of coffee with him. "A hazelnut trim latte and a spinach frittata for the best boss in the world." He laid his gifts on the counter, hurried over to Clarissa, who'd just emerged from her office, and squeezed her.

"Guh," she gasped. "Can't breathe, Leo."

He rocked her back and forth. "I'm so ecstatic to see you. Please never leave me again. I need you here. The world ceases to make sense without you."

Despite the overwhelming weekend, she laughed. "That might be the nicest thing anyone has ever said to me." When he didn't release her, she added, "You can let go now."

"Thirty more seconds."

She counted them down in her head, while he clung to her like a limpet.

When he finally backed off, he asked, "So how'd the nuptials go? Was the dress divine? Were there any handsome single men?" He must have seen something in her expression because he clapped and exclaimed, "There *were*. Tell me. I want to know everything."

She hesitated, preferring to keep her emotions private, but with the look in his eye, she knew he'd pester her until she told him whatever he wanted to know. "You remember Mark Talbot?"

"You mean Lawyer McHottie?" he asked, his eyes going wide. "Don't tell me he was there."

"As a matter of fact, he was."

He gasped. "How, what, when, where, why? Also, drink." He grabbed the coffee and thrust it into her hand.

"It turns out that he works for the groom. He was best man at the wedding."

"That must be the world's biggest coincidence or one hell of a message from fate."

"*Or* not a coincidence at all," she said. "The bride was the one who recommended his podcast to me, but she failed to mention she knew him."

"Ah, I see." The puzzlement faded from his face, replaced by disappointment. "I was so hoping for fate."

"Don't be so glum. It was actually really nice to see him again."

"After you shot the poor guy down last time."

She rolled her eyes. "Who I date, or don't date, is my business."

"I know." He sighed. "But I don't want you to end up alone in a granny flat with twenty-seven cats."

"I'm allergic to cats."

He threw up his hands. "There's no hope for you."

She felt bad for teasing him, but it wasn't often she had juicy gossip he wasn't privy to. "Here's the thing. We danced, and then we kissed, and then…." She trailed off suggestively and chuckled at the way his face went slack.

"*Then?*" he demanded, impatient.

She shrugged. "The weekend ended."

He groaned and dragged a hand through his carefully styled hair. "You're torturing me. Please say you arranged to see that delicious hunk of man again."

She grinned. "He's going to call."

"Yusss!" he crowed, tapping out a happy dance with his feet. "Praise the Lord, my girl has got some game."

She didn't join his celebration. She was optimistic, yes, but she didn't want to get too carried away. That would no doubt lead to disappointment.

When he'd finished his dance, he said, "Seriously, though, I'm so proud of you for putting yourself out there, boss lady."

Her chest squeezed, and her eyes watered. "Thanks, Leo." She wasn't sure if she was truly ready to dip her toes into the piranha-infested waters of the dating world, but she was considering it, and it was nice to have her bravery noticed.

She cleared her throat. "So, did you run into any problems while I was away?"

"Nothing I couldn't fix." He went to the counter and speared a fork into her frittata.

"Hey!"

"Friends share." He chewed defiantly. "Did you doubt me?"

"Of course not. I just wanted to know if there is any work I need to tackle immediately."

He swallowed and waved the fork in the air. "We have two new clients for custom dresses and half a dozen brides who ordered dresses off the rack."

"Fantastic. Timelines?"

"No rush jobs." He set the fork down. "Now, no more distractions. I want to see the photos."

She'd expected he would and already had them open on her phone. She handed it over and watched as he skimmed through.

"What a gorgeous bunch," he said, pausing on a photograph of the bridesmaids. "You're the stunningest, of course, but the others are knockouts too."

"I don't think 'stunningest' is a word."

"Oh, shush. I just invented it. Say, who's this sexy creature?" He pointed at one of the photos with his fingertip.

"That's Evie. And, yes, she knows she's a ten."

"How could she not? Even I want to do her." He stopped again, studying a shot of the entire bridal party. "The bride looks flawless in that dress. Not that she could possibly be anything but." He tilted his head, moving from Aria to Eli. "She did well for herself. That's one handsome fellow, all dark and commanding. Which of these men are her brothers?"

Clarissa took the phone and zoomed in on Cooper and Justin. "Those two."

"Huh. She got all the 'tiny' genes in the family, huh?"

"Her brothers are enormous."

"Single?"

"No." She zoomed out again. "The blond one is dating Sophie, the bridesmaid nearest the bride, and the other is dating the florist who made the bouquets."

Leo nodded and peered at the flowers. "A talented

117

woman, weaving together all of those different colors so effectively. Who were the other two groomsmen?"

"One was the groom's sister's boyfriend, and the other was one of the groom's friends."

"Was he as charming as Mr. McHottie?"

"No." She didn't even have to think about it. Much as she liked Sterling, there was no comparison. "Not charming, but very interesting. He's the chief operating officer of a business, so we had a lot to talk about."

"Oooh." Leo's eyebrows waggled. "Any sparks?"

"Not a single one. The only sparks were with Mark." A fact that frightened and excited her in equal measure. She sipped the hazelnut latte, enjoying its sweetness and the fact that she hadn't even had to leave the building to get it. "Thanks, by the way. You're amazing."

He grinned, dimples forming. "I know. So what is it about McHottie that makes you want to shed that invisible chastity belt you've been carting around since I met you? Besides the obvious, of course."

She swallowed and set the latte down, her throat suddenly too tight to drink any more. What *was* it about Mark that made her want to throw caution to the wind when no other man had roused more than a flicker of her interest? She considered her answer carefully, and Leo pinned her with deep brown eyes that were similar to Mark's, but so different too.

Leo knew what a big deal it was for her to even think about letting someone into her life. He was encouraging her, but she sensed protectiveness concealed beneath his breezy attitude. He wanted the person she eventually fell for to be the right one, almost as much as she did.

"He's patient," she said, her tongue sticking to the roof of her mouth, which had turned dry. She didn't like to talk about this type of stuff, but Leo was her friend, and outside of Itirangi, she didn't have many of those. "He's kind and gentle. Maybe it comes from being raised in a house full of women, but he's sensitive without being a pushover. I like that."

"He must be smart too," Leo added. "Surely that's a prerequisite for getting a law degree."

"He is," she agreed, still exploring exactly what it was that made her want to moon over Mark. She sighed. "To be honest, a lot of it probably stems from listening to his podcast, watching the livestream, and interacting with him by email. When I met him, I felt like I already knew him. Not all of him, obviously, but my heart told me he was a good person. I don't usually spend enough time with men to feel that way." A thought occurred to her. "Did I tell you he walked me home one night?"

"No." Leo leaned forward, expression eager. "What happened?"

She didn't want to tell him the full story and have to explain her complicated relationship—or lack thereof—with her family, so she paraphrased. "We ran into each other at the local bar. I wanted to head home early, and he didn't want me walking alone at night, so he went with me right up to my friend's door, then turned around and left." She smiled at the memory. "He's a gentleman." Though he'd been less than gentlemanly when he'd kissed her. She pressed a hand to her cheek to mask the blush spreading over it.

"Oh, my." Leo fanned himself. "Are you sure you want him? Friends share, you know."

She laughed, grateful for the reprieve from her tumultuous emotions. "You can share my frittata, but that's where I draw the line."

"I suppose I can live with that." He took her hand and doodled a heart on the back of it with a marker. "Are you going to give him a fair chance?"

"I want to." She tapped her lower lip, her insides quivering with uncertainty. "But I'm not 100 percent sure I trust him yet. Anyway, how would it work? I'm down here, and he's up in Auckland. But…." She trailed off.

"But?" Leo prompted.

"I really like him," she admitted in a small voice.

He squeezed her hand. "Then be the brave woman I know you are and give him the chance to woo you before you go letting the details get in the way."

"I'll try," she said, then repeated it more firmly. "I'll try to channel you. You're not afraid to go after what you want." And she didn't want to wake up one morning, cold and alone, overcome with regret. She just hoped her judgment had improved from when she was seventeen.

"That's my girl." He patted her cheek and released her. "Let's get to work. There are brides who need to look fabulous."

13

_____

$\mathcal{M}$ark rehearsed what he wanted to say to Clarissa under his breath. He swung around to face the office window, the midafternoon sun in his eyes as he waited for the call to send. After ten rings, it went to voice mail. *Damn.* She must be busy. He floundered as he heard a beep.

"Hi, Rissa," he said, exhaling on a rush of air. "It's me, Mark. I'm calling, just like I said I would." *Brilliant strategy, stating the obvious.* "It was great to spend time with you this weekend. I wish we'd had longer together." He cringed. Did that sound too clingy for how long they'd known each other? Oh well, too late to take it back. Besides, it was the truth.

"Are you at work today? I'm sitting in my office at the moment. It's a lovely day up here, but I've been run off my feet this morning. Sterling has his pants in a twist about a property he wants to buy, and he's decided to make it my problem too. All my other work built up while I was away. I suppose it's the same for you."

He was an addle-headed idiot, having a one-sided conversation with an answering machine. *Wrap it up, Talbot.* "I, uh, well, I suppose I'll—"

"Mark?" The voice caught him off guard. He hadn't noticed her pick up.

"Hey!" he exclaimed, blood rushing to his cheeks, which were no doubt a violent shade of crimson. "I thought I'd missed you."

"I could tell." A smile warmed her tone. He tried to focus on the positive. At least he amused her. "I was busy with a client, but I got back to my office just as you were leaving a message."

Turning to the wall, he knocked his forehead against it. *Dolt.*

"How are things today?" he asked, desperate to change the topic. "Was everything as you left it?"

"More or less. And you? I know how your day has been, but what did you do after you got home last night?"

He loved that she sounded genuinely interested. Like she wanted to know the minutiae of his life. "I had a quiet night. Needed to recover from the weekend. It was just me, a book, and a couple of fingers of whiskey."

"Sounds blissful."

He laughed, taken aback. "A lot of people would call that boring."

She sighed. "Not me. I'm an introvert, and I like my quiet time. We should probably get that out in the open now."

As if that would put him off. "Rissa, sweetie, I know who you are, and if that were a problem, I wouldn't be talking to you, so put your mind at rest."

He thought he heard her exhale softly. A sound of relief? Or was he imagining things?

"Which book?" she asked, clearly done talking about herself. "Was it the one you were reading the other night?"

"No, I finished that on the plane and started a new one. *A Rogue by Any Other Name* by Sarah MacLean. I'm not totally sold on the hero yet. He's behaved pretty poorly so far, but I have faith that he'll pull through. Sarah always writes a good story, and I adore her heroines." He paced by the window and gazed out over Auckland, the familiar towers and the harbor behind them all. "What do you like to read?"

"Crime thrillers," she replied. "Police procedurals, mostly. Some mysteries and psychological suspense, but I prefer the ones where I know the bad guys will be put away in the end."

He gaped, then pulled himself together and clapped his mouth shut. That answer did not gel with the mental image he was building of her.

"I'd never have expected that," he admitted.

She chuckled, apparently not offended that he'd stereo-typed her reading material. "Most people don't. I used to love the classic romances. Mansfield Park, especially, but I don't read them anymore. I don't like the way they build up expec-tations to a standard that real life can't possibly live up to."

His brows drew together. It sounded like something had happened to disillusion her with romance, which wasn't particularly surprising given how reticent she'd been with him, but he disliked the thought of any man hurting her. In fact, while he wasn't prone to violence, he'd happily do harm to anyone who'd made Clarissa feel less than perfect. He wanted to ask about this theoretical man from her past but didn't want to push too far too soon. If he frightened her off, there was very little he could do to win her back, so he held his tongue.

"How about movies? What's your favorite?" Before this conversation, he'd have guessed *Dear John* or something else based on a Nicholas Sparks book. Now, he had no bloody clue.

She didn't answer for a long moment. "Promise not to laugh?"

"Cross my heart." How bad could it be?

"It's *Underworld*."

It took a moment for his brain to process this. "As in,

vampires and werewolves locked in an eternal battle, terrible special effects, bucketloads of blood? That *Underworld?*"

"You said you wouldn't laugh!"

He didn't, but it was hard. "I'm not laughing, I swear." He sucked in a breath. His stomach ached from the effort of controlling his laughter. "You love *Underworld.* That's, uh, totally understandable. I know, um, people who—"

"I know it's ridiculous," she muttered, saving him from digging himself into a deeper hole. "That's part of the reason I like it. It's a form of escapism."

He'd never heard gory horror flicks described that way before, but if it worked for her, who was he to disagree?

"Your turn," she said, her tone verging on petulant. "What's your favorite movie? And if you say *Underworld*, I'll know you're lying."

"Fine." He had no problem sharing. "It's *Titanic.*"

"And *you* judged *me*? There was plenty of room on that door for both of them."

"Hey," he cautioned, "I didn't say anything about the dubious science of vampires. Let me have Rose and Jack's tragic love story without bringing your logic into it."

The cell phone on his desk, which was reserved for work use, vibrated. He went over and checked the screen. It was Sterling. He sighed, if he didn't take this, there'd be no living with the boss.

"Sorry, Rissa, I have a call on my other line. I've got to go."

"Oh, okay then."

A stupid grin spread over his face because she sounded as reluctant to end the call as he was. "Can I call again tomorrow?"

"Sure," she said, quickly enough to be considered eager. "But evening would suit me better. Can you call after eight?"

"Absolutely. Have a wonderful day."

"Bye, bye."

He ended the call and picked up the other phone, raising

it to his ear. "No, Sterling, I haven't acquired that property yet."

Sterling grunted. "Keep working on it."

"Yes, sir." He saluted in the direction of his friend's office, regardless of the fact that no one could see. Then he looked up the name of the woman he needed to persuade to part with her beloved piece of land in order to appease his boss. Katarina Hopa. Poor Katarina had no idea what was coming to her.

~

"HI, GORGEOUS."

Clarissa smiled when Mark's greeting filtered through the phone. "Hi, flatterer."

It was Sunday, a week after they'd last seen each other, and Clarissa adored Sundays. They were her one day free of customers and business concerns, when she could embrace the creative aspect of her job. She was sitting cross-legged on her apartment floor and had been leafing through a stack of the latest bridal magazines, snipping out images of dresses or accessories that captured her imagination, when Mark had called. At present, she was surrounded by photo clippings, the center of her spartan living room in disarray.

"Am I interrupting anything?" he asked.

She put the phone on speaker and set it on the coffee table beside her. "No, I'm just doing some industry research. I can keep going while we talk."

"Oooh, that sounds interesting. What does 'industry research' involve for a wedding dress designer?"

"It comes in lots of different forms," she hedged. "But at the moment, I'm cutting and pasting designs I like into a brainstorm notebook."

He chuckled. "You're doing arts and crafts?"

She bristled, but he wasn't far off. "And I suppose you're

using your Sunday more productively?" If she sounded snippy, so be it. She knew he was teasing, but she was used to people belittling her work, and she wasn't about to take it on the chin. Not from him. Not if she wanted to build a relationship with him based on mutual respect, and she thought maybe—just maybe—that might be where this was going.

"On the contrary, I rolled out of bed an hour ago, had a coffee and a shower, and all I plan on doing later is making a trip downstairs to the gym." He hummed, a deep, contented sound. "I might not even leave the building. Oh yeah, and I've got a podcast to record. Will you be listening?"

"Of course. I hope you answer the question I sent. I much prefer hearing you talk to me during the livestream to reading an email after you're done."

"And why is that?"

It was her turn to laugh. "Why do you think? I like the sound of your voice, and I like seeing your face and knowing you're thinking about me, even if it's only peripherally." Saying these things to him was easier when she couldn't see him. It removed the visual barrier, making her confession seem safer.

A beat of quiet followed her statement. "Have you always felt that way?"

She shrugged, then remembered he couldn't see her. "Maybe."

"Clarissa," he said, his voice rumbling from low in his chest. "I need you to be completely honest with me."

She nibbled her lip, hesitant to agree without knowing what he'd say next. "I'll do my best."

He needn't know her fingers were crossed behind her back.

"Before we met, when I was just some guy you listened to online, did you have a thing for me?"

She squirmed and contemplated hanging up, but that would be childish. "Just a little one."

"Clarissa Mitchell. You had a crush on the teacher."

She blushed ferociously. "Okay, okay, I did. Stop tormenting me."

He was instantly serious. "I'm sorry, I didn't mean to upset you. I go a little too far sometimes."

"It's fine," she replied. "I'm just embarrassed."

"Don't be. It's sweet."

Sweet. Exactly how she wanted him to think of her.

"Easy for you to say." The words were out of her mouth before she could stop them.

"What do you mean?" he asked.

Fantastic. Let's see you wiggle your way out of this one, Rissa. "Erm. Just that you've probably got a lot of experience with women, and things like that don't faze you. I haven't had many boyfriends." Understatement. "It's hard for me, getting close to someone. Opening up. Sharing things like a silly crush."

"It's not silly," he said. "And sure, I've dated my fair share of women, but each person is different, and none of them has been you."

Her downturned lips twitched up. How was it that he knew just the right thing to say?

"Thank you." She swallowed. "I've just…." She trailed off, then tried again. "The experience I do have, it made me a little wary. I don't trust easily. You might have to be patient with me."

"It sounds like you've had the wrong men in your life, honey, but I can absolutely give you whatever time and space you need to work through things. If you want to talk, I'm here for that. If you fumble sometimes, I'll never think less of you for it. I'm guessing you wasted your time on an idiot who wasn't worth it, and I want to show you that not all men are like that. Is that all right with you?"

She nodded. "Thank you." She spoke so low she wasn't sure whether he'd heard her, but she carried on. "I don't know what I've done to make you interested in me, but I want you to know that I don't take it lightly." She screwed up her courage and forced herself to continue. "You mean something to me, and even if nothing more happens between us, I want to thank you for being so kind."

It cost her a lot to open up, but a weight lifted off her shoulders. She'd been so repressed for so long that letting go of some of the things she kept tight to her chest was as freeing as it was terrifying.

"It's no hardship at all," he said, and she thought his voice sounded gruffer than before. "You're the kind of woman who makes a man want to better himself."

If only that were the truth.

"You're clever and humble, and you deserve all the goodness the universe has to offer," he went on.

If he kept going, she might cry. "Thanks."

"Who was he?" Mark asked. "The man who hurt you."

Her heart sputtered like a backfiring engine, and she went cold. "I can't tell you that yet."

It would take more than a week of phone calls and a couple of kisses for her to air out that particular baggage.

"No pressure. You tell me when you're ready."

She exhaled roughly, but didn't say anything. They shared the silence, and she listened to his even breathing, waiting to see if he'd make the next move. When it became clear he wanted her to do so, she shook off memories of the past.

"Mark?"

"Yes, honey?"

She grabbed the double-sided tape and focused on cutting it into even lengths. "It seems only fair that since you've complimented me, I return the favor."

"I'd like that."

She turned a couple of cutouts upside down and added bits of tape around the edges. If she distracted herself enough, perhaps she wouldn't notice how much she was splaying herself open, putting herself out there, with the potential of being shot down.

"I like the sound of your voice. I like how professional you are with your podcast, and how much you go out of your way to help people. I like that you dote on your mum, but maybe my favorite thing about you is that you have a good heart."

"Thank you," he said softly. "Your good opinion means a lot to me." He was quiet for a moment, then added, "You know what else? Most people would say I'm too close to Mum. They don't understand it." His voice was thick with emotion.

She ignored the tightening in her chest. "I do."

Because she'd never had that bond, but she'd wanted it. She'd been the rebellious daughter. The constant disappointment. The mess her parents needed to fix. If she'd had the bond with her mother that Mark had with Rose, she'd have held onto it for dear life.

"Speaking of Mum," he said in a lighter tone, "how's her dress coming along?"

She latched onto the change of topic, eager to cast aside her increasingly gloomy thoughts. "It's fantastic. We've agreed on the final design, and I sent it to one of my seam-stresses to begin work. I'm so excited for her. I hope the wedding is everything she's dreamed of."

"I'll make sure it is," he assured her. "She deserves the best."

"Why?" The question blurted out, and only when she heard herself say it did she notice how rude she sounded. "I mean, every woman deserves a special day, but it seems like there's a particular reason you want Rose's wedding to be perfect. Why is that?"

Twenty seconds ticked by, and she begun to think he wouldn't answer, but then he did, in a most unexpected way.

"My dad died from a heart attack when I was twelve. He was young, and the doctors weren't sure why it happened."

"I'm so sorry," she murmured, her heart hurting for him.

"Thanks. Anyway, Mum raised my sisters and me alone after that. She was a working, single parent, and we weren't exactly angels. It can't have been easy, but she did it anyway. She put herself through law school as an adult. Life never handed her anything, but she would've given us everything that was in her power to give. That's why I want to do whatever I can now to make things good for her."

Clarissa sniffed. "That's so sweet." Her voice sounded watery to her own ears.

"Are you crying?"

"No." She sniffed again. "Maybe a little. She sounds amazing, and I think it's wonderful that you appreciate her."

"Well, uh, thanks." She could tell she'd taken him by surprise again. "Tell me about your parents."

And just like that, her constricted throat threatened to suffocate her. The flow of her tears ceased. "Another time."

Preferably, never. Her parents weren't a suitable conversation topic when trying to impress a man. If she told him the truth, she might scare him off. Either that, or he'd pity her. Neither option appealed. She needed to change the subject. Fast.

"Has the hero in your book redeemed himself yet?"

*T*onight.

Mark was going to ask her tonight. He and Clarissa had been speaking every day for more than three weeks, and by now she might be open to his idea. Their phone calls had morphed into long evening conversations on FaceTime, so they could see each other face-to-face and talk properly, without either one of them needing to hurry off to a meeting or appointment.

When he arrived home from work, Mark changed into his running clothes and pounded out ten kilometers on the treadmill in the gym. Then he showered, munched on a chicken salad, and poured a glass of wine. By that time, it was past eight. Clarissa would have made her way upstairs to her apartment and eaten whatever tidbit Leo had saved for her. He sipped the wine and topped it up, needing fortification. Then he FaceTimed her.

"Hi, you."

Her smile and the fondness in her voice made his palms sweat and his heart pitter-patter madly. With how much he'd battled to get past her initial barriers, he hoped he was reading her correctly when he guessed she'd take his suggestion well. He didn't want to damage their fledgling relationship.

"Hello, sweetie." *Baby steps, Mark. Work up to it.* "Did you encounter any bridezillas today?"

She laughed, the sound like tinkling bells. "No bridezillas. They were all lovely."

"You make it easy for them."

"And you're buttering me up. I thought we'd passed that stage."

He'd meant every word. She didn't seem to realize that brides responded well to her because they could tell they had her complete attention and that she wanted to bring their dreams to life. Having been the subject of her focus, he knew it was heady. Addictive.

"You haven't seen flattery yet." He had plenty to say about her clear blue eyes, sweet pink mouth, and the impertinent tilt to her chin, but he sincerely doubted she wanted to hear it. Compliments about her physical appearance seemed to make her uncomfortable. He'd discovered she preferred to be recognized for her business savvy or her personality, which only served to make her more likable.

As if she needed help in that department. Sure, she was a little distant at first, but she was like a coconut, all sweet nectar on the inside once you cracked the outer shell.

"Clarissa," he said, exhaling long and slow.

"Yes?"

He gathered his courage and took a sip of wine to wet the inside of his mouth. "I'd like to see you again. In person. Can I fly down and visit this weekend?"

A furrow formed between her brows, and she cocked her head. "You want to stay with me?"

Ah, shit. Had he miscalculated? Her frown would indicate so. Should he back down? Rescind the offer? *No.* Everything inside of him rebelled. He wanted to see her again. Badly. He

132

wanted the chance to hold her. To kiss the spot at the base of her neck and find out whether it was as soft as it looked.

He nodded. "Yes, I do."

"Okay."

"You—wait. Okay?"

"Yes," she said simply, showing him a glimmer of white when she smiled. "You can stay with me. I think I'd like that. Just don't expect any intimacies. I'm not there yet."

"I'll sleep on the couch, or even book a hotel room if it makes you comfortable," he said. "You've made me the happiest man. I'll buy the flights tonight." Before she had time to talk herself out of it. "If I let you know my arrival time, can you pick me up from the airport?"

"Sure. You can text or email me the details. And—" She scrunched her nose up cutely. "—don't book a hotel room. It won't be necessary. We can work out something here."

Was it his imagination or had her voice become as breathless as his? He certainly hoped so. He'd been growing more nervous with each passing hour today, but now he could look forward to a weekend spent with her. Thank the heavens.

"You won't regret it," he promised. "I can't wait to see you."

She laughed. "You're seeing me right now."

"You know what I mean." He couldn't stop grinning like a goofball. "I'm glad you said yes." Being this excited to see a woman was a new experience for him, and those were few and far between. He savored the sensation. It felt right, at a gut level. Impulsively, he said, "I'll make you dinner on Saturday."

Hell, why not? He liked good food, and she seemed to share his taste.

"I'm going to hold you to that," she told him. "Don't make offers you don't mean."

"Never. I'm going to buy tickets now. Good night, sweetie."

She bid him farewell, and he hung up and pumped his fist. The conversation had gone better than he could have dreamed.

～

CLARISSA'S HEART was aflutter as Mark stuck his head into her office, grinning boyishly. "Hey there."

"Hi, handsome." She'd promised herself she'd take this weekend as it came and give him a real chance. She believed him when he said he wouldn't push her into anything she wasn't ready for, which was the main reason she'd managed to convince herself to drive to the airport and pick him up, rather than wussing out as she'd been tempted to do. Besides, being a coward wouldn't have solved anything. He'd just have taken a taxi and been annoyed by the time he arrived. Either that, or he'd have gotten on the first plane back, and she'd have lost out.

"I can't believe it," he said. "The boutique is so pristine, you'd think there was an army of elves hiding in the corners, but in here, it's like a hurricane passed through." He spread his hands wide, mimicking an explosion.

She giggled at the analogy, well aware of the contrast between the two areas. Leo commented on it regularly, but he also knew she needed her creative space.

"Is it Leo that keeps the boutique tidy?" he asked.

"No, it's both of us. The customers see that space, so it needs to be well maintained, but back here is my territory, so I can be as messy as I like."

He winked. "I like this messy side of you."

And she liked him. Far more than she'd be comfortable admitting. She adjusted her bun, tucking away a couple of strands that had fallen loose. His eyes tracked her movements, narrowing slightly, making her conscious of the severe hairstyle and bland makeup she usually wore when working. For the first time she could recall, she yearned to wipe it off, let her hair down, and see a man's eyes light with appreciation for her physical being.

He stepped toward her. "You know, you're so put together that sometimes I just want to muss you up."

"Not now," she said, sounding less firm than she'd have liked. "I have an appointment with a client soon."

His eyes lit. "But later?"

"Perhaps." She wasn't about to make any promises. "We'll see."

He leaned on the edge of her desk, his jean-clad legs crossed at the ankles. His dark cashmere jersey looked so soft, she itched to touch it. Touch *him*. But she didn't. She couldn't. Not yet.

If he noticed her perusal, he gave no sign of it. "So, what's the plan for the day?"

"I've taken the afternoon off. The boutique is open until evening, but Leo can run the show. I need to give him more room to spread his wings, and I thought it might be nice for us to spend some time alone."

"Fantastic." He clapped his hands, and her heart thunked erratically in response. "I want to see all your favorite places in Dunedin."

Her smile softened. "That sounds wonderful. How about—"

"No." He held up a hand. "Don't tell me. Surprise me."

Clarissa cocked her hip. "Did anyone ever tell you you're bossy?"

He grinned and picked up a design she'd been working on earlier that morning. "How many of these do you do at a time?"

She tried to snatch it from him—it was still a concept, not complete enough for anyone to view it—but he held firm. She pulled. He gave a shit-eating smile. Frustrated by the answering tug in her lower belly, she replied, "There's really

135

no limit. I might work on designs for up to ten dresses at a time, but when you include the ones in different stages of creation, there could easily be fifty."

One of his fingers traced the line of the skirt. "Impressive."

She grabbed for it again, this time successfully. "I've only got a little more to finish up. If you head upstairs or hang out with Leo for half an hour, I should be done."

Hopping off her desk, he dropped a quick kiss on her cheek, so airy she barely felt it, yet her feet rooted to the ground and the words died in her throat. She watched as he left, her cheek burning in the spot where his breath had caressed it.

"Work hard, sweetie," he called over his shoulder. "I'll be waiting for you."

No more than three seconds after he closed the door, Leo breezed through it, looking positively ecstatic. He edged around her desk, took her hands, and jumped up and down excitedly.

"Yay, you," he exclaimed. "I'm so happy for you. That man got even more gorgeous since last time, and he seems to really like you." He stopped bouncing and whispered, "Which is a sign of his good taste because you're a smart, sexy, independent woman."

She laughed. "Thanks. Hopefully he likes me as much at the end of this weekend as he does now."

"Aww, Riss. How could he not? You're fabulous. He's lucky to be here. We both know how many men have set foot upstairs."

None, barring Leo and tradesmen.

He squeezed her hands. "And if he doesn't appreciate you, then he's not worth your time, and you and I can have a date to get over him. Because, honey, I'll need the recovery drinks too."

On impulse, she hugged him. She hadn't initiated a hug between them before, but he didn't hesitate to embrace her.

"You're a great friend," she said. "Thank you."

"No problem, boss lady." He held her at arm's length, smiling proudly. "Now, I'm going to go keep that hunk of yours company so you can finish working and get to the important stuff."

"Go." She shooed him. "Sell some dresses."

15

"So, where are we going?" Mark asked, feeling like a kid on a road trip. "Will it take long to get there?"

His impatience wasn't feigned. He desperately wanted insight into Clarissa's mind, and touring her favorite places seemed one of the most efficient ways to get it. He also hoped it would relax her, so she'd be comfortable opening up to him. He was beginning to know her, but her history remained shrouded in mystery.

"Be patient," she said. "It's only five minutes down the road."

He watched her out of the corner of his eye. After she'd finished working, she'd let her hair down so it curled around her face. He reached over and tugged a curl. It bounced back into place, and she glanced at him curiously.

He shrugged. "I wanted to see if it felt as silky as it looked."

She accepted his explanation at face value. He brushed the back of his fingers through her hair again, reveling in the slide of the silken strands over his skin, enjoying a moment of satisfaction. Everything was going better than he could have dreamed. He'd worried she might stand him up at the airport, but she'd been right on time, the purse of her lips the only thing that gave away her hesitancy. She liked him, but she was wary of him, and damned if he didn't want to know why.

He paid no attention to the traffic flowing past their window, thinking back to her apartment. In complete contrast to her chaotic office, her living room was bare except for a sofa. He'd sat there while she changed and studied the white walls. If he had to guess, he'd say the office best reflected her personality, while the apartment only contained what was necessary to survive. Unlike his own, which while minimalistic, was also luxurious.

"We're here," she announced, pulling into a park next to a barred fence that barely restrained a wilderness of dense green shrubbery. "The botanic gardens."

A garden. As he'd had no idea what to expect, he was neither surprised nor disappointed. She jumped out of the car, and he joined her at the entrance.

"I like to come here during spring if I need inspiration," she said. "It always refreshes me and cheers me up. Come on."

Caught in her enthusiasm, he strolled next to her, close enough for their arms to touch. Cherry trees in bloom bordered the path that meandered through the garden, and beneath the canopy of blossoms, yellow daffodils blanketed the earth. In short, it was stunning. A sublime example of spring, with new life budding around them and bright colors dancing under a blue sky.

"Wow," he breathed.

"Isn't it something?" Her eyes sparkled as she spun in a circle, arms outstretched. "I love it here."

"I can tell." His voice came out husky, and he cleared his throat. "Spring is a pretty special time of year. For a few weeks, it's like everything has reset itself and the world is ready to start over again."

She stopped and stared at him. "What a fantastic way of phrasing it. I totally agree. It's my favorite season. It makes me feel hopeful for the coming year." She touched the tip of her finger to a blossom. "It's also one of my busiest times. Brides love spring weddings."

"No wonder when they can get married in a place like this. It's perfect for a wedding. Imagine it." He pointed to the rotunda at the far end of the path. "You'd have the ceremony over there, with the bride approaching through the daffodils, the flower girls trailing blossom petals. Upbeat music. There would be canapes served outside and waiters handing out champagne flutes."

When she didn't say anything, he looked around. Her mouth opened and closed soundlessly.

"Clarissa, what is it?"

She shook her head. "You missed your calling. You should have been a wedding planner. You could sell that wedding to half of the brides who come through my boutique."

He smiled. "You ever think about planning weddings?"

"No, that's not really my thing." She twisted a luminescent blue ring on her finger.

"Nice ring."

She glanced down as if she hadn't realized she'd been fiddling with it. "Thanks. Avery gave it to me when we graduated high school."

"That's sweet." He lifted her hand to study it. "You two are close, huh?"

Her eyes filled with warmth. "She's my best friend. She put me back together when I needed it most. Gave me this ring to remind me to breathe when things started getting to be too much." She rubbed a thumb over the surface. "It still calms me down."

"That's a good friend," he said. "Hold onto her."

Clarissa dropped her hand and offered him a smile. "I will. Come on, let's go to another of my favorite places."

As CLARISSA LED Mark past a group of students lingering outside a cafe, down toward St. Clair beach, the spring breeze stirred her hair and carried with it the scent of the ocean. She breathed it in.

Mark took her hand as they skirted around a bunch of kids on scooters and tucked her into his side. She liked it. Liked the feeling of the hard planes of his body bumping against hers as they walked, his body heat radiating through her jeans as if nothing separated them. For a moment, she wished the layers between their skin would vanish, so she could discover what his body felt like without the barrier.

She sighed. This would be so much easier if she could be someone other than herself.

"What's up, buttercup?" he asked. "That was an awfully big sigh considering how pretty the view is."

She glanced up. While she'd been occupied with her thoughts, they'd reached the deck that overlooked the beach. Below, the sea lapped at the sand, leaving trails of white foam behind. The blue of the sky blended into the blue of the water on the distant horizon. Faced with such a view, her black thoughts lightened.

"It's nothing," she said, dismissing his concern. "Nothing a paddle in the waves can't fix, anyway."

It will be nothing, she decided. *I'll make it be nothing.*

Mark wasn't like Heath. She'd known that from the start, on some level. She owed it to both of them not to let her past hold them back.

He touched her cheek and gazed into her eyes. She held his gaze, unwavering, taking a moment to appreciate the flecks of light brown in his dark irises and the way the color lightened to a tawny shade near the pupils. Then he dropped his hand and tugged her toward the stairs.

"What are you waiting for?" he asked, swinging their

linked hands jauntily as they headed to the water. She hadn't held hands with a man before. Heath hadn't been the hand-holding type. In hindsight, that should have been a red flag. One of a million she hadn't noticed.

She slipped her shoes off, tucked her cell phone inside one, and left them on the sand, waiting while he did the same. Minutes later, they sauntered along the shallows. When water rushed up her ankles, she squeaked in shock at the arctic cold.

Mark burst out laughing. "What kind of a noise was that?"

"It's not normally so frigid," she said defensively, eyeballing a pair of surfers out on the waves. "They're totally nuts."

"Agreed."

Then, to her horror, he knelt, cupped his hand in the water and splashed her. She saw it coming, but nothing could prepare her for the icy droplets that soaked her lightweight blouse and beaded on her face.

"Oh, you—"

Another volley of cold water cut her off. She sputtered indignantly, wiping her eyes so she could glare at him.

He grinned, unrepentant. "What are you going to do about it?"

She wanted to wipe that smug expression off his face. She wanted to destroy him.

She wanted to *kiss* him.

But instead, she swung the edge of her open palm toward the surface of the water, sending a spray in his direction. He leaped back, but too slowly to avoid her retaliation strike. Before he could react any further, she splashed him again, giggling when a few drops entered his gaping mouth, and he spat it out.

"Weren't expecting that, were you, tough guy?"

He didn't swear or grouch. His grin simply widened. "It's *on*." She backed up a step. The gleam in his eye promised retribution. "Yeah, you'd better run. You're in for it."

She started to back up more, but she'd only taken two steps before his arms wrapped around her waist and they both crashed into the waves, water flying everywhere.

Clarissa fell on her ass, in water up to her waist, her hair drenched, blouse clinging everywhere it ought not to. Her nipples contracted—because of the chill, not the way Mark, who'd landed safely on his knees, was staring at her like she was a tasty morsel he wanted to devour. She shivered. No one had ever looked at her that way before. At least, not someone who didn't make her skin crawl.

"I can't believe you just did that," she gasped, shoving his shoulders so he flopped into the surf beside her. "I'm soaked." Not to mention that her hair would morph into an afro as it dried.

"I can see that." He sounded strangled.

She frowned. "Are you okay?"

"Uh." He coughed and fixated on something beside her right shoulder. "Fine. Let's say I didn't think this through."

She laughed. "How could you think it would end well?" Then, because she was wet anyway, she lay back and gazed up at the sky. The water was freezing, but the sun warmed her front, and now that she was half-submerged, it didn't feel so bad. A shadow passed overhead, blocking out the sun.

Mark's face appeared in her line of sight. "You're crazy."

"Come in," she murmured, yanking on his collar. "The water is fine."

He collapsed onto her, his hips settling over hers, creating an intense contrast between the cool water and his hot body. Tingling started between her thighs, and she shifted to relieve the tension. As she did, heat flared in his eyes and his jaw tightened. She knew that look. He was about to kiss her.

Yes.

She wanted this. But at the same time, her nerves

screamed at her to get out from beneath him and save herself. The two urges warred within her, but the choice of action was taken away when he rolled to his side and hopped up, pulling her with him. He kissed her temple, feather-soft, and wrung out his soaked jersey.

"Shall we head back to your place to dry off?" he suggested.

She nodded, relieved, but also strangely disappointed at the same time. "Smart idea," she muttered. "But let's stop for coffee on the way."

~

HIS BELLY full of the delicious Thai curry he'd cooked for dinner, Mark slipped into his boxers and pulled on an old T-shirt while Clarissa changed in her bedroom. He was torn between hoping she wore a lacy negligee and praying she didn't. He'd promised to be on his best behavior, after all.

When she emerged wearing cute summer pajamas—not an ounce of lace in sight—he breathed a sigh of relief. The shorts revealed legs pale enough to be termed translucent, and toenails that were painted pink, the fourth toe of each foot bedazzled with silver glitter. Her toenails were a total contrast to the invisible polish on her fingernails. A clear example of the juxtaposition between the person she was inside and the one she revealed to the world.

"Ready for bed?" she asked. He noticed she had a duvet tucked under her arm. Presumably meant for him when he slept on the couch.

"Yes, and I'm more than happy to sleep out here. The couch is plenty comfortable," he said, lounging back on it. "But I'd really like to hold you for a while, if that would be all right with you." Just holding her, he promised himself. Nothing more. A ripple passed over her, turning her to stone.

"It's okay if that's too much for you," he added, a little hurt

144

that she looked like she'd rather stick pins in her eyes than let him touch her. Surely she could trust him not to take advantage of her by now. "You set the boundaries."

He didn't want to ruin this when everything had been going so well. But then she unfroze and took a small, deliberate step toward him, offering him her hand.

"Just for a while," she said. "Hands in PG places only."

"Okay, thanks." He released the breath he'd been holding and smiled. "I would never touch you anywhere without your permission. Do you believe me?"

She watched him, the clock on the wall marking the seconds. Finally, she nodded. "I do."

Thank you, Jesus.

She padded back to her bedroom. "Turn off the light behind you."

She was inviting him in? He'd expected her to curl up beside him on the couch. He followed her, a little tentative. As he passed through her bedroom door, the scent of lavender greeted him. He couldn't tell if it was coming from her or from something else. He daren't try too hard to figure it out.

If he'd expected her bedroom to be similar in style to the living room, he couldn't have been more wrong. Tucked in the corner nearest the door, opposite a small window, was a queen-size bed covered by a purple patterned duvet. Closets and cupboards occupied the remainder of the walls, leaving no free space.

Cosmetics crowded the surface of the cupboards, lined up in rows and ordered by type and color. She had a veritable treasure trove of lotions, perfumes, and lipsticks. Here, Mark knew he was seeing the real Clarissa. She wasn't empty and ordered like the rest of the apartment, or chaotic like the office downstairs, but somewhere in between.

"I like it in here," he said. "It's very you."

She looked around, brow furrowed as if taking notice of

her surroundings for the first time in a while. "Thank you, I think."

"Definitely a compliment."

She slipped between the sheets, careful not to untuck them. He followed her example.

Once in, he wriggled toward her. "Do you mind if I spoon you?"

"Go ahead."

This might go down in history as the most stilted, formal conversation he'd ever had in a woman's bed. He scooched over, draped an arm around her waist, and pressed the length of their bodies together so his chest covered her back and his lap cradled her ass. Despite that, he kept his hands in proper places, as she'd requested. There would be time to explore her body later. For now, she trusted him not to overstep, and he valued that trust.

It *was* her who smelled like lavender. He nuzzled her hair and inhaled deeply.

"Did you just sniff me?" she asked.

"Mm. You smell good."

He worried he'd said too much. Keeping his toe on the acceptable side of a boundary hadn't always been his strong point. But then she relaxed in his arms.

"You do too. Whatever cologne you're wearing, I love it."

16

The dark emboldened Clarissa, made her nearly brave enough to admit his cologne smelled so good she wanted to lick his pulse points until she found the source of the scent. Her core throbbed with frustrated desire. Normally, if she felt this way, she'd have a quick session with her vibrator and sleep it off, but she could hardly do that with Mark here, so she endured it. The fact his body was encasing hers didn't help.

Despite the lust heating her blood, she enjoyed the novelty of a man in her bed. She'd been afraid she'd panic when he touched her, but his embrace brought comfort. Security. The last time she'd been this close to a man, it had been the worst day of her life, hands down, but Mark was different. Safe. She snuggled closer, and his hand curved around her ribs and dragged her firmly against him, so close she heard the steady beat of his heart.

"This is nice," she whispered into the dark.

"Mmm," he murmured, the vibration rumbling up his throat and tickling the back of her neck. "I could hold you here forever."

She was okay with that. In the warmth of his embrace, she fell asleep in a matter of minutes.

～

MARK AWOKE with a start as something solid thumped him in the gut. Wheezing, he curled protectively around his stomach just in time for another blow to hit him in the shoulder.

"Whoa!" he gasped, raising his hands to block the strikes. Unfortunately, the next whack came from below. A knee thrust into his balls, squishing them so high he'd be singing soprano for a week.

"Ugh." He groaned, rolled out of the way, and fell off the edge of the bed. Above him, Clarissa continued to thrash. Breathing heavily, he cupped his abused balls and waited for her to run out of steam. But when she stopped lashing out, she began whimpering. Heartbreaking whimpers of fear, with a few decipherable words dispersed between them.

"No. Please, no. Stop."

Mark had heard enough. He clambered to his feet, perched on the end of the bed, out of reach of her flailing limbs, and crooned, "Easy, love, it's only a dream. You're safe. I'm here, and I won't let anything hurt you. Wake up now. You're safe. It's only a dream."

The whimpers died away, but she didn't wake and her breath echoed harshly off the walls. Damn, he needed to do more for her. Girding his loins, he inched toward her, then reached over and flattened his palm over hers, interlocking their fingers.

"It's all right, sweetie."

His thumb stroked rhythmically back and forth, feeling a tremor in her hand that spread up her arms. Within seconds, her entire body was convulsing. He eased his hand from hers

148

and the shaking slowed. Leaning over, he kissed her forehead.

"Wake up, love." He spoke full volume, and it had the desired effect. Her eyes flew open and her pupils contracted as she focused on him.

"Mark?" she croaked. "What's going on?"

"You had a nightmare," he told her, reclaiming her hand now that she didn't seem to wish him bodily harm. "It was intense. How do you feel?"

"A bit shaky," she admitted.

His heart squeezed. After what he'd witnessed, he couldn't blame her. What he'd seen and heard made him suspect she'd understated things when she'd said she had a sketchy history with men.

"Poor darling," he murmured. "You stay here. I'll make you a hot chocolate."

She looked like she might argue, but he ducked out before she could. He searched the kitchen for what he needed and, as a bonus, discovered a dark chocolate bar stashed in the cupboard. He returned to her, drink in one hand and chocolate in the other. Setting the cup on the stool beside the bed, he handed her the chocolate. She eyed it dubiously.

"It will help," he said. He didn't know that for certain, but it couldn't hurt, and given the bar had been hidden out of sight, it was probably her guilty pleasure.

She chewed slowly, then lifted the mug. Her hands trembled, so he helped steady them while she sipped. When the drink was done, she rolled over and faced the wall.

"Can I hold you again?" he asked. He ached to comfort her, but she may not welcome him, especially if he'd triggered her nightmare. He touched her shoulder. Like lightning, she spun around and shoved his hand away.

"No," she muttered. "Please, just go away."

Her rejection was like a knife to the heart. He swallowed the metallic taste in his mouth and tried not to take it personally. She was upset and her emotions were running high, but she'd come around in the morning. He fetched the duvet she'd left folded on the floor and paused in the doorway.

"I'll be right out here if you need me. Don't hesitate to wake me up. I'm here for you."

Then he lay on the sofa in the empty living room, his mind a whirl of questions and turmoil, until sleep finally claimed him.

~

THE SECOND TIME CLARISSA WOKE, it came upon her slowly. First, she became aware of the unusual scent of cologne on her bedsheets. Then she registered soft snoring coming through the door.

Oh, God.

All in a rush, she remembered: the nightmare, Mark's face puckered with concern, the way she'd shoved him.

"*Shit,*" she muttered, burrowing beneath the blankets. If she just stayed here, could she pretend none of it had happened? Perhaps if she waited long enough, he'd pack his bags and leave so she wouldn't have to see him.

She cringed at the thought of explaining herself. He'd treated her with care and respect, and in return, she'd assaulted him during his sleep and told him to take a hike. What was wrong with her? Shame burned low in her gut. Why couldn't she be normal, just once? Why had she never been able to do the right thing? She hated being this way, but couldn't seem to stop.

Lifting the blankets, she peered out. The bedroom door was ajar. He must have left it that way when she chased him out. She listened to his snoring, wishing she could see his face. Did he sleep with his mouth open? Drool? Knowing him, he'd be as adorable asleep as he was awake. The man couldn't be less than perfect if he tried.

Maybe she could slip outside, leave him a note, and come back after his flight.

No. She refused to take the coward's way out. Screwing up her courage, she threw back the blankets, pulled a brush through her hair, and tied a bathrobe on. Tiptoeing through the living room, she discovered Mark did indeed sleep with his mouth open, hair curling over his forehead.

His lips wiggled as he made a soft snuffling sound, and she stifled a nervous giggle. Then she hurried past and started the coffee brewing. She heated croissants in the oven and assembled breakfast on a platter. It was the least she could do to start his day off well, considering the episode in the early hours of the morning.

Mark sat up straight when she came over and rubbed the sleep from his eyes. "Is that coffee I smell?"

"Sure is." She lowered the platter onto his lap and sat at his feet. "And croissants, fruit salad, and yogurt. I didn't know what you preferred."

His eyebrows shot toward his hairline. "Do all of your guests get this treatment, or am I special?"

She nibbled her lip and fiddled with the end of the belt cinched around her waist. "I'm sorry," she said, battling an overwhelming surge of humiliation. "This is an apology for last night."

Breath hissed between his teeth, and he gripped her hand. "Don't you dare apologize for that. Not to anyone, ever, okay?" His tone was vehement, and he held her hand tightly. "It's obvious that something awful happened to you. You had a nightmare. You were frightened." Releasing her, he sat back. "Can you trust me enough to tell me what it was about?"

She battled down a surge of terror at the prospect. He wanted an explanation, and she owed him that much. The thing was, she'd only verbalized the events of that night once, to Avery. She hadn't even come clean to the rest of her friends, and as far as she was aware, Avery was still the only person who knew the truth.

It was long overdue for her to stop holding her fear so close to her chest, but she was afraid that if she acknowledged it at all, she'd break down. So she recited the facts as unemotionally as possible, like she was reading last week's grocery list.

"First, you need to understand something about my parents. They're very religious and conservative. I was raised to be a good God-fearing girl."

He nodded encouragingly.

"Actually, calling them only 'religious' is an insult to open-minded, loving people of faith. They were zealots. I constantly disappointed them. I was too rebellious, too flirty, too much like the other girls at school. The ones who were destined for Hell."

Mark scoffed, but he didn't interrupt.

"During my senior year of high school, I dated a guy named Heath Shaw. You might be able to guess that my parents didn't want me to have a boyfriend, so I saw him in secret. I thought sneaking around with him was sooo romantic." She rolled her eyes. "I wasn't even very good at it. One of my parents' friends saw us kissing and told them. They grounded me for a month and forbid me from seeing him again."

"I can't imagine you took that well."

"I didn't." She sighed. "I was supposed to be going to the school dance with him that month, and they weren't going to let me."

He rubbed the back of her hand soothingly with his thumb. "Let me guess, you snuck out?"

She nodded. "I picked a fight with Jen so it wouldn't look suspicious when I locked myself in my room. Then I climbed out the window, and Sophie and Evie picked me up and dropped me off at Heath's place. In the end, we only went to the dance for a while. We left early because he wanted to go for a moonlight stroll by the lake, and I was stupid enough to go with him."

When he simply watched her, no sign of judgment in his expression, she continued, "We went down by the water and started kissing. We hadn't gone very far before then, and I hadn't planned to change that." She shrugged helplessly, remembering the silly girl she'd been. "All I wanted was to have a little fun, free from my parents. Apparently those weren't the vibes I was giving out. Maybe it was because I agreed to leave the dance with him, or maybe I was just naïve about how things worked between girlfriends and boyfriends, but—"

"No." For the first time, Mark interrupted. "Don't you dare blame yourself for anything. I'm getting the impression that if there's anyone to blame in this situation, it was your boyfriend. What happened next?"

She took a deep breath, because the next part was the hardest to tell. "He started groping me. Kept trying to get my clothes off. I asked him to stop, but he didn't. He thought I was playing hard to get or some shit like that. Anyway, I started to fight him, but he pinned me to the ground and pulled down his pants. He was so much bigger than me. I—" She hiccupped back a sob. "I knew he wasn't going to stop."

"What did you do?" Mark asked, deceptively calm. But she saw his white knuckles where he clenched the duvet in one fist.

"I headbutted him. I just about knocked myself out, but it got the message across."

"He stopped?"

"He was furious. He punched me in the face, got in his car, and left."

Mark's eyes narrowed to slits. "He just abandoned you

there?"

"Yeah." She nodded and struggled to keep her breathing even, wanting to get the full story out before she broke down. "We'd been miles out of town, around the side of the lake, and it was a cold night. My nose was bleeding, and I thought it might be broken. I didn't know what to do. So I called Mum."

The same mother who'd supported her father in grounding her. For some reason, she'd thought her disobedience wouldn't matter when her parents learned of the situation she'd landed in.

"She came and got you?" Mark asked quietly.

"No, that's just it. She wouldn't even listen to me. She gave the phone to Dad." He'd been livid, and she'd thought he would direct his anger at Heath, but he'd screamed *at her*.

"Please tell me he tracked the bastard down and shot him."

"Uh, no." *Facts*, she reminded herself. *It's ancient history.* But God, it hurt. "Dad told me it was my fault. That I'd been asking for it by sneaking out to see a boy and by dressing the way I did." The words spilled from her lips like she'd been storing them up behind a dam and the floodgate had opened. "My clothes had been a bone of contention between us for ages. He'd long since stopped giving me money to buy them, but I just made my own. It infuriated him. He told me I wasn't the daughter he'd raised. That I had the devil in me and he wouldn't harbor me under his roof anymore. He said I wasn't welcome in his house. That I wasn't any blood of his."

She'd been left in the middle of nowhere on a cold July night in her ripped party dress, without anything except her purse and her phone. She'd sat there for fifteen minutes, waiting, honestly believing he'd change his mind, that he couldn't be so mad he'd cast her aside. Who would do that to their child?

She'd been wrong.

17

*M*ark had never wanted to wring someone's neck so badly in his life. "Your *dad*"—he emphasized the noun for the man who was supposed to protect her and love her—"just left you there after you called him for help? He actually kicked you out after your *boyfriend*"—the other male who should protect her—"attempted to rape you."

"Yes."

The distant tone of her voice didn't fool him for a minute. She was hurting. She'd been hurting for years, and no wonder. The most important men in her life had betrayed her and let her down. The fact she'd welcomed Mark into her bed showed the strength of her character.

She amazed him.

But that didn't stop him from wanting to hunt down her ex-boyfriend, shut him in a concrete box, and throw away the key. It didn't stop him wanting to drive to Itirangi, knock on her father's door and shove a Bible down his throat.

He needed to hear more. All of it. The full story. "And then?"

She shrugged. "I called Avery. She left the dance and came

to get me. Gave up her own night of fun because I'd made a hideous mistake. She took me to hospital, and I moved in with her until the end of the year."

His mouth dropped open. "Your parents didn't change their minds?"

She shook her head. "I never heard from either of them. I saw them in the street a few times, but they'd leave as soon as they saw me. Although...."

"Yeah?"

"You remember that night you walked me to Aria's place? I'd just run into my sister. A few days later, she and I talked. She wants to reconnect, but I'm not there yet. She never called or texted or emailed after Dad kicked me out. Sometimes, I think that's what hurts most of all. Knowing that even with how close we were, she believed whatever rubbish Dad told her."

He couldn't believe what he was hearing. "I *hate* your family."

To his surprise, she laughed, though the sound was bitter. "Join the club."

"But I think I love Avery. She really came through for you." He noticed her twist the blue ring on her finger, and his brow furrowed as things fell into place. "That's why she gave you the ring. To help you cope."

"She did. I had panic attacks, and having something physical to focus on really helped." She took a shuddering breath. "Avery was there when I needed her, and I'll never forget that. When Gareth broke her heart, I was a little relieved, to tell the truth, because it gave me an opportunity to support her at least a fraction of the way she supported me."

He drew her close and kissed the top of her head. "Please tell me you don't believe that bullshit line your dad fed you about it being your fault."

"It was," she whispered into his chest. "At least a bit. There must have been signs that Heath wasn't a good guy, but I ignored them. I liked feeling special. But I shouldn't have defied my parents. Yeah, their rules were stricter than most, but they were there for a reason. I put myself in a vulnerable position. I was an easy target, and that's on me."

"Shh, shh, shh," he soothed. "I don't want to hear any more of that, okay? All you're guilty of is being a teenager with an infatuation and bad taste in men." She sniffled. "You didn't do anything to make that asshole attack you. That's on him. Maybe you broke your father's rules, but what kid doesn't? Most don't get disowned for it. That's child abuse and neglect. I could have both of them arrested. Would that make you feel better?"

She shook her head, her face still buried in his chest. He ran his hands up and down her back, reminding himself that she was here. She'd *survived*. Everything was fine. Or at least, as fine as it could be. She sucked in another shuddering breath.

"Let it out, love," he murmured against her hair. "Let it all out. It's all right. I'm not going anywhere."

Her chest heaved, and then she was weeping. He held her until she calmed, glad he could provide a shoulder to cry on, but feeling utterly useless that he couldn't do more. He couldn't go back in time and fix everything for her, and that just plain sucked, because for once, he cared enough about someone to want to conquer the world for her.

And all he could do was mop up her tears.

～

"THERE'S an improv comedy based on *Pride and Prejudice* showing at the university today," Mark said from behind his laptop. He sat cross-legged on the end of Clarissa's bed, looking perfectly at home, while she was propped at the head, drinking tea. They'd rescued breakfast after she'd finished her explanation; then he'd suggested they move somewhere more comfortable.

Perhaps he pitied her—she couldn't tell—but he'd taken the whole sordid story well. Now, sneaking glances at his handsome face, creased with concentration as he read something on the screen, he didn't seem bothered at all.

"What's an improv comedy?" she asked. She'd never gone to any of the shows at the university, even as a student, unless Aria had dragged her along. She'd been too busy proving to her parents that she could make something of herself without them.

"It's when the actors play a certain role and the plot is meant to loosely follow a well-known story, but there are no set lines. They make it up as they go, and if one actor throws something crazy into the equation, the others have to work with it."

"Sounds interesting." And like it could get wacky fast.

"Let's go." He put the computer on the floor and sprawled beside her, resting his chin on his palm. "Improv is hilarious, and it's a good way to forget yourself for a while."

So much for him not being bothered by her revelation. But it was sweet of him to want to distract her. "What time is the show?"

"11:00 a.m."

That gave them an hour to get there. Plenty of time. "Okay, let's do it." Clarissa's friends teased her about not being impulsive, but she was proving them wrong this week.

"Yeah?" He looked delighted, a grin tugging at his lips. "Fantastic. You'll love it, I promise."

Acting on impulse again, she kissed the corner of his mouth, and just like that, his grin flickered and changed into something darker. Needier. She thought he might pounce on her, and wasn't opposed to the idea, but then the expression vanished and he pecked her on the cheek. Like a sister. Brilliant. She hadn't shared her story because she wanted him to lay off—quite the opposite.

A while later, they sat in the back row of a theater on the university campus, in an old building she'd never been in before. A handful of others dotted the theater, but it was largely empty.

A single spotlight illuminated the stage, where half a dozen actors in Georgian-era costumes played out a farcical version of the opening scenes of *Pride and Prejudice*. She'd familiarized herself with the classic novel in her early high school years and could quote it almost line for line, but she'd put it out of her mind after senior year, convinced that romantic love was for fools or people purer than her. Ridiculous, perhaps, but her teenage-self had sworn never to read another romance and, justified or not, she'd kept her word.

Mark held her hand. She closed her eyes and focused on the delicious sensation of his palm pressed into her own. His hand was warm and larger than hers, which were delicate, well-suited to needlework.

He ducked his head to murmur in her ear, "Mrs. Bennet is such a treat. She's one of my favorites. After Mr. Darcy, of course. No one can top him."

Normally, she kept her mouth shut during entertainment of any kind, preferring not to disrupt anyone, but no one was sitting near them, so she replied, "I always preferred Mr. Bingley, except for the part where he lets himself get talked into ignoring Jane. Bingley is a much nicer man, and he knows how to have a good time."

His lips quirked. "Interesting."

She couldn't help herself. "What's interesting?"

He tapped a finger on his chin, watching the action on stage. "I'm piecing together what your type is. Now I can add a crush on Mr. Bingley to the equation."

"I don't have a type." She couldn't possibly. She hadn't dated enough for that.

"Everyone does."

He pulled his hand free and looped it around her shoulders. She laid her head on his shoulder and breathed in the scent of his cologne and the wool of his jersey, which was damp from the rain. "There must be some traits that attract you to a man, whether you act on them or not."

"Maybe." But she tended to think not.

The rest of the show passed quickly, with Mark narrating it quietly in her ear, adding quips that made her laugh more often than the actors' antics did. He touched her constantly—held her hand, hugged her to his side, rested his palm on her thigh, kissed her cheek when she laughed at something he'd said. His attention was heady, making her feel like the only woman in the room. She loved it.

When it was time for him to leave, she wished they could spend another night together, one she wouldn't waste by throwing a hissy fit over an old memory. They drove to the airport in companionable silence, and she waited while he checked into his flight and dropped off his suitcase. Then he returned to her.

"I've got to go now, sweetie."

"I know. Thank you for coming. I had a wonderful time."

"I'm glad." His hands came up to her shoulders. Without thinking, she leaned forward and kissed him, short and sweet. He smiled against her mouth. "I could get used to goodbyes like that."

She smiled back. "I hope you had as much fun as I did. Sorry about the awkwardness last night."

He heaved a dramatic sigh and buried his face in his hands. "What did I say about apologizing?"

"Don't."

"That's my girl." Opening his hands, he kissed the tip of her nose. "I loved every minute with you. And I'm hoping," he added, retrieving a small square of paper from his pocket, "that you might come to this art show with me next weekend."

Next weekend? Her heart soared, and she took the paper from him with trembling fingers. "This show is in Auckland."

"Exactly. Come visit me, love. You showed me your favorite things yesterday, and I want to share mine with you."

"But...." She trailed off. But what? But visiting him in Auckland made this seem more real? It would put her squarely outside of her comfort zone. "I don't know," she hedged.

"It's my birthday this week," he said, widening his eyes until he resembled a begging puppy. "Seeing you would be the nicest birthday surprise I can imagine."

"But it wouldn't be a surprise," she said, her lips curling up. "Are you emotionally blackmailing me?"

He grinned, utterly shameless. "If that's what it takes."

She tapped her lower lip. "Surely you already have something planned with your family or friends. I don't want to intrude."

"Nothing at all," he said solemnly. "I don't like to make a fuss of my birthday, but if it'll convince you to come, I can make a big deal of it. Pretty please." He batted eyelashes that should be illegal on a man.

"Okay," she agreed. "If you're sure."

"I am." He hugged her, but not so tightly that she panicked, just enough to feel warm and safe. She realized with a sinking feeling that she would miss him this week. Calling and texting weren't enough. She wanted more of this.

"I'll see you then," she murmured.

"I'll be counting the days." He planted one final kiss on her lips and sauntered away. She watched him go, a surge of affection welling within her. She'd bared her soul to Mark Talbot, and now she was in danger of falling in love with him. She hoped to hell he felt the same way.

n Wednesday morning, Clarissa received a text from Mark.

Can't call tonight.

That was all. No explanation. No "Good morning, sweetie." The text lacked all of his characteristic Mark-ness.

It was his birthday, she reasoned, so perhaps he was busy. He'd said he didn't have plans, but that seemed unlikely. Maybe his mum had called, so he'd been distracted when he fired off a quick text, or maybe his friends had planned a party this evening and that was why he couldn't call.

She considered texting Aria to see if she knew whether Eli had been involved in any birthday plans, but she knew her friend would ask too many questions.

She hoped his friends *had* planned a party. He deserved it.

But what if there were women at the party? What if there were women who had a history with him or who were bolder and less damaged than her? They'd never discussed exclusivity or even whether they were officially dating. Her stomach tightened uncomfortably. She didn't know whether she had any sort of claim on Mark, but she wanted to.

He's a good guy, she told herself. *He wouldn't have come here if he weren't serious about me.*

That didn't help her messy insecurities. As she brewed coffee, she hit speed dial for Sophie's number.

"Mmph." Sophie answered the phone with a muffled grunt.

"Morning, Soph," she said brightly. "Are you awake enough to talk?"

More grunting, shuffling noises, then a sleepy, "I am now."

She winced. "Sorry about that."

"No problem, Riss." Sophie's voice was thick. "What's up?"

She hesitated. She trusted Sophie more than any of her other friends to be nonjudgmental, but regardless of that, she hadn't talked to any of her friends about men in years—not seriously—and opening up was harder than she'd expected.

"I need your advice about something."

"About what?" Sophie yawned. "Sorry, I'm not at my best before coffee."

Clarissa chuckled, pouring her own drink. "I sympathize." She took the plunge. "About a man."

All noise on Sophie's end ceased. Then she asked cautiously, "A man? Would this be the same man you danced with at Aria's wedding?"

"It would be," she admitted.

"Eli's tasty best man," Sophie mused.

"Hey," Cooper protested in the background.

Sophie giggled. "He knows I'm kidding. Kind of. Anyway, what's the story? Are you guys sleeping together? Wait—doesn't he live in Auckland?"

"Yes, he does, and we aren't." She hoped Sophie wouldn't think that too strange. "But he came to visit me last weekend. It went well." She flushed at the memory of whispered words exchanged in the back of the theater. "Really well. He invited me to visit him this weekend, but it's his birthday today and

163

he sent me a text earlier to say he can't call. It worried me. We've been talking every night, and he didn't seem like himself."

"I understand." Her voice was full of empathy. She'd had plenty of insecurities and a couple of bad experiences of her own before she'd started seeing Cooper.

"What if he has a party and there are other women?" She loathed the whiny tone of her own voice. "I don't even know if we're officially dating."

"Oh, honey," Sophie said. "If he wants another woman, there's nothing you can do, whether you're officially dating or not."

Clarissa's heart sank. "That's not what I wanted to hear."

"I said *if*," Sophie stressed. "I'm speaking from experience, babe. Evan and I were dating exclusively for years, and he still cheated on me." A fact that made Clarissa want two minutes alone with Evan to slap him around. "The big question is: do you trust Mark? If you do, then you have nothing to worry about."

Clarissa relaxed immediately. She did trust him. Maybe it had taken time, but they'd gotten there. He wouldn't have been so sweet and thoughtful and patient with her if he didn't care.

"Thanks, Soph, you're right. I have faith in him. I just need to be patient. I'm sure he'll tell me all about it tomorrow."

"Damn right, he will," Sophie said. "So tell me how this started. I need to know everything. Details, girl. Am I the first to know it could be something serious?"

Clarissa laughed. *Girl talk*. This, she could do. "The first except for Leo. Unless Mark has told Eli, but I'm sure I would have heard from Aria if he had."

"Yus!" Sophie was fully awake now. "I love being the first to have a piece of juicy gossip. But don't worry, I won't say a word until you give me the all clear. Now, spill."

Clarissa told her all about the podcast and about designing Rose's dress, the wedding, the phone calls, and finally, their weekend together—excluding the part where she tried to kill him during the night. Getting it off her chest was a relief, and hearing Sophie's excitement made it feel less like a dream. By the time they'd hung up, her typical levelheadedness had returned, and she was thankful she'd called.

Girlfriends rocked.

As a way to relieve her stress, she started a sketch of Mark, shirtless, guessing at the lines and contours of his body based on what she'd felt through a layer of clothes. Sometime soon, she'd have the chance to confirm whether her imagination had captured him accurately. She looked forward to it.

ON HIS BIRTHDAY, Mark woke, ate breakfast, went to work, came home, and burrowed into bed. He'd have slept for the whole day if he could, but that would have meant taking leave from work, which would clue his colleagues into the significance of the day.

He hid in his warm, dark space beneath the blankets until someone began pounding on the door. Groaning, he pulled the blankets tighter and ignored it. Then the yelling started.

"Mark! We know you're in there. Open up!" His sister Mikayla's voice. Maybe if he stayed quiet, she'd get bored and leave.

"Mark, please let us in." His mother's voice joined her. He winced. Mikayla had brought in the big guns.

"It's your thirtieth birthday." Megan added her voice to the chorus. "We need to celebrate."

No, they damn well didn't. Another birthday brought him another year closer to death, especially if he had inherited that genetic predisposition to an early heart attack. He'd rather not acknowledge the passing of time.

Finally, a deep male voice rumbled through the walls, "For God's sake, son, open the door. I don't want to be stranded in the hall with these three. Help me out." Joe, his mum's fiancé. The family had turned up in force.

He guessed he wouldn't be sleeping the evening away. Reluctantly, he dragged himself from bed, yanked on a pair of trousers and a T-shirt, and headed to the door. He didn't bother checking the mirror. They were lucky he'd dressed at all. It would have been fitting to greet them in his birthday suit.

"Go away," he snarled at their overly perky faces. "I'm not in the mood to celebrate. Mum can stay. The rest of you, I'm sure there's a bar open nearby."

Mikayla, a five-foot-nothing dynamo, ducked under his arm and hugged him from behind. "Cheer up, grumpy-pants. We brought Thai, and Meg baked a cake."

"Cake?" Whatever his uncharitable thoughts toward his family, that tweaked his interest. "What flavor?"

"Champagne with strawberry buttercream frosting," Megan replied, handing him the box.

Where Mikayla was petite and high energy, Megan was reserved and softly spoken, but as sweet on the inside as the cakes and slices she made for a living.

He lifted the lid and sniffed, salivating. "Is it as amazing as it smells?"

Megan shrugged. "Beats me. This is the trial run."

Well, now. He couldn't say no to that, could he? Standing aside, he allowed them to file into the room.

Rose gathered him in an embrace when the others made for the kitchen. "This is a milestone birthday, you need to celebrate it." She pinched his cheek. "It makes me sad thinking of you holed up in here every year."

"It's only one day, Mum."

She looked unconvinced, but she followed the others into the kitchen. He sighed. This wasn't over. He'd be hearing her opinion on the matter.

In the kitchen, his family had opened a selection of containers and were serving themselves. Mikayla thrust a plate into his hands and shoved him toward the couch. He sat. Far be it for him to question his sister. Joe and Rose sat next to him, while Mikayla and Megan took the armchairs.

"This is good," he said of the food, the closest he'd come to thanking them.

"Say, Mark," Mikayla said, slurping down a spoonful of curry, "I saw a ticket to an art show on the fridge. What's that for?"

He twitched. He should have left the ticket in his wallet. "There's a new up-and-comer displaying some work at a gallery across town on Saturday. I thought I'd go and have a look. Birthday treat to myself."

There, that'd satisfy them.

"You need company?" Megan asked. "I can get off work early and join you."

"No, no, I can't ask you to do that."

"It's no hassle at all. I'm owed some time off in lieu."

He bit the bullet. "Actually, I'm already going with someone."

Everyone froze, spoons halfway to mouths, dripping fluid. Eyes widened incredulously.

"Who?" Mikayla demanded, dropping her spoon with a clang. "None of your friends like art galleries."

He shrugged. "I made a new friend."

Megan's eyes went from wide to narrow in the space of a blink. "You're being evasive. Are you seeing someone?"

He begged the floor to disintegrate beneath him and save him from this ordeal. He'd have no problem telling his family about Clarissa, once he was sure she was in as deep as he

167

was, but he didn't want to get their hopes up prematurely. "Yes, as a matter of fact. You know her, Mum."

"Ooh, I do?" Her hands fluttered excitedly. "Who, dear? Wait—do I like her?"

"I think so." It was now or never. "Clarissa Mitchell, the woman who's designing your wedding dress."

Rose gaped. "Clarissa? Why didn't you say so? She's lovely. I adore her. How long has this been going on? Were you already seeing each other when we went down there?"

"No." He waved a hand. "It's very new."

"I knew you liked her," she said slyly.

He felt his face heat. "She wasn't sure she felt the same."

"But you changed her mind?"

Mikayla and Megan watched the chat go back and forth like it was a tennis match.

He shrugged. "Maybe. I'm not sure yet. I flew down to visit her last weekend, and she's going to come here this weekend."

"When can we meet her?" Mikayla asked. "Is it serious?"

Mark held up his hands. "Slow your roll. I don't know if it's serious yet, but she's pretty skittish, so I'd appreciate it if you all respected our space this weekend. If she agrees to come back a second time, you can interrogate her then."

Mikayla snorted. "You're no fun." She nodded to their mum. "What do you know?"

"Like Mark said, she owns a wedding boutique in Dunedin and she's designing my dress. She's a creative genius. Very sweet, but quiet. Probably not the juicy details you were after, sorry."

Mikayla growled in frustration. "Is she short? Tall? Brunette? Blonde? Twenty? Thirty? Forty?"

Mark rolled his eyes. "Are we really going to do this?"

"We want to know," Megan said firmly. "She could be our new sister-in-law."

He sighed and rubbed his eyelids. The sooner they found

out what they wanted to know, the sooner they'd leave him in peace. "She's maybe 5'5, blonde, blue eyes. I haven't asked her age—that's rude, you know." He stared at them meaningfully. Megan had the decency to hang her head in shame, but Mikayla met his stare head-on. "If I had to guess, I'd say mid-to-late twenties. Most importantly, she's an amazing woman. Clever, funny, and damned determined. A bit relationship-shy though."

Mikayla guffawed. "Oh, that's just the greatest."

His sisters exchanged glances.

"Priceless," Megan agreed. "The eternal bachelor falls for a commitment-phobe."

He raised an eyebrow at Rose and Joe. "Can't you do something about them?"

Rose smiled widely. She liked the girls having fun at his expense. "They're your sisters. They're happy for you."

"If you say so." If he had his way, they'd be a little less so. But he knew just the way to shut up smart-aleck Mikayla. "How'd your date with the surgeon go?"

Mikayla glared daggers at him as Rose gasped. "You didn't tell me about that."

He winked at his sister. Easy as pie.

19

*C*larissa second-guessed herself as she packed her bag. She second-guessed herself as she checked in at the airport, and then again as she was tossed into a sweaty stranger during turbulence. Most of all, she second-guessed herself as she crossed the arrivals area at Auckland airport, hauling a suitcase that weighed nearly as much as she did, scanning the crowd for a familiar face and coming up short.

Had he forgotten her?

But no, she caught sight of him behind a gorilla of a man, and her heart notched up a gear. She rushed toward him, afraid he might disappear like an apparition if she was too slow. The gorilla moved out of the way, and Mark waved and grinned widely. All thoughts of playing it cool went out the window. Attraction zapped between them as she launched herself into his arms.

Catching her, he stumbled backward, laughing. "Where's the fire, sweetie?"

She clutched him and buried her face in his chest, reveling in his nearness. "You're here."

His lips grazed the top of her head. "Where else would I be?"

She looked up and drank in the sight of him, as devastatingly handsome as usual, with his mouth tilted up and his eyes dancing with merriment.

"For a moment, I thought you'd forgotten me."

He shook his head, dismissing the notion. "I could never forget you. I've been looking forward to seeing you all week."

She could tell he meant it. Realizing she still held him captive, she released him and grabbed for her suitcase, but he beat her to it, trundling toward the exit with far more ease than she had.

"Did you pack up your entire apartment and bring it with you?" he asked over his shoulder.

She blushed. "I couldn't decide what to bring. Packing light isn't my strong point. You should see it when I travel overseas for fashion shows. I can easily fill three bags this size."

"But I bet you don't have a bevy of men to carry them around for you."

She imagined three identical copies of him, in various stages of undress, waiting on her hand and foot, and her libido fired. "Sadly, no."

They drove across town to his apartment, and she had to wipe her palms on her skirt as she strode down the corridor by his side. Her first time in a man's apartment. It shouldn't be a big deal, but it was. She wondered what it would look like. Hopefully, it smelled of his cologne. If not, she'd have to hunt it down and spray it everywhere.

He opened the door, and she looked around, sniffing happily. It did smell of his cologne. The room they'd entered had modern décor, the walls and carpet white, furnishings deep blue and green. The living area was open plan, and they passed a kitchen with a long bench that arced around it, separating it from the lounge, which was dominated by an enormous sofa.

Four plush armchairs were arranged in a semicircle, and a

glass coffee table was at the foot of the sofa. A bookshelf adorned one wall, crammed with colorful novels—romances, she assumed. Above the bookshelf was a liquor cabinet, and she could see a king-sized bed through a door across the room. The sight of it sent shivers of anticipation down her spine.

"Nice place."

"I like it."

"Of course you do." Spacious, masculine, comfortable. Exactly his style. She wondered how many other women had been here.

Don't go there.

"Drop your bag in my bedroom, and we can walk to the gallery."

His bedroom. She approached it cautiously, noting that the massive bed had plenty of room for both of them, and there didn't seem to be a spare bedroom. Goose bumps prickled over her skin. They'd be sharing a bed again. Hopefully with more success this time than last.

She set her bag down, and they left the apartment together, his arm around her. The sun filtered through the clouds overhead as they walked to the gallery.

"Have you been to an art show before?" he asked, steering her inside once they'd reached their destination.

"A few," she replied. "I knew a lot of art majors when I was studying. Visiting the galleries was just a typical Saturday for them. I tagged along sometimes when I wasn't too busy. Have you seen this artist's work before?"

"A couple of pieces. His style is quite abstract. I'm interested to hear what you think of it." His hand rested on her hip as they stopped in front of the first painting, a haze of pinks and purples with splotches of black.

"Simple, but appealing," she said.

The next piece was a twist of blues and greens, like the currents of an ocean. Dark navy notes hinted at depths, while pale yellow shimmered like light on water. She couldn't look away.

"You love it, don't you?" he asked. "Wait—don't answer. I'm willing to bet that no matter how many other paintings we see tonight, none of them will speak to you the way this one does."

She wanted to scoff, but based on the way she lingered over the painting, tracing its curves with her eyes, she suspected he was right. They worked their way around the gallery, stopping at each painting. When she didn't find any she liked better, she turned and smiled up at him. "How did you know that the second one would be my favorite?"

He smiled back and gently tucked a curl behind her ear. "I remembered how much you love the beach at St. Claire. That painting is like an underwater vision, so it stands to reason you'd like it. It brings back positive memories."

She inclined her head and nibbled on her lip as she considered this. "Very insightful."

His smile turned cheeky. "Do I get a reward for being clever?"

A faint puff of laughter escaped her; then she looped her hands behind his neck and pulled his face down to hers. He met her lips with a sweet kiss. Bright starbursts of light flashed behind her eyelids. Neither of them deepened the embrace. She wanted to, but this wasn't the place.

"Come back to my apartment," he murmured, his lips moving against hers, like he couldn't bear to distance himself from her even for a moment.

Everything within her stilled. Was he asking what she thought he was? Her brain short-circuited. If it had been a computer, it would have frozen, ten different tabs open, the cursor spinning in circles.

"Only if you want to, Rissa." He kissed her again, and her body melted into him of its own accord, her curves conforming to the ridges of his chest and stomach. "I

173

promise I won't push you into anything, but I want to have you all to myself."

In the end, she couldn't bring herself to say anything but yes.

~

CLARISSA AND MARK raced down the corridor together, hand in hand, giggling like teenagers. They tripped through the door to the apartment and fell on the couch, Mark on the bottom, Clarissa straddling his hips. His chest heaved beneath her, and his eyes darkened to the color of rum and cola, black near the pupil with flecks of gold.

He *wanted* her.

Satisfaction tightened like a fist in her gut. Propping herself on her elbows, she aligned her body with his and kissed him full on the mouth. Once, twice, then as if they'd planned it, their mouths both opened and tongues entwined. His stroked along hers, robbing her of the ability to think.

Though a novice at kissing, she responded enthusiastically, hoping to make up for her lack of experience. His hands framed her face, the tenderness of the gesture making her feel exposed—vulnerable but also cherished.

He stroked down her neck, over her ribs, to the flare of her hips. Their lips never parted. She wrenched herself away and spanned his shoulders with her hands, caressing his pecs, following the line of his collarbone. She wouldn't be denied the opportunity to study his body, but she didn't know how to ask him to strip. She tapped her finger on the corner of her mouth.

"Stop overthinking," he ordered. "What do you want? Whatever it is, I'll give it to you."

His palms came up beneath her blouse to cup her breasts, thumbs stroking her nipples through the sheer lace of her bra. They pebbled to his touch and her breasts felt heavy. Her back arched, pressing them forward, and a mewling sound spilled from her lips. She gasped, startled by the noise, quite sure she'd never made one like it before.

"You like that," he said, as much to himself as to her.

He continued the exquisite torture, exploring her through the fabric of her blouse as though they had all the time in the world.

"*Yesss*," she hissed, gyrating on him when lust speared downward. "But…."

"But?" he asked, stopping immediately.

She groaned in frustration. "I want to see you," she admitted, shocked by the thready quality of her voice. She sounded like a woman who wanted to be ravished. "Just your chest. Please."

"Your wish is my command." He yanked the shirt off and tossed it away.

She feasted on him, first with her eyes, then with her fingertips. His head fell back onto the cushion, his breath coming in pants.

"You're harder than I imagined," she told him. The lines that grooved the sides of his abdomen and those that were etched into his chest cut deeper than she'd expected. For a man with a sedentary job, he clearly took care of himself.

"You don't say?" he choked.

"I sketched you," she continued. "But I had to guess what you looked like. Next time, I'll know for sure."

His brows lowered in confusion. "You sketched me?"

She leaned forward to whisper in his ear. "That's my dirty little secret. I like to sketch shirtless men."

Unburdening herself to him felt good, and right. Judging by the way he growled deep in his throat and shifted, brushing his hard shaft against her core, he liked it too.

"I have to say, I never expected to hear those words from your mouth. Do you ever sketch nudes?"

"Not yet, but I'm open to experimenting."

He pulsed against her. "We'll have to explore that now that you've seen me," he said tightly. "Can I see you?"

Adrenaline blasted through her veins as she wriggled out of her blouse. He flicked her bra open, faster than she ever had. "Impressive."

He didn't reply, his gaze roving over her torso. He touched her reverently, smoothing his hands over every inch of exposed skin, but when he jackknifed upward and licked the sensitive nub of her nipple, warning sirens blared in her head, louder than if someone had held a foghorn to her ear. Without conscious thought, she found herself standing on the floor two yards away.

"Are you okay?" His voice sounded rusty.

"Um, I'm not sure. Hang on. Give me a moment to think." She bolted to the bathroom, or to what she hoped was the bathroom, and slammed the door behind her.

What was she doing? She'd almost gotten there. So close, and she'd run away.

She planted her hands on the vanity and stared at her reflection, trying to understand herself. Mark didn't scare her. He wouldn't do anything she didn't want. So why was she here and not on the sofa kissing him silly?

Because of that night, all those years ago.

Not the part where she'd struggled with Heath—although that *had* been awful—but the part where her father had assassinated her character. When he'd told her she had the devil in her and that she'd brought everything down on herself. When he'd disowned her and left her alone with her shame and guilt.

He'd been wrong to do that to her. Logically, she knew that. Kids acted out, and their parents got angry, then moved on.

Not her father.

He'd rejected her, and his rejection had scythed her spirit, making her feel like there was something wrong with her.

But she hadn't done anything Sophie and Evie hadn't, and she didn't look down on them or consider them to be worth less because of their mistakes. Besides, look at her now. A virgin at her age. Her father certainly couldn't accuse her of having loose morals, but no matter what she told herself, she worried she'd feel dirty if she went through with this.

Her pocket vibrated, scaring the bejesus out of her. *Her phone.* The screen showed a text from Mark asking, once again, if she was okay. She swiped it to the side and speed-dialed Sophie. Her friend answered immediately.

"Help me," Clarissa begged. "I'm hiding in Mark's bath-room. We were half-naked on his sofa, and I freaked out and shut myself in here. What do I do?"

"Why did you freak out?" Sophie asked, getting straight to the point. "What's going through your head?"

Blast, in her panic, she'd forgotten Sophie didn't know the truth, and Clarissa didn't want to rehash it now.

"So, here's the thing, Soph, I'm a virgin."

"You're a... whew." She whistled. "Really? You've never...?"

"Never," Clarissa whispered. "Dad slut-shamed me when I was younger, and I'm struggling to get past it now." She stuck to the root of the problem. No point getting into the other stuff. "I keep hearing his voice in my head, telling me I've got the devil in me."

"Aww, I'm so sorry, babe. You know that's not true, right? And even if you'd slept with every man you'd met, that wouldn't justify him saying that to you."

"It makes no sense to believe it, I know."

"Okay, okay." Sophie gathered her thoughts. Clarissa appreciated how quickly she was processing everything. "If you want to have sex with Mark, that's nothing to be ashamed of. There's absolutely no reason why you shouldn't be with a man you care about. But don't let him pressure you. Do you know what you want, Riss? Think about it. What do *you* want?"

With startling clarity, she knew. She wanted Mark, naked and hot, inside her.

"Thanks, Sophie. Love you!" Blowing a kiss, she hung up, pocketed her phone, and unlocked the bathroom door.

"There you are." He'd retrieved his shirt while she'd been gone. "Would you like a cup of coffee? I started it brewing."

Any doubts she might have had disappeared. Mark—the perfect, patient man—smiled at her, happily pretending she hadn't taken off as though the hounds of hell were on her heels. He'd never pressure her, and that's why she could do this.

Keeping her hands at her sides despite the undeniable urge to cover herself, she stalked up to him and kissed him. "I'm sorry for panicking."

His eyes never left her face. "I can wait as long as you need."

"I'm done waiting." She took his hand and tugged him closer, then dampened her lips with her tongue, barely able to believe what she was about to ask. "Please, make love to me, Mark."

20

*M*ark felt like he'd been waiting his whole life to hear those words spoken in her sultry bedroom voice. Even sexier than the words themselves was her certainty. Whatever had frightened her earlier, she'd gotten past it, and now she wanted him. He felt like a king. But he had to be sure.

"I won't be upset if we don't have sex today," he said, willing his body not to make a liar of him. "We can take it slow."

She swung around, and his palms itched to cup her breasts again. "I've had enough of waiting. Please make love to me. I don't think I can ask again."

He nodded. Never let it be said he did anything to cause a lady distress. She padded into his bedroom, her unbound hair cascading down the sleek lines of her back and brushing the top of her rounded bottom—a bottom he desperately wanted to sink his fingers into.

"So sexy, sweetie," he murmured, sliding his arms around her from behind. The skin of her stomach was velvety smooth, and he dragged her into the shelter of his body, pressing his hardness into the globe of her ass. She wriggled against him, and he groaned. "God, I love the feel of you. So soft. I just want to sink into you. Would you like that?"

She purred with contentment, then tilted her head to the side to give him access to her elegant neck. He scattered kisses from her collarbone to her jaw, learning her reactions, finding the most tender spot. When he did, he sucked—hard —and she gasped.

"Good or bad?" he asked into the junction of her shoulder and neck.

"Good," she breathed. "Definitely good."

"You have such a sexy voice," he told her between kisses. "I could come just listening to you."

She sagged into him, and he supported her weight, dropping more kisses along her neck. Then, without warning, he scraped his teeth over her skin. Her throaty moan told him she'd enjoyed it.

"If I do anything you don't like, tell me, and I'll stop straightaway. Promise?"

"I promise," she said, twisting to face him. The desire blazing in her eyes melted his insides. "But I think you could do anything and I'd like it."

He wanted to test that. Damn, how he wanted to test it. But not this time. It hadn't escaped his notice that she'd asked him to *make love* to her. He was 90 percent sure this would be her first time, and he'd do everything within his power to ensure she had no regrets.

"Kiss me," he said, because she seemed in need of instruction. Lifting on her toes, she did as he said. Mark sank under her spell, giving himself permission to take her breasts in his hands and worship them the way they deserved. He lathered them with attention, smoothing his palms along the underside, his thumbs smoothing over the tips.

Her head fell back. "Please, don't stop."

"Never, love."

She stroked his abdomen, and his muscles contracted. She then gripped the bottom of his shirt and yanked it over his head. Their skin met again, and they both sighed with pleasure. Her questing hands roved over his back and dipped into the waistband of his jeans, but his belt blocked them from going lower.

"Take these off."

He unsnapped his belt and shucked the jeans, standing before her in his silk boxers, which tented and barely concealed the burly length of his erection.

"Oh, my," she murmured. He wondered if the mechanics of sex concerned her, but then she licked her lips. His Clarissa had other things on her mind, and if she did what it looked like she wanted, it would all be over. He distracted her by unbuttoning and unzipping her jeans, slowly, so she could stop him if she wanted. She didn't. She watched him with a lazy expression as he eased them down and over her hips.

When he saw her underwear, he dropped to his knees. "You slay me."

The lacy pink thong begged to be ripped off. Later. For now, he ushered her to the bed and spread her thighs. Then he drew the thong to the side, held it there, and gave a long, slow lick from her opening to her clit. She squirmed under him.

"Oh, oh, *wow.*"

He repeated the action, then played her with his tongue and fingers, stringing her tighter and higher. She tasted tangy and perfect. Like aroused woman. *His* woman. He might be the first man to ever taste her. That thought wound him tighter. No one else had ever seen her like this—legs splayed, cheeks flushed, breasts heaving. He was *first.*

Clarissa gripped fistfuls of his hair and pinpricks of pain burned his scalp, but he didn't hesitate. He tested her with a finger. Finding her slick, he slipped into her, up to the knuckle, twisting to stroke her tight passageway. His tongue batted her, and she shuddered.

"What are you doing to me?" she asked.

"Pleasuring you. Is it working?"

"Oh, yes. But I want you. I need you. I need to come. *Please.*"

He withdrew his finger and sucked it clean. She watched him, thighs trembling. She was ready for him. He took a condom from the bedside table and rolled it on. They shifted fully onto the bed, and he dragged the head of his penis through her wet folds and notched into her entrance.

"This might be uncomfortable," he said through gritted teeth. "But I'm going to take it real slow."

Clarissa had other ideas. She dug her heels into his butt, and he slipped easily into her.

"Oh, shit," he cursed. "Wasn't expecting that."

"I've spent a lot of time with a vibrator," she panted as he fought not to explode inside her. "You won't break me."

That statement didn't help. He squeezed his eyes shut. "So hot."

She rocked beneath him, trying to take her own pleasure. He latched onto her mouth, kissing her as he thrust again. He was the first man to be inside her. He wanted to crow his victory from the rooftops, but instead poured everything he had into pleasing her with deliberate, rolling strokes. She whimpered and drew her knees up near her elbows.

That marked the end of his finesse. He pounded into her, no longer concerned about taking it slow. She was accepting everything he could give and demanding more with soft gasps and moans. He grasped the flesh of her ass and lifted her to meet him.

"Oh my God," she groaned. "So good. So good. Please don't stop."

"You feel like heaven," he said, burying his face in the crook of her neck. Tingles started at the base of his spine, but he held on until she started shaking wildly beneath him. Then he let go, following her over the edge.

~

THAT WAS what she'd been missing out on?

Clarissa let out a satisfied laugh. If sex was always that good, she should have done it years ago. But she suspected the man she'd made love with had made all the difference. Mark knew how to play her body like a violin. God, she was already halfway in love with him. Whether that was good or bad, she'd yet to determine, but for now, she was too sleepy and sated to question it.

She rested her head on his shoulder and snuggled into his side. He held her close, and she could hear the erratic thumping of his heart slowly ease back to its normal rhythm.

"You're good at that," she said, tilting her face up to smile at him.

He bent to kiss her. "I'd love to take credit, but I think it must be you, sweetie. It's never been quite like that for me."

Did that mean he'd want to do it again later? She certainly hoped so.

He must have read her expression because he chuckled and said, "Soon, minx. I need recovery time."

She settled in and closed her eyes. She must have dozed off because when she opened them, dusk had stolen over the city. Mark snored softly beside her, and she didn't want to disturb him so she stayed where she was and replayed the day over on a reel in her mind, analyzing how she felt about it.

The truth was, she'd experienced none of the shame she'd feared she would. She didn't feel dirty or sordid. Quite the contrary, she was refreshed and optimistic. Wonderfully so. Right now, she could take on the world. Skydiving, jet-boating, roller coasters... you name it, she was ready to take the plunge. If Mark had woken up and suggested they catch a flight to Paris, she would have asked when they departed.

Instead, her stomach grumbled, protesting the lack of lunch.

"What was that?" Mark mumbled without opening his eyes.

"Nothing," she assured him. It growled again.

"Nothing?" He blinked blearily and raised an eyebrow. "It sounds like the beast from the abyss demanding a virgin sacrifice."

"Guess it better look elsewhere," she quipped. "No virgins here."

He laughed and kissed the tip of her nose. "No regrets?"

"None whatsoever."

"Good."

The third time her stomach growled, she sat up and rubbed it. "I suppose I'd better feed the beast. Is it all right if I raid your kitchen?"

"Go for your life," he said, then paused and added, "Actually, why don't we order takeout?"

"Delicious food and more sex. Sounds sublime."

He groaned. "I've created a monster."

"Pizza?" she asked. "I'll call and order for us."

He gave her his order, and she googled the number of a local pizza shop and asked if they could deliver.

"Forty minutes," she said when she finished with them. "That gives us plenty of time for other things." She studied Mark. He lay sprawled on the bed, his hands behind his head, his gorgeous body on display, completely unselfconscious.

"What did you have in mind?" he asked, watching her through hooded eyes as she noted the details she hadn't earlier—the light dusting of hair that speared downward from his belly button, the angle of his narrow hips and proud jut of his erection, which was growing beneath her gaze. Her eyes darted up to his and found they'd darkened and narrowed to slits.

She plucked up her courage. "Earlier, I wanted to taste you, but I didn't get a chance."

His throat bobbed as he swallowed. "You have one now."

She smiled, but also hesitated, unsure where to start. She was a complete novice, and he was probably accustomed to women with experience.

Remember. You're ready for anything.

She crawled up his body and knelt over his groin. Then, holding herself up on one elbow, she licked him from root to tip. He bobbed against her face. She tried to remember what she'd read in *Cosmo* and took a firm hold of him, sucking the crown into her mouth and cupping his balls with her other hand. She swirled her tongue around the head and must have done something right because he groaned.

She loved the sound, throaty and desperate, so she did it again. Then she took him as deep as possible and slid back, stroking him with her hand and her tongue at the same time. His hips bucked, and he lodged in the back of her throat.

"Sorry, love," he panted, withdrawing. "Lost control."

"I liked it," she said, but her reply was muffled, her mouth was full of him. His legs shook. She released him with a pop and repeated herself. "Do it. I don't mind."

"Angel," he breathed. And when he looked at her like she'd painted a Picasso on his body, she believed him. She struck up a rhythm, and his hips moved in tandem, mating with her mouth. His breathing grew ragged, and he thrust one last time, stopping with apparent effort.

"That's enough for now, sweetheart. I'm so close."

"Give me everything," she instructed, refusing to budge.

A pained expression crossed his face. "Are you sure?"

She nodded. She wanted every part of him. "Absolutely."

"Do you know what you're asking for?"

"*Yes.*" Exasperating man.

He relaxed. She licked, sucked, and tasted him as though her life depended on it. When he came, with her name on his lips, she swallowed every last salty drop. And when he collapsed, wearing a satisfied smile, she'd never seen a more wonderful sight.

21

*M*ark had just finished repaying Clarissa for the incredible orgasm she'd given him and was basking in the glow of her admiration when someone knocked on the door.

Her slumberous eyes snapped open. "Oh God, there's someone here and we're—"

"Naked as the day we were born," he declared, feeling rather proud.

She scrambled off the bed, searching frantically for her discarded clothing. "We look like we just had sex."

He crossed to her, tucked her into his chest, and hugged her tight. She wriggled at first, trying to escape, then calmed. He kissed the top of her head. "We *did* just have sex. Don't worry, I'm sure they've seen worse. If it makes you feel better, you can hide in here while I get the pizza."

The tension eased from her body. "Yes, please."

"Okay. Kick up your pretty feet and relax. I expect to find you naked when I return." He waggled his eyebrows suggestively and went to fetch his robe. He paid the pizza guy and chose a bottle of wine from the kitchen to accompany the food. An evening like this, with good company and good conversation, deserved good wine as well.

Back in the bedroom, Clarissa had set up a wall of cushions at the head of the bed and reclined on them with the duvet pulled up to her waist. Her lush breasts remained uncovered for him to peruse at will.

Hot damn, he was a lucky man.

He handed her the box of pizza, placed two wine glasses on the bedside cabinet, and poured a generous serving of deep red Sangiovese into each. He handed a glass to her and sipped from the other, savoring the intense flavor that would pair nicely with the fattiness of the pepperoni pizza. He watched her mimic his actions, swallowing delicately. The column of her throat rippled, reminding him of the pleasure he'd found there earlier. She'd sampled him as though *he* were a fine wine.

Now, knowing she would taste of Sangiovese and sex, he couldn't resist stealing a kiss. Her mouth opened to him immediately, and his tongue danced with hers, tasting the spice and longing for more. At least, until her stomach rumbled and he remembered her priorities. They'd have time for lovemaking after.

He drew back and sat cross-legged on the opposite side of the bed. "Food now, kissing later."

"Probably a good idea," she agreed.

They chowed through the pizza, and he lay back, full and warm on the inside. He was used to wringing the joy from life, but even so, he knew for certain he'd never felt as perfectly content as he did now. He and Clarissa were side by side, sharing space, but not touching. He fixed that, brushing the tip of his index finger against hers. She went a step further and intertwined their fingers so their palms pressed together.

Her simple sweetness undid him. Tears gathered in his eyes, and he blinked them away, smiling to himself like a goofball. He'd questioned whether they'd ever get here, whether she would ever want anything to do with him, and now that she'd given herself to him so freely and with such reckless joy, his heart felt so full it could burst.

He needed her to know it, to understand how much being with her meant to him.

"Clarissa?" he said gently.

"Yes, Mark?" Even the way she emphasized the "r" when she said his name made him want to slide the blanket back to expose her body again.

"The way I feel about you, I've never felt about anybody before." The confession stripped him bare. "This is all new to me, but I want you to know that I care about you and I want to see where it goes." And, preferably, ignore the sword hanging over his head for as long as possible.

"I feel the same way," she whispered. "It's a first for me too. We can find our way together."

Damned if that didn't sound just perfect.

CLARISSA TIPTOED across the luxurious carpet and opened her suitcase, searching for the pretty sundress she'd brought to wear today. As she lifted it out, a gift-wrapped parcel dropped to the floor with a quiet thud. Mark's birthday present.

With everything that had happened yesterday, she'd forgotten to give it to him. She slipped the sundress over her head, gathered the gift up, and knelt beside the bed to wake him with a string of soft kisses from his forehead to his mouth. When she reached his lips, he grabbed the back of her head and deepened what she'd intended to be a chaste kiss. Their tongues grappled, and before long, their breath came in puffs.

He hummed in the back of his throat. "You can wake me up like that any time you want."

She kissed him once more for good measure. With sleep blurring his expression and his hair mussed, he was too yummy not to kiss. Then she placed the gift next to him. "I brought you something for your birthday."

As if she'd flipped a switch, his playful mood vanished. He didn't physically move, but she sensed him emotionally shift away from her. "Thank you," he said stiffly. "You didn't have to do that."

"I know, but I wanted to."

He held the gift like it was a foreign object, one that might contain radioactive material. Did no one ever give them to him? Had she freaked him out and made too many assumptions about their relationship?

No, after their conversation last night, she didn't think so.

"Open it," she urged, to break the awkward silence.

His fingers fumbled with the paper, and he carefully unpeeled each bit of tape she'd used to wrap it. She cringed just watching. Most of her friends would simply rip into it without regard for the wrapping, and she didn't know what to make of his caution.

When he held the book in his hands, no excitement showed on his face. He didn't light up the way she'd hoped, just stared at it like he had no idea what it was.

"It's the next book in your series," she explained. "*One Good Earl Deserves a Lover* by Sarah MacLean. It comes after *A Rogue by Any Other Name*, which you've been telling me about."

"Oh," he said, as though he knew she expected a response, but she'd spoken in German and left him as clueless as before. "Thank you."

She told herself it was only a present, that it didn't matter, but his lack of enthusiasm felt like a rejection. She'd never bought a gift for any man before. Apparently, she should have kept it that way. A suspicion sneaked through her mind. Had he feigned interest in romance novels because he thought that appealed to her?

No, she dismissed the notion. She couldn't believe it. She knew him better than that. But for whatever reason, her gift had fallen flat.

He placed the book on his bedside table and looked at her, finally seeming to realize she was disappointed by his reaction. "I like it," he said.

She shook her head slowly. "No, you don't. But that's okay, though I'd like to know why."

"Of course I like it," he repeated, baring his teeth in a semblance of a smile that fell far short of its usual brightness. "But I like you more."

He stood and stalked toward her like a predator, grinning when her gaze fell helplessly to his naked body, memorizing the way the shadows and light played across it as he moved. She could go through an entire scrapbook sketching Mark in all his glory and still never capture his soul. He cupped her face in his hands and kissed her hard. Despite her reservations, she softened and accommodated him with her body.

Then she accommodated him a whole lot more.

It wasn't until the airplane had taken off that evening that she realized he'd never answered her question.

CLARISSA FINISHED DRAWING a mermaid-style wedding gown and started to input the design into her computer. It was the Saturday following her weekend with Mark, and Leo had taken control of the boutique to give her some much-needed creative time because she'd fallen a little behind. Fortunately, she'd managed to finalize designs for two dresses and start on a third before her phone rang. She checked caller ID.

"Hi, Avery, how are you?"

"Excited as hell. Aria's water just broke." She got straight to the point, as per usual. "Gareth and I are on the way to the hospital. Sophie too. Eli's frantic. Called an ambulance, but I think she's doing well."

Clarissa's eyes widened, and the breath rushed from her lungs. "Oh my God." She jumped on the spot, waving her free hand. "That's so exciting! I can't believe it's really happening."

The door swung open, and Leo rushed in, mouthing, "What is it?"

She shook her head. She'd explain soon.

"How long does it take to give birth?" she asked.

"How the hell should I know?" Avery demanded. "I'm not exactly maternal. Hang on." She spoke to someone, but Clarissa couldn't make it out. "G says it took Caro three hours to have one of the girls and fourteen to have the other. Apparently, it can vary a lot."

Clarissa winced at the thought of trying to push a baby out for fourteen hours. "Let me know as soon as it's born. I can't get away from work today, but I'll drive down tomorrow." She paused. "Do you think Aria will want company?"

"It's Aria, she always wants company. If she doesn't, you and I can go for drinks at the bar and celebrate."

"You're on." Clarissa blew her best friend a kiss. "See you tomorrow."

The moment she hung up, Leo pried the phone from her hands. "What's the goss?"

"You know that wedding I went to a month ago?"

"With the beautiful pregnant bride?"

"That's the one. Her water broke. The baby is on its way."

He clapped. "How sweet! Who doesn't love a baby? They're darlings."

"Little bundles of joy," she agreed wholeheartedly. One day, Clarissa wanted a posse of children, and she'd shower them with all the kindness and acceptance her parents hadn't given her. "I've been working on a selection of gender-

192

neutral baby clothes, because they chose to keep the gender a surprise. It's my first time making anything for a baby." It had been such fun.

"I expect to see photos," he said.

"I'll take so many you'll beg me to stop."

The rest of the day breezed by. Later that evening, she assembled the tiny clothes, plus a few goodies for Aria, and packed her bags for another weekend away.

When Mark messaged with the news that he'd be visiting Itirangi too, she wanted to dance for joy. Though he hadn't been able to call because he had to prepare a podcast ahead of time, he conveyed his enthusiasm with five smiley face emojis and a string of kissy lips. Perhaps she shouldn't read anything into those emojis, but she grinned until her cheeks ached. She massaged her jaw, not regretting a thing

She couldn't even bring herself to be annoyed when her eyes were gritty in the morning because she'd been so excited she couldn't sleep.

She sang at the top of her voice all the way to Itirangi.

---

22

*M*ark met Clarissa outside the hospital, as they'd arranged the previous evening. In her signature colors of baby blue and white, with the wind ruffling her curls, and her lips painted pastel pink, she was irresistible. He swept her into his arms and kissed her laughing mouth.

"I missed you," he murmured, punctuating each word with a kiss. "Got. To. Kiss. You."

She returned his kisses, softening in his embrace, her lush curves pressing into him in all the right places. Feeling her melt against him was a welcome relief. He'd worried he'd upset her by not being enthused enough about her sweet gift, and that she'd pull away from him. The simple truth was she'd reminded him of his birthday and the passing of time, which he preferred not to dwell on. When she moaned, he peeled away. It wouldn't pay to get too eager this early in the day.

"I love kissing you," she said. Music to his ears. "But I also really want to meet the baby and see if Aria is okay."

"Visit me later," he said. "Room 206 at Eli's motel."

"I'll be there."

They walked into the hospital side by side, maintaining at least a foot of space between them by unspoken accord, like friendly strangers. No need to cause a stir. This wasn't their day. Today was for Eli, Aria, and their little girl.

All the same, Mark longed for the day to end so he could take Clarissa to his rented room and unwrap her, layer by layer.

～

JUST A FEW MINUTES after kissing Mark outside the hospital, Clarissa fell in love. The recipient of her affection, a gurgling cherub with a thatch of dark hair and eyes the color of an ocean in the tropics, blinked slowly up at her.

"Hi, gorgeous," she cooed, rocking the baby in her arms. "Hi, Lauren. Aren't you just the cutest thing I've ever seen?"

Aria, who was propped on a mountain of snowy white pillows, beamed at them. Violet shadows circled her eyes, but she looked radiant. Eli sat beside her, clasping her hand, unable to tear his gaze from his daughter. Lauren utterly captivated him.

Clarissa gave Lauren a final kiss on her chubby cheek and handed the baby to her mother, who cradled her. Eli leaned over and smiled down at them, his adoration obvious to anyone who looked—a far cry from the baby-phobic man he'd been when Aria first announced her pregnancy. Clarissa was relieved for her friend. They'd had a whirlwind romance, and she'd worried he might leave her in the lurch once the baby arrived. But based on his expression, he wouldn't leave the room, much less the relationship.

Clarissa sought out her own man. Mark lounged on the wall near the door. They shared a private smile that warmed her all the way through. She stopped herself from blowing him a kiss before she gave them away and thrust a bag from the floor at Eli, like an offering.

"Here. I made a few outfits for Lauren. They won't fit for a while because I wasn't sure how big she'd be, and I overestimated."

In an uncharacteristically affectionate move, he kissed her cheek. "Thank you, that's very kind. We know how busy you are."

"It's no big deal," she replied, blushing. "Nothing is more important than friends. Besides, it was fun."

He lifted the items one at a time to show his wife.

"They're darling," she exclaimed. "Thank you so much, Riss."

Clarissa nodded, then wriggled into the tight spot between the wall and the bed to hug Aria.

Aria turned to Mark. "Do you want to hold her?"

MARK THOUGHT he'd been prepared for the baby. He'd been wrong.

He was totally blindsided by the image of Clarissa with a sleepy infant in her arms. He'd watched her fall in love with the little girl, and all he could think was: *I want that.*

He wanted Clarissa and babies and a home together. A place where he could relax at the end of a long day, share his evenings with the woman of his dreams, and raise a few miniature humans to fill his life with color and noise. He yearned to see her hold their own daughter in her arms. He could picture the little girl perfectly in his mind's eye—with Clarissa's blonde curls, his dimples, and a smile he'd never grow tired of. He wanted to be there for her first steps. To teach her to say "Daddy." He wanted a family of his own to belong with, as Eli belonged with Aria and Lauren, and that terrified him.

The simple fact was, no matter how much he wished for children, they could never be more than a pleasant dream.

He couldn't risk passing on defective genes that would sentence them to an early death. Even if he didn't mind taking a chance that they'd turn out fine, what if he died young and left them fatherless? His sisters didn't remember their father much, but Mark did. He especially remembered the way their mum had gone to pieces when he died. The entire family had fallen apart, and it had taken years for them to grow strong again.

Mark's heart ached with the grief of lost opportunities. If he shared the same gene that may have been responsible for killing his father, he couldn't bear to worry every day about the pain it would cause his wife and children if he suddenly dropped dead. A wife could choose to be with him, regardless of the risk, but children had no say in whether they were born to a time bomb of a father, and it was irresponsible of him to even contemplate the possibility.

So, no, he didn't want to hold the baby. Didn't want to smile down at her tiny face and be reminded of the daughter he'd never have. But he couldn't find the right words to explain that when faced with Clarissa's expectant expression and Eli's encouraging smile. His throat tightened to the point where he couldn't speak, could only make choking noises, so he held out his hands and took Lauren with care. She was heavier than he'd expected, but so much more fragile.

He held onto her cautiously, afraid he might break her. She was so delicate, with a sweet snub of a nose like her mama's. His heart swelled with protectiveness, but at the same time, a voice in his head screamed at him to hand her back and run far, far away before the yearning unfurling in his heart became any stronger.

"She's a beauty," he said, praying no one heard the way his voice wavered. "She'll be turning heads in no time."

"Better not be," Eli muttered.

He cuddled the baby for barely more than a minute, then handed her back to her parents. Letting her go was hard, but holding on would only do more damage in the long run. He couldn't allow himself to want and hope for his own baby. "She's an angel."

"For now," Aria said. "Just wait until she's hungry."

Eli smoothed a hand down her back, providing casual comfort that belied the panic Mark had heard in his voice yesterday. This guy in front of him had it all together.

Baby Lauren gurgled, and the women cooed. The noose around his heart tightened. He had to get out of there.

"Right," he said. "I don't want to overstay my welcome after everything you two have been through, so I'll go get a coffee from the bakehouse. See you later." He took a step toward the exit, then paused. "I'm happy for you."

He left, but as he passed through the hospital foyer, his phone buzzed with a text.

I'll be at your hotel room at 7:00 p.m. XO

Guilt flashed through him, along with a side serving of self-pity. He'd have to tell her tonight. She clearly adored babies, and it wouldn't be fair to let her fall in love with him if his decision not to have children was a deal breaker. She deserved to know; then she could decide whether she wanted to stay with a man who would never give her a family and might drop dead at any time.

Judging by the tenderness in her expression when she held Lauren, he thought he knew where she'd fall in this equation. The hot coals in the pit of his stomach told him he'd be sleeping alone tonight.

~

Life was truly wonderful.

Clarissa practically floated onto Avery's front path, pausing to smell the blossoms as she crossed the yard. Avery had wasted no time in transforming the garden after she and

198

Gareth had moved in a few months back. It was bursting with flowers in every shade of purple and yellow.

Clarissa glided inside and greeted her friend with a hug. "Thank you so much for letting me stay here."

Avery grinned lopsidedly. "Any time." Then she cocked her head, and her grin stretched wider. "You look great. Really happy. Do you have some good news?" She gestured at Clarissa's face and clothes. "And have you done something different?"

Sometimes Clarissa forgot how observant her friend was. Observant and suspicious by nature. Perfectly suited to her career as a scientist.

"I dug out some clothes from the back of my wardrobe. I got so used to wearing work clothes that I was just doing it all the time, but I decided I want to enjoy my personal fashion choices again."

"Are you sure there isn't anything more going on?" Avery quizzed, staring at her, unflinching.

Clarissa met her gaze. Okay, perhaps she'd hoped to impress Mark, but so what? The key with Avery was to not give any quarter. "Not that I can think of." She wasn't comfortable sharing yet. Not with her most skeptical friend, even if she'd recently become somewhat of a romantic, in her own way. "Hey, do you mind if I pop into the spare bedroom and make a call?"

"Knock yourself out."

Clarissa showed herself into the spare bedroom and scrolled through her contact list until she found the one she'd added this morning. *Jen.* She'd woken up feeling strong enough to contact her sister. It was time. Without an ounce of hesitation, she hit Send.

Immediately, the call icon appeared, and a few seconds later, a woman asked, "Who is this?"

"It's Clarissa," she said, jumping right in. "Jen?"

She thought she heard a sniffle. Then she definitely heard a sob.

"Are you okay?" she asked, with a growing sense of unease.

"You called," Jen said, her voice thick with tears. "You *actually* called. I never thought you would. You can't believe how good it is to hear from you."

Actually, Clarissa *could* believe it, because she felt the same after so many years apart. They'd been more like friends than sisters, and despite their complicated past, she wanted that back.

"It's about time we talked," she said. "We're both adults now, and our parents can't rule our lives anymore. Would you like to get cake and a coffee at the bakehouse? Say, in half an hour?"

"I'd like that more than anything," Jen replied. "I'll see you in half an hour, Rissa."

The fact Jen had remembered her preferred nickname told Clarissa all she needed to know. She was making the right decision. They hung up, and she spent a few minutes catching up with Avery, then refreshed herself in the bathroom and changed into a pair of ballet flats to walk to the bakehouse.

On the way, she tilted her face up to enjoy the sun. Fluffy white clouds hovered overhead, and the town bustled, the tourist season already picking up. She took her time, glorying in the cheerful atmosphere and bright spring colors, meandering from the paved streets down to the lakefront, where she gazed out over the glistening water. When she reached the shore behind the bakehouse, she straightened her back and marched up through the French doors.

The bakehouse was packed, as always. She searched the throng and spotted a familiar blonde head ducked over a coffee in the corner. When she got to the table, she noticed a second drink waiting.

"Hi, Jen." She slipped into the seat and nodded to the second coffee. "Is that for me?"

"Yeah." Jen pushed it toward her. "Caramel latte. I remember you used to love them. I'm not sure if you still do...." She trailed off awkwardly.

"I do," Clarissa assured her, stirring and taking a sip. "Thank you."

"No problem."

Silence descended, and Clarissa glanced out the window toward the lake. "Beautiful day, isn't it?"

Jen nodded far more eagerly than small talk about the weather warranted. "Sure is. It's meant to be like this for the next week."

"Great." Clarissa swirled her spoon through her latte and fished for something to say. Across from her, Jen rubbed a stain on the tabletop with single-minded focus. "You didn't want a brownie or anything?"

Jen nodded toward the throng queuing at the counter. "And wait in line all over again? No, thanks."

"I could go." It would give her another ten minutes to gather her wits.

"No, no. Don't worry about it. Unless you particularly wanted something?" She raised a brow.

"No, I'm fine." Truth be told, she wasn't even sure she could stomach the coffee, let alone anything solid. "So, what have you been up to today?"

Her sister shrugged, as if it didn't matter. "Spent a couple of hours rowing on the lake with a friend."

"You row now?" Like Clarissa, Jen had never been especially athletic.

"It's a new-ish hobby. How about you? What brings you to Itirangi?"

"Aria had a baby." Since they'd all gone to school together, Jen would know who Aria was.

"Good for her," Jen smiled, though it seemed strained. "What's the baby's name?"

"Lauren."

"That's cute." The smile became a little more genuine. "How big is she?"

"Born six pounds, ten ounces."

"Oh, yeah. Average size, give or take."

Clarissa drank her latte. The cup was almost empty, as was her well of topics that were safe for discussion. She sighed. They'd have to get around to the hard stuff eventually, if they truly wanted to bridge the gap between them. But did *she* have to be the one to broach the subject? Hadn't she done enough by reaching out? She heaved a sigh and toughened up.

"So," she said, "we should talk."

Jen scraped a hand down her face. "God, I know. Look at us. We're being ridiculous, tiptoeing around everything. Like that's going to get us anywhere."

"It's hard, though," Clarissa said. "It's been so long since we really talked that we don't even know each other anymore."

"Hey, that's not entirely true," Jen protested. "I know you still like wine and caramel lattes. I know you're still the more fashionable sister, and you're a decent human being because you're here and willing to try. That says a lot, when I know how you feel about me."

Clarissa swallowed. It was time to get real. "Jen, you should know that I don't blame you for what Mum and Dad did." It was true. She didn't. Although it would have been nice to have had some kind of support. A conversation, a text message, a telegram—heck, she'd have settled for a smoke signal.

"Yeah, you do," Jen said. "At least a little. And that's okay. But answer something for me. Why didn't you fight back when Mum and Dad kicked you out?" She leaned forward on her elbows, her eyes a shade lighter than Clarissa's own and intense in their focus. "You were always the rebel. Dressing in cool clothes, dating behind their backs, drinking with your friends. Why did you just lie down and play dead?"

Whoa. If Jen had slapped her, it couldn't have stung more. Clarissa had done battle in the years after she'd left home, determined to show her parents up. She'd hadn't rolled over and let them win.

"Is that what you think I did?"

"I *know* you did. You didn't yell or kick up a fuss. You just... left. One night you were there, and the next morning, you'd gone."

"Because Dad told me I wasn't welcome under his roof." She'd never forgotten the way he'd said that. He'd meant it, 100 percent. "After what happened with Heath, I didn't have the energy to fight."

Jen frowned, her confusion evident. "What happened with Heath? Dad said you'd disgraced yourself with him, but I never saw you two at school together after that night."

"Ha." Clarissa laughed derisively. "What happened is that Heath assaulted me, but I got away from him and called Dad for help. I begged him to come and get me, and he just left me there. He fucking disowned me because I broke his stupid rules." Her voice had risen. Becoming aware she was attracting unwanted attention, she stopped speaking.

Jen's hand flew to her mouth, and her eyes watered, tears threatening to spill. "Oh my God. That's *awful*," she whispered. "I'm so sorry. I had no idea."

"That's because Dad wanted it that way, and he always gets what he goddamn wants." She was on a roll now. "I've made peace with it. He thinks I've got the devil in me, and you know what? I don't care anymore. His opinion means nothing to me."

Twin tears trickled down Jen's cheeks and dripped onto

the table. "I can't believe that happened and I never knew about it. You had to go through it alone."

She shrugged, uncomfortable with her sister's tears. "I had Avery."

"It's not the same." Jen flushed with anger. "I knew Dad could be an asshole, but I never imagined he'd do that. I just figured you got in a fight over your boyfriend and you'd had enough of him so you left. I didn't realize...." She choked up, her expression tortured.

"Hey, it's okay. Everything worked out for the best." Clarissa reached over to pat her hand. Then she finished her drink, giving Jen a moment to compose herself. They'd both dealt with enough emotional baggage for one day. "Anyway, now that we've got that cleared up, what are you doing with yourself these days?"

Jen wiped her cheeks with the heels of her hands. "I work at the information center, helping out the tourists." She shrugged self-consciously. "It's not anything fancy, but it pays the bills, and I like helping people."

Recalling the earnest, sweet sister from her childhood, Clarissa said, "That sounds perfect for you. What about romance? Is there anyone special in your life?"

Jen blushed a delicate pink. "There is, actually. I live with my partner. You might have seen her playing pool with me at Davy's. Her name is Maya."

Clarissa read the subtext. Jen was gay—another cardinal sin in the Mitchell household. No wonder she was not on good terms with their parents. Their father had kicked Clarissa out for sneaking off with boys and disobeying him. He'd never tolerate a lesbian daughter.

"I remember," she said. "She's gorgeous."

"A total babe. I'm a lucky woman."

"That can't have been easy on you, though."

"It wasn't." Jen drained the remainder of her coffee and set the cup down firmly. "I never had half the backbone you did,

204

but I had to find it after you left. It took a while, but I got there. I don't see Dad anymore. As far as I'm concerned, he can take his talk of eternal damnation and shove it up his ass."

Her outburst shocked Clarissa into laughter, and she knocked her empty cup over. "I'm sorry," she gasped, hurrying to right it. "I wasn't expecting you to say that."

"I know." Jen grinned wickedly. "But it feels good. How about you? Any men in the picture?" She must have seen something in Clarissa's face because she gasped excitedly. "There is!"

"Shh!" Clarissa hissed, motioning for her to keep it down.

Jen looked around guiltily. "Sorry."

"It's *very* new. I'm not sure if it's even official yet, but I like him. He makes me happy."

"Then he has my vote. Is he anyone I'd know?"

She shook her head. "No, he's from Auckland. He's friends with Aria's husband."

"Is he good-looking? What's he do?"

"He's a lawyer, and, yes, he's handsome."

Jen waggled her eyebrows. "Oooh, a lawyer."

For a while longer, they traded stories. Then they walked together until the roads that lead to Avery's house and Jen's flat forked. They hugged and separated, promising to meet again soon, so Jen could introduce Clarissa to Maya.

She'd never expected they'd reach this point so soon after such a long estrangement, but they'd both suffered from the separation and wanted to move forward however they could. It wouldn't be easy, but Clarissa was committed to rebuilding their relationship, and she knew Jen was too.

Somehow, despite the emotional upheaval of the day, she felt even better now than she had earlier.

23

*W*hen Clarissa approached the door of Room 206, she noticed it was ajar. She smiled, and anticipation rushed through her. She couldn't wait to be alone with Mark again. Seeing him so soon after last weekend was a wonderful, unexpected surprise.

Pushing the door open gently, so as not to startle him, she let herself inside and called out, "Mark? I'm here."

"Clarissa, hi." He entered the living area through one of the attached doorways, his hair damp and curling up at the edges. She laid down her handbag and went to hug him, but he held himself stiffly and brushed a chaste kiss over her cheek rather than giving her the knee-knocking lip-lock she desired.

She pulled back, frowning. "What's wrong?"

He sighed and sifted a hand through his hair, sending droplets of water flicking away from his head. "Have a seat. There's something I need to tell you."

"Uh-oh," she said. "That doesn't sound good." She didn't move to take a seat. She was afraid of getting comfortable and then having the rug pulled out from under her. If this was him trying to let her down easy, or if she'd done something to upset him, she'd rather be standing when she found out. It helped her feel in control of the situation. She rolled her shoulders back. "I'm fine here. What is it?"

"Are you sure?" he asked, his brow creasing with concern. "What I'm about to say might come as a shock."

"I'm sure," she said, digging her toes into the insides of her shoes because it helped ground her. She waited for him to speak. She wouldn't beg him to spit it out and put her out of her misery. Whatever was going on, she still had her dignity.

"Okay. You might not need the support, but I do." He crossed to the couch and sat. "Do you remember me telling you that my dad died when I was young?"

"Yes." It was official. She didn't have a clue where this was going.

"He had a heart attack, and it was very unexpected," he continued. "Mum never discussed it with me or my sisters. Perhaps it hurt her too much to talk about, or perhaps she thought it would be too overwhelming for us, I don't know. Anyway, I overheard her on the phone with my aunt one night, after we were supposed to be asleep, telling her the doctors thought there may have been a genetic factor at play, something that predisposed him to the heart attack."

A chill coursed through her. *Genetic.* Meaning Mark could have the same predisposition.

"I was only twelve, but I was afraid what that might mean for me."

She moistened her lips. "Did you ask her about it?"

He shook his head. "No, and I didn't mention it to Megan or Mikayla either. They were so young, and I didn't want to burden them with the knowledge that something might be broken in their DNA."

Clarissa crossed to sit beside him and rested her hand on his knee. Sorrow for the scared boy he'd been squeezed her heart. "So you kept all your fears to yourself to protect everybody else?"

"Yes." His voice cracked. "Now I can't help wondering, what if it happens to me? Dad wasn't much more than a decade older than me when he passed away."

"It won't happen to you," she told him, stroking little circles on his leg. *It couldn't.* That would be too cruel.

"You can't know that," he said, not unkindly. "No one can. It took me a while to get used to the idea of my own mortality, but I did. At least, as much as it's possible to do so."

"You were a little boy," she said, tears prickling hotly behind her eyes. "You shouldn't have had to."

He shrugged like it was no big deal, but she could see through him. The fear had permeated his life. She wanted to turn and take him into her arms, to hold him tight.

"There's more, and I'm afraid you won't like it."

As if she *liked* anything that had come out of his mouth so far. What kind of person would that make her? But she didn't interrupt.

"I saw how hard Dad's death was for our family, and because I might carry the same defective gene he did, I made a decision not to have children. I don't want to put my family in a position where they have to grow up without my support, and I won't risk sentencing my own child to an early death." He swallowed. His jaw was tight, and the cords of his throat stood out. Even though he was so close, he seemed remote. "So that's it. All my cards are on the table. If you want to be with me, you'll never have children. I can't risk it."

His words sounded so final, but they hadn't quite sunk in yet. Clarissa replayed them in her mind, sorting through them, trying to make sense of them.

"Surely there's a test they can do to find out whether you carry the gene or not." She didn't know who "they" were, and she didn't know much about science, but it seemed like that was the kind of thing medical professionals ought to be able to do.

He shook his head. "Maybe one day, but technology isn't there yet."

"But there's tests for everything these days. And the chance of you passing on the gene must be—what?—fifty percent, at most. Say there's a fifty percent chance you inherited it, that's only a twenty-five percent chance your child would. And that's assuming genetics were a factor at all."

"We don't know how it works," he said. "Assuming your basic math is right, twenty-five percent is still much higher than I want anyone to have to live with." He crossed his arms and stared at her. "I made up my mind years ago, Clarissa. I've been through all of the arguments from every possible angle. I'm not budging on this. You need to decide if it's something you can live with or whether it's a deal breaker for you."

She shook head slowly from side to side, unable to accept what he was telling her. She wished she could wind back the clock until before she'd come in and start over. Except next time, she'd kiss him before he had a chance to say a word.

"I don't…." She tried again. "I'm not…."

"It's okay, you don't have to decide right now. Take some time and think it over." He looked up at her, and his eyes were brimming with emotion. "When I saw you with Lauren earlier, it was like a punch in the gut. I wanted so badly to have a future with you and a baby of our own, but it also reminded me that I can't have that and that it wouldn't be fair of me to lead you on without giving you all the facts."

Clarissa clutched at her last shreds of hope. "But there are all kinds of options these days. I'm sure there's something…." She trailed off because his expression said he wasn't discussing the matter further. He'd made his position clear, and she needed to figure out whether she could handle it.

She swallowed hard. She'd always wanted to be a mother

one day. The how and when had been a bit fuzzy, but now she realized that in her heart of hearts, she'd believed she'd filled in the "how" part of the equation with Mark and his kind, dancing eyes and velvety voice that would be just perfect singing lullabies to their baby. Now she had to reevaluate.

Not only that, but she needed to decide whether she could handle being left alone, holding everything together if he died young. The thought of facing abandonment, in whatever form, soured her stomach. But he could be wrong. The heart attack that killed his father might not have been caused by bad genes. He'd been a child when he overheard that phone call, and it seemed like he'd accepted the information without ever questioning it.

"I need some time," she told him, her gaze sinking to the floor. Time to figure out her own values. Time to investigate the science of heart attacks and whether any advances had been made in understanding them since he was a boy. "Is that okay?"

She wished she could smile and tell him the answer he wanted—that it didn't matter, that she'd be with him no matter what, but she felt like something had slammed into her from behind, knocking the wind out of her, and she couldn't do anything except gasp for breath and crawl into a dark corner to think.

He scooted across the couch and reached over, clasping her clammy hand that hung uselessly at her side. She sniffed and realized her nose was running.

"Take all the time you need. I know it's a major decision, but I just want you to know that I think about you every day, and I want you in my life. Look at me." She raised her eyes and met his. They were dark and intense. "I don't want there to be any misunderstanding. I'm falling in love with you, Riss, but I want you to take the time to think about your options."

"I-I'm falling for you too, Mark. But I need time and space. Actually," she rose on shaky legs, "I think I need to go. I need to clear my head. Will you be okay here by yourself? I can send someone over for you."

"No." He let her go and waved a hand. "I don't want to bother anyone, especially not when there's a new baby to look after. I'll be fine. None of this is new to me. I'll just miss you." He stood and kissed her. He tasted bittersweet, like he'd already given up on them. "Let me know what you decide."

"I will," she promised, kissing him again. "Take care, all right?"

It was only when she left the room that her tears began to fall. A sob ripped from her chest. She'd started the day on such a high. How had it gone so wrong?

THE SATURDAY FOLLOWING his heart-to-heart with Clarissa, Mark woke early and trudged to the office. He couldn't spend any longer moping around home, waiting for her to make up her mind, so he had no choice but to work. He fixed himself a coffee and was catching up on his emails when Sterling rapped on the door.

"Go home," he ordered.

"A bright and cheery good morning to you too," Mark replied.

Sterling looked down his nose at him. "I can't call it a cheery morning when you're in here looking like you sucked a sour grape."

"I'm at work at the weekend. You can't expect me to be Mary Poppins."

"And whose choice is it to be here?" When Mark didn't reply, he sighed and smoothed a hand over his slicked-back hair. "I'm not sure what's going on with you, but you're bringing everyone down."

Mark glanced around. The office was empty, except for them.

Sterling grunted. "You know what I mean. Pull your head out of your ass and fix whatever it is that's making you miserable." He paused, looking downright uncomfortable. "I've never seen you like this. I need you bringing your A game on Monday, so go and drink wine, look at art, or flirt with a pretty woman, whatever you need to do in order to recharge. I'll see you in a couple of days." He fidgeted with his expensive watch, avoiding eye contact.

"Are you worried about me, Sterling?"

He snapped to attention. "Don't be ridiculous. I need you on point to achieve the bottom line."

Mark smiled. "You *are* concerned about me. I can see it in those shark's eyes of yours."

The aforementioned eyes, which had infamously caused a competitor to faint when they'd stared each other down across a boardroom table, glinted like steel under the artificial lights. His lips thinned.

"Don't you try that hard-ass act on me," Mark warned, reclining in his chair. "I see through you."

"Yeah?" he asked. "Well, I see through you too. Something has upset you, and you're trying to suppress it. I hate to break it to you, but that approach isn't working. Try something else."

"Well, you would know about suppressing things." He could see from Sterling's expression that he'd gone too far. His friend's posture stiffened, his shoulders squared, and he spun on his heel and stalked away.

"Go home," he called back.

Mark didn't argue. He could tell Sterling wasn't in the mood, and frankly, neither was he. His entire future hung in the balance, and he had no idea which way it would tip, or whether he should do something to prompt it one way or the other. He hung his head and groaned.

$\mathcal{M}$ark was three glasses into a bottle of wine when Mikayla breezed into the apartment unannounced.

"Hey, big brother," she chirped, coming to an abrupt halt at the sight of him. "Oh, hell. You're a mess."

"I'm not that bad," he protested, even as he took stock of the takeaway wrappers strewn around the room and the dirty dishes he hadn't cleared away. Perhaps he should have tidied up before he started on the wine, but he'd been agitated from his encounter with Sterling and not thinking straight. Though he couldn't blame the mess on that. It had accumulated over a week.

"Uh, yeah, you are." With a heavy sigh, she tossed her purse on the sofa and began gathering wrappers and stuffing them into the rubbish bin. Once she'd finished, she collected the glasses and stacked them in the dishwasher. While she cleaned, Mark changed out of his robe into jeans and a T-shirt.

"Why didn't you answer your phone?" she asked, wiping her hands on a towel.

"It didn't ring." He grabbed it and pressed a button. It was dead. He showed her the black screen. "Oops, sorry. Didn't think to check."

"Pull yourself together, Mark."

She made it sound so easy. As if he hadn't been trying desperately to do exactly that. "It's not that simple."

Mikayla crossed her arms and raised a doubtful brow. "It kinda is."

"Screw you and your judgmental attitude," he said, his ire rising. "You don't know what's going on with me."

"So tell me."

He looked at the floor, afraid that if he maintained eye contact, he'd see sympathy. Or worse, disdain. He was indulging in a fit of self-pity, after all. "I may have lost someone I really cared about. I've never made a connection like that before, and I probably never will again."

"What happened?" She was listening intently now. He was tempted to cuss at her until she left him alone, but he didn't have the heart. Not when she'd gone quiet and was nibbling on her lower lip, a telltale sign she was genuinely worried about him, though he doubted she'd ever admit to it.

He collapsed on the sofa and puffed out a heavy breath. "I haven't heard from Clarissa in a week." He dragged a hand over his face and felt the weight of the secrets he'd kept like fifty-pound sandbags strapped to his shoulders. How much of a relief would it be to set them aside for a moment?

He eyed Mikayla. She was a woman now. An adult. She deserved to know the truth, and she was strong enough to handle it. "I told her I can't offer her children because of what happened with Dad."

She tilted her head to the side, lips pursed. "You mean his heart attack? What does that have to do with anything?"

He patted the cushion beside him. "Come over here, Mickey Mouse."

Her eyes narrowed. She'd always hated that nickname, but he hadn't meant it meanly. It reminded him of the girl she'd been, all spindly arms and legs and pigtails. She sat, and he put an arm around her.

"There's something you should know about Dad's death. The doctors thought there might have been something in his genetic makeup that made him vulnerable to it." He hesitated, weighing up his options, and decided to throw caution to the wind. "Something that could have been passed on to us."

"Oh." Mikayla's expression darkened. "Are you sure? Who told you this?"

"I overheard Mum talking about it a couple of days after the funeral. As to whether I'm sure," he shrugged, "I'm sure of what I heard, but it's impossible to be certain what the implications are for us."

She swatted him hard enough to hurt, then buried her face in her hands, and he noticed they were shaking. "I can't believe you knew this for years and never said anything."

"It's not like we ever talked about it. We all just brushed it aside and focused on surviving."

She sighed and dropped her hands to her lap, meeting his eyes. Hers shone with unshed tears. "We really didn't, did we? Maybe we should have talked." Her voice cracked. "God, how could Mum not say anything to us about this? It kind of affects us, don't you think?" Her fear seemed to be giving way to anger. "We deserved to know." Burning with renewed energy, she stood and slung her handbag over her shoulder. "I'm going to talk to her about it."

"Wait, Mik." She paused, studying him with a wary expression he hated. He'd royally screwed up this entire confession, and rather than having a weight taken off his shoulders, it seemed to have multiplied. "I should talk to her first. Think you can wait a couple of days?"

Her shoulders slumped, and she flopped back onto the sofa, folding into herself. "Okay. I'll give you one day." She rested her head on his shoulder, and much as he knew he'd done the right thing by coming clean to her, he wished he could resurrect her peppy spirit.

"I'm sorry about Clarissa," she said. "Do you mind if I stay here a while? I need to process this, and I think we're long overdue for a talk."

He laid his cheek on the top of her head. "Stay as long as you like."

~

"Oh, Mark."

A soft hand stroked through his hair. Gentle. Comforting. A hint of cinnamon in the air. Only one person smelled like that.

"Mum?" Mark rolled, but a hand caught him before he fell off the sofa. He blinked, trying to clear his head. He remembered leaving a message for her to call him, then crawling beneath a soft blanket. After that, everything faded to black.

"Yes, darling. I'm here."

Rose's angular face came into view above him. He grabbed her cheeks and planted a kiss on one. "I'm happy you're here."

She stroked along his hairline again. "I came as soon as I got your message. You sounded upset. What's happened, darling?"

Sitting up, he rubbed the sleep from his eyes and then grabbed a glass of water from the coffee table and gulped it down. This conversation should have happened a long time ago, and he'd need all of his faculties to pull through it.

"Ma, there's something we need to talk about."

"Are you moving?" she asked.

"What? No." He frowned. "This has to do with Dad."

"Oh." Her eyes dropped to the ground, and her lips pressed together. He sighed. This was exactly why he'd never mentioned anything to her. Talking about his father seemed to cut her as deep now as it had eighteen years ago. "Okay, I'm ready."

He ignored his misgivings. They had to get this out in the open, or Mikayla would confront Rose herself, with all the tact of a bulldozer. The trouble was, he didn't know where to start. He'd been silent for so long that verbalizing his fears seemed wrong.

He tried a different angle. "I think I went and fell in love with Clarissa."

She was completely still. "What does that have to do with your father? And how is it a bad thing? She's a nice girl. Shouldn't you be happy?"

Something tickled the tip of his nose. He swiped at it and felt moisture. Damn, he was crying. So much for manly stoicism. "I think it might be over, and the reason for that has to do with Dad."

She rubbed her chin. "I'm afraid I don't understand."

He could tell she wanted to, but she just wasn't making the connection. "I heard you on the phone to Aunt Florence, a little while after he died."

Her expression remained blank.

He sucked in a deep breath and took the plunge. "You said the doctors thought the heart attack might have been a genetic thing. That he might have been predisposed and it could be hereditary."

Rose's eyes widened, and she raised a shaky hand to her chest. "I remember," she whispered, tears brimming in her own eyes. "I didn't realize you were there. You never said a thing."

"I know."

"But you must have been so frightened, hearing that and having no one to console you." The first tear spilled onto her cheek. "Why didn't you come to me?"

He ducked his head to hide his wet face. "I knew how hard it was on you. I thought it would hurt less if I kept it to

217

myself." He swallowed. "It's not like talking about it would have changed anything anyway."

She wrapped an arm around him, rested her head on his shoulder, and took an uneven breath. "I'm so sorry, Mark. I had no idea you heard that or that you'd been bottling all of this up inside you. I didn't say anything about the heart attack to you or the girls because the genetic factor is only one possibility, and I knew that a new medication might be developed before you even grew up. That knowledge isn't the type of thing any child should be burdened with."

He couldn't fault her logic. It was a similar line of reasoning to why he hadn't confided in his sisters. "There was no way you could have known that I heard you."

She scoffed, the sound watery. "Of course I could have. I *should* have. What kind of mother doesn't notice her son is struggling?" Her arm around him tightened. "We should have talked. It was a mistake for me to act like everything was all right. I just…." She fought to find the right words, and he waited, eager to know what she would say but also wary of it. "I thought that if I made sure you had a roof over your head and food in your bellies, nothing else would matter. I didn't think you'd forget your father, but I suppose I believed you'd follow my lead." She laughed without humor. "Looks like you did, but I led you down the wrong path."

Mark turned to embrace her fully. "You did the best you could. No one ever teaches you what you're supposed to do in a situation like that. We all grew up knowing we were loved, and we're all happy and healthy now."

"Happy?" Rose drew back, wiping her eyes. "This doesn't look like 'happy' to me. Tell me what happened with Clarissa."

"I saw her with Eli's daughter and panicked," he admitted. "I liked the sight of it too much. She looked... I don't know—right?—with the baby, and that scared me because I can't have a family, Mum. I can't. What if my heart is bad like Dad's was and I die early and abandon them? What if I pass on some kind of fatal genetic defect? I can't risk doing that."

As he spoke, tears welled hotly and streaked down his cheeks. It was like she'd uncorked his bottled emotions, and words exploded from his chest. "I won't do that. Surely you understand. You remember how it was. How torn up the girls were and how hard it was to keep us all together. I've been so afraid for so long. I don't want anyone else to have to live with that fear."

"Oh, honey." Then they were hugging and crying together, tears dampening each other's shoulders. Mark's body shook as he finally let out all the anguish he'd contained since he was twelve years old.

Finally, they separated. Rose exhaled. She looked like a shell of the vibrant woman she usually was, and he hated that he'd done this to her, but their shared grief was also cathartic.

"I didn't realize you remembered everything so clearly," she said, her voice scratchy. "Or that it had such an effect on you. I'm so sorry."

"Not your fault." His own voice was rusty too.

She continued. "We were all devastated when your Dad died—"

"I—"

"Hush, don't interrupt." She straightened and caught his eye, pinning him with her gaze. "Yes, I was devastated, but the time I had with him was precious. I'd never trade it for anything, and I'd like to think you and the girls wouldn't either."

She twisted her hands in her lap, turning the ring on her right hand over and over. The ring from her first marriage, which Joe had never asked her to stop wearing.

"You might not know this, but you children were what got me through his death. If I hadn't had you, I don't know

219

how long it would have taken me to recover or where I'd be now."

They sat in silence for a moment, Mark digesting her words, wondering if they made any difference in the scheme of things. Wondering if, perhaps, he'd raised his fears with Clarissa the way he had—firmly and without warning— because deep down he preferred to do that than face the possibility of having something real with her and losing it.

But wasn't it her choice if she wanted to be with him? And if she did, shouldn't he accept that rather than trying to make the decision for her?

"Is this the reason you've never had a serious girlfriend?" she asked. "You're afraid to leave her alone in the world? Afraid she'll end up like me?"

"*Mum.*" His cheeks stained red. This topped the list of things he never wanted to discuss with her. Also featured were orgasms, his birth, and that time he'd spent a weekend hugging her toilet, suffering from food poisoning.

She didn't let him off the hook. "Well? Is it?"

"Not exactly," he hedged. "Any woman would be lucky to turn out like you, but you've had a hard time of it. I don't want the same for the woman I love. Not if there's something I can do to prevent it." Still, he couldn't help questioning, in the light of things, whether it was actually his job to prevent it.

Rose just nodded, as if his answer didn't surprise her, but she looked so weary with her gray pallor and red-rimmed eyes that perhaps nothing would be able to shock her now. "And you're afraid to have children in case they inherit this gene you may or may not carry?"

He felt two feet tall when he said, "Yes."

She ruffled his hair like she'd done when he was in primary school. "I wish you'd told me this sooner, Mark. We didn't see your Dad's heart attack coming. There was no reason to expect it, so he never bothered with medical

220

checkups. He was a typical kiwi guy in that regard. But you're forewarned. You can be proactive. Monitor your health well and visit a specialist; it's not as though you can't afford it." She took his hands in hers and squeezed. "Medicine is improving every day, and unless there's something else you're not telling me, there's no reason not to hope."

Mark's eyes closed briefly, and he drew a deep breath in through his nose. It felt like the fifty-pound sandbags on his shoulders had been split open, their contents pouring out onto the ground, lightening his load in fits and starts.

Could it be possible his mother was right? That he might be able to do something to lessen his risk rather than growing increasingly anxious as each birthday passed him by, waiting for the inevitable?

He was afraid to hope. Hoping meant facing the possibility of disappointment. But she'd planted a seed, and he couldn't seem to smother it.

Maybe he could be with a woman. He still couldn't give her children—at least, not unless the day arrived when medical technology was advanced enough to give him the all clear—but maybe Clarissa would decide he was worth the risk. Maybe she would love him anyway.

"You've given me a lot to think about," he said.

Rose stroked her thumb across the back of his hand. "Don't write off a relationship with Clarissa. I know you've got to make your own decisions, but I'm your mother and I want you to be happy. If she makes you happy and you make her happy, you can figure out the rest later."

"Maybe." If anything, he was more confused than he'd been earlier, but that little seed of hope had settled in his mind and taken root. Dozens of thoughts whirled though, and he tried to catch each one, but he was too exhausted to focus. Opening himself up had drained his energy. "Thanks, Ma. I love you."

"I love you too, silly boy." She leaned over to kiss his

cheek, her breath warm against his skin. "Do your sisters know?"

"About Dad?"

She nodded.

"I spoke to Mik yesterday. She's probably talked to Meg by now."

"Right." Rose disentangled herself from him, squared her shoulders, and reached for her phone. "We need to have a family meeting."

~

"HEY, BOSS." Leo bustled into the shop, balancing two coffees and a paper bag. The heavenly aroma of pastry reached Clarissa's nostrils when he placed a coffee on her desk and slid the paper bag over to her. "Chocolate Danish, cream-filled donut, pecan pie. Take your pick."

Her mouth watered, but she was suspicious. "What are you up to, Leo?"

He put the other coffee down and threw his arms around her. "You've been a misery-guts all week. I know something happened to upset you. Maybe I can't help, but I can supply you with treats and coffee."

She was touched by his gesture. "Thank you." She selected the pecan pie and dug into it as he bit into the cream-filled donut and groaned with satisfaction.

"The first bride of the day is due in five minutes," she said, her tone conveying her lack of enthusiasm.

Leo took the pecan pie from her and replaced it with coffee. "Bottoms up. That's instant motivation right there."

She sighed. "It'd be better if it were wine."

"Tell you what. As soon as that Closed sign goes up, you and I head upstairs for a couple of glasses of sav and some banter. You can tell me what's on your mind."

"Can we do all of that *without* the talking about my feelings part?" She really didn't think she had it in her. As it was, every waking minute she was turning over the "Mark plus baby equals not going to happen" equation in her mind. Add to that the "Mark might die" dilemma, and she was going crazy.

She'd watched the livestream of his podcast earlier in the week, agonizing over his paleness, and the circles etched beneath his eyes, hating that she might be responsible. Guilt piled on with every hour that passed without her contacting him. She was leaving him in limbo, and it wasn't fair. But she hadn't been wallowing in inaction, every waking moment she wasn't working had been spent googling heart attacks and research articles in the desperate hope she might find something to prove his beliefs to be false.

A bell chimed as the door swung inward. A petite Japanese woman entered, followed by three tittering friends and two older ladies in button-down jackets. Clarissa suppressed a sigh. She had a rule limiting the number of visitors to four per group, but it wasn't uncommon for brides to ignore the fine print.

"Good morning," she said with a brightness she didn't feel. "Ayano?"

The petite woman nodded. "Clarissa," she replied, her accent lilting and soft. "It is lovely to meet you in person."

She put her worries to the back of her mind. Or at least, she tried to.

*A*fter Leo left and she was alone with her thoughts, Clarissa didn't sleep a wink. She tossed and turned all night, replaying her conversation with Mark. She didn't know what to do. Throughout her hard times, she'd visualized the future when she'd have a husband, a beautiful baby, a thriving business, and a white picket fence.

Forget choosing between work and family, she'd wanted it all, and she'd clung to that image, to the wonderful normalcy of it. She couldn't fathom casting it aside.

But she wasn't prepared to lose the man she was falling in love with either. She rubbed a hand down her face, sat up, and switched the light on. She checked her phone. It was before midnight, which meant that Avery would probably still be awake. She needed practical advice ASAP. But she cringed even thinking about how to explain herself. If Avery had kept a secret like this from her, she'd be furious, and her friend wasn't the type to pull any punches. Clarissa would have to take it on the chin.

"Hey, Riss." Avery answered on the first ring.

"Hey, Ave." Without further ado, she launched into an explanation, afraid she might chicken out otherwise.

Avery listened, hmming occasionally. Clarissa stumbled when she got to the part about how they'd set up a date in Itirangi but ended up each going their separate ways instead. When she finished, Avery was quiet, but Clarissa knew from experience that the cogs would be turning in her friend's brain, running through options and odds.

"What should I do?" Clarissa asked.

"First of all," Avery said, "I can't believe you didn't tell me this was happening. Aren't we supposed to be best friends?"

"I know, and I'm sorry," she moaned. "I don't know why I didn't say anything. It was all so new, and I guess I was afraid it was too good to be real."

"Sounds like you should have listened to your instincts." Avery sighed. "If you want a baby and he doesn't, my advice is to call it quits. That's not a hurdle you can get over."

Everything inside Clarissa stiffened in denial. *No. She couldn't lose him.* The prospect of never being with Mark again filled her with sorrow and brought tears to her eyes. She ached right down to her bones to see his gentle smile. To be held by him and experience that same glorious sense of belonging and safety she'd had after their weekend in Auckland. There had to be a way around this. One that satisfied them both.

"You okay there, Riss? You're awfully quiet."

"I'm okay. I just...." She couldn't give voice to the doubts flying through her mind.

"You don't want to let him go, do you?" Avery asked slyly.

"No," she admitted, the most honest she'd been herself all week.

"Then go tell him that," Avery said like it was obvious. "I only suggested letting him go because I knew you'd instinctively agree or disagree, and that would give you your answer."

She'd been Jedi mind tricked by her best friend. "You—"

"Don't thank me now. Thank me after you've got your man."

"I don't even…." She huffed. "That doesn't solve the problem."

Avery huffed back. "He doesn't want a biological child, right?"

Clarissa nodded. "Yes."

"Does he have anything against a nonbiological child?"

She frowned. She hadn't considered that. "I don't know."

"Well, maybe you should find out. And while we're on the topic, how do *you* feel about them?"

She'd never given it much thought. "I'm not opposed."

"Great. Problem solved. I assume you've heard of adoption. Artificial insemination. Foster parenting. The choices are endless."

Clarissa felt like she'd been staring at a code that didn't make sense and Avery had just shown her the key. Everything clicked into place. "Oh my God. How did I not think of that?" She blinked rapidly, staring at the wall, imagining a baby in her arms. One she hadn't birthed but who needed a loving home. Could she care for a child that didn't share her blood?

She remembered the warmth that had infused her as she held baby Lauren and knew the answer. *Yes, beyond a doubt.*

As far as the possibility that Mark would leave her a young widow? She'd take it. She'd rather be with him for a while than without him forever.

"Love you, Ave. I have to go now."

Avery chuckled. "Bye, Riss. Give 'em hell."

Clarissa glanced at the clock and began to formulate a plan.

~

CLARISSA RACED across the airport parking lot, cursing her high-heeled sandals. If she'd been less concerned with looking her best, she'd have made better time as she rushed to make the first flight of the day to Auckland. She ran through the front entrance and scanned the departure list, noting immediately that boarding began in fifteen minutes at Gate 16.

She hurried to the security checkpoint only to be stopped by a guard.

"Miss, do you have a boarding pass?"

She fished around in her bag. "Uh, I have a ticket."

"That's great. You'll need to go over to one of those machines," he gestured behind them, "and print a boarding pass. You can't pass through until you have one."

"Okay, thanks." She teetered over to the machine and scanned her ticket, waiting while it printed a pass. The damn thing took an eternity, and she didn't have time to waste. She didn't want there to be any possibility of her missing this flight. She grabbed the boarding pass and dashed back to the security checkpoint. This time, the guard let her through without comment. She glared at his back, hoping he could feel the sting of the imaginary dagger she'd lodged there.

Once she'd made it through, she hesitated.

God, this was crazy.

She'd never done anything so impulsive, so completely out of character. But nothing this frightening and wonderful and exhilarating all at once could be wrong.

Calmness descended over her. Being with Mark was *right*. She felt it in her gut.

When she reached the gates, they hadn't opened, so she browsed the minimart in the departure lounge. She scanned the titles on the bookshelf, pausing on a selection that looked to be romances. The spine of one read "Tessa Dare." She'd heard Mark mention the author, she was certain of it. On a whim, she purchased the book and tucked it into her handbag. A voice over the intercom announced boarding, and she took a deep breath and embarked on what she hoped would be the journey to her future.

~

STANDING outside the glass and chrome high-rise, Clarissa hoped she wasn't about to make a fool of herself. She inhaled, counted to four, and exhaled. Her thumb went to her touchstone ring and rubbed its smooth surface; then she strode through the automatic glass doors and checked the list of tenants on the panel beside the elevator until she found Lockwood Holdings. When she did, she took the elevator to the top floor.

She stepped out into a modern office space, the kind that was open plan, the few offices having glass walls so anybody could see what the managers were up to. Good for hierarchical transparency, she supposed. With false confidence, she marched up to the receptionist.

"I'm here to see Mark Talbot."

"Do you have an appointment?" the receptionist asked, without looking up.

"Yes," she lied. "Clarissa Mitchell. You can call him to check, if you'd like."

Now, the woman did look up, taking in Clarissa's formal attire. "No need for that. Go right on through, Ms. Mitchell. Mark's office is the third on the left."

Unaccountably self-conscious, she passed by the desk and counted off the doors, reading the name plates as she did so. She knew when she'd reached Mark's, not just because the door said so but because he was inside, his familiar disheveled head bent over paperwork, his back to her.

She knocked.

Please, universe, grant me courage.

He turned, running a hand through his hair, and froze when he saw her. A grin split his face from ear to ear. He stood and tripped over his own feet as he crossed the carpet to pull the door open. Heedless of the people working around them, she threw herself into his arms, knocking him backward. His embrace tightened around her. She buried her face in the crook of his neck and breathed in the spicy scent of cologne and Mark. They held each other for eternity, fitted perfectly together like complementary pieces of a jigsaw.

"I missed you so much," she said.

"I missed you too," he replied. "You didn't call, and I thought perhaps that was all the answer I'd get."

"I'm sorry." She drew back but didn't release him. "I've been thinking myself in circles, and I didn't want to say anything until I was sure where I stood."

"That's okay. I'd have waited however long you needed. Here, come into my office." His lips twisted. "It's not exactly private, but at least no one will overhear us."

Her cheeks warmed at the reminder of the onlookers. She'd all but forgotten they were there.

"Am I to take the fact you're here as a good sign?" he asked as he ushered her inside. "Or did you come in person to let me down easy?"

The door clicked shut. She swallowed, her mouth dry. It was time to tell him why she'd come. To say the words desperate to trip off her tongue.

All in, she reminded herself. *Have faith that it'll work out.*

"You're the most amazing man I've ever met," she said, the words she'd rehearsed on the plane coming out in a rush. "I love you. You're all I can think about. If you don't want biological children, I can accept that, as long as you're willing to explore other options. As far as the possibility of something happening to you…." She swallowed. "I've decided I'll take that risk. I'd rather have years of fond memories with you than be without you and spend my whole life wondering 'what if.'"

His mouth opened, then closed. He turned away, and Clarissa thought she might faint from the blood thumping in her head. Was he rejecting her? But then he turned back, his eyes shining and wet. He had the look of a person who was afraid to believe his own ears.

He cleared his throat. "When you say 'other options,' what do you mean precisely?"

"Adoption or fostering." She ticked the options off on her fingers and wished she'd had a glass of wine before airing the last possibility. "Or perhaps you'd like to go the route of artificial insemination from a donor. This is all hypothetical, of course." She was babbling now. "Assuming you still want me and assuming we last for the long haul and mutually make the decision that we both want children. You're not opposed to children in general, are you?"

"No, not at all." Mark wondered if he'd fallen asleep at his desk and this was all a lovely dream, but he replied anyway, on the off chance it was actually happening. "I love children, and I think you'd be a wonderful mother. But are you certain you won't regret it if you never experience pregnancy? If you never go through childbirth?"

She shook her head. "I'm sure those experiences are wonderful, but what I want is a family. Or at least the possibility of one. I don't mind how I get it."

Neither did he. The vision of a little girl, hand in hand with Clarissa, swam before his eyes. The little girl he'd always wanted and feared he wouldn't have. He didn't care how she came to him. Her very existence would be a miracle.

"What if I have a heart attack myself?"

"We'll cross that bridge if we come to it." She smiled. "I'm willing to take the chance if you are, and we can figure everything else out as we go along."

Mark considered that. She'd echoed what his mum had suggested almost word for word, and after hearing that Rose had no regrets despite how things had ended with his father, he was far more open to the idea than he'd been previously. Especially since the cardiologist he'd seen yesterday had said all the evidence pointed to him having a healthy heart, which he could maintain by eating well and cutting back on wine. He'd booked in for an echocardiogram to double-check, but there was no reason not to be optimistic. There was no reason to push Clarissa away, if she was willing to take a chance on him.

And she was. She really, truly was. He pinched himself. It stung, and he grinned.

He was soaring, his decision already made. Everything in the world ceased to exist beyond him and the beautiful woman who was offering him everything he'd ever wanted on a silver platter. He'd hardly dared to hope he'd ever hear the sultry sound of her voice again, but here she was, bravely offering him her heart in a glass room surrounded by spectators. All she asked in return was that he be open to the possibility of raising a child with her who didn't share his defective DNA.

She was so courageous. So generous. So lovely. He cupped her face in his hands and stroked her cheekbones with the pads of his thumbs. She shivered, her deep blue eyes holding his, and he couldn't hold back the words bubbling up inside him.

"I love you," he said, vowing to himself to never give her any reason to doubt her choice. His life mission would be to make her the happiest woman alive. Nothing less would do. She deserved every bit of goodness he could squeeze from the world on her behalf. "I know it's soon, but I think I've loved you since I kissed you at the wedding. You're unlike anyone I've known, and I want you in my life every day and every night."

Her eyes shone, and her lips curved up at the corners. "Will you hurry up and kiss me already?"

"Gladly." He kissed her again, his hands sliding down her

sides, grabbing her ass, desperate to get closer. He plundered her mouth, reveling in her whimper of submission. But then he remembered where they were and why he couldn't strip her naked on the desk like he ached to. He softened his mouth and kissed her again. Once, twice, sweet and undemanding. "I can't believe you're here."

"Believe it." Her tone was dead serious. "I'm not the impulsive type, so I don't plan on disappearing anytime soon."

He'd thought he couldn't possibly soar any higher, but he'd been wrong. His heart swelled with happiness. "Did I tell you that I love you?"

She laughed, but it subsided when he covered her mouth with his own.

A throat cleared. "Ahem." They turned to face Sterling, who stood in the door with a stony expression but lips that twitched at the corners. "Take the rest of the day off, Mark. You've worked enough overtime, and Clarissa deserves to be taken out on a date." Then he winked.

By the time Mark's shock had worn off, Sterling had gone. "I think that's his subtle way of asking us to leave. Would you like lunch?"

She leaned closer. "Later. For now, take me to your place." Her breath tickled his ear. "I want to be closer to you than I can get in public without being arrested."

A jolt ran through him. He grabbed her by the elbow and tugged her to the elevator. Once inside, he pressed her against a wall and imprisoned her between his forearms. "Have I told you how much I love you?"

She laughed, light and airy. "I'll never get tired of hearing it."

"I love you," he said, punctuating the statement with a kiss. "I." Kiss. "Love." Kiss. "You." Kiss.

"I'm so happy," she murmured into his mouth, looping her

fingers at the back of his neck. "Promise me this is real, Mark. Promise me this is forever."

"I'll love you forever, sweetie," he vowed, eyes twinkling down at her. "I've never been so certain of anything in my life." He caressed the length of her throat, coming in for another slow, sweet kiss. "But this long-distance thing is going to be hard. I've missed your kisses. Your touch. I can't be without you all the time. We need to think about how this is going to work."

"I'll move to Auckland." She sounded so certain, as if the decision wasn't a difficult one, and he fell in love with her all over again.

"I can't ask you to do that. Your whole life is in Dunedin."

She shook her head. "My life is with you. At least, I hope it will be. I'm not suggesting I move now, but maybe in a few months, once we've seen where this goes."

He grinned. "What did I do to deserve you?"

"You taught me to trust again. To believe in happy ever after."

His heart sang. He dipped his head and kissed her. Each time, she tasted a little sweeter. He could never get enough. "Everything you worked for is in Dunedin."

"It's just a place." She put her hands on his chest and pushed him back as the elevator dinged to signal they'd arrived at the bottom. They exited hand in hand, and he guided her to a corner of the lobby. "I can expand my business," she continued. "Keep the Dunedin boutique but promote Leo to manager. He'd need some training, but it would be a great opportunity for him, and he's been doing more and more on his own lately."

She'd given this some thought, he could tell. "And you? Would you start over?"

"Starting over wouldn't be as hard as starting from scratch." She smiled, the expression full of mischief. "Besides,

I'd have unrestricted access to one of the foremost legal authorities on small businesses in the country."

"Ah, I get it." He nodded knowingly. "You're using me to further your career. Now everything makes sense."

She swatted him. "Don't be absurd. It's a fringe benefit, but I want you for more than that."

"I know, sw—"

"Shh," she said. "Don't interrupt."

He mimed zipping his lips.

"If you'd asked me six months ago, I would have said I'd never trust a man again, but then you came along and made me question everything I've been telling myself for years. For some crazy reason, I believe we're meant to be together. I don't know exactly how it will play out, but I trust that we'll make it happen. I have faith in us."

He believed her. Because, God help him, he'd never been more certain of anything either. She'd talked about never expecting a happy ever after, but neither had he. He'd never imagined any woman would want him enough to compromise or that he'd accept her decision if she did. He'd always been the guy women loved to date but didn't want to keep. And, yeah, perhaps some of that was his fault, for playing the part of the charming companion, refusing to let anyone too close because some part of him feared they wouldn't want to take a risk on him. But here he was, madly in love with someone who'd been just as cautious about love as he had.

They could be each other's happy ending.

"I will never, ever let you down," he promised. "I'm yours unreservedly. Now, what do you say we buy a box of artisan chocolate, a bottle of red wine"—which he'd learned was healthier for the heart than white—"and head over to my place? Unless… you don't have to fly back, do you?" If he had to part with her again so soon, he might just follow her to Dunedin.

"No, I didn't buy a return ticket. I'd like to stay for the rest of the week, if you don't mind."

"If I don't...." He stared at her, incredulous. "As far as I'm concerned, you can stay forever." He entwined his hand with hers and placed it over his heart. "This is all yours, okay? My heart is your heart. My home is your home. Now, come on. Let's go home."

EPILOGUE

CHRISTMAS, A FEW WEEKS LATER

*C*larissa swerved into a car park outside the home Aria shared with Eli, Lauren, and Teri, getting out just in time to see Gareth slide a ring onto Avery's finger and kiss her full on the mouth.

"Eeek!" she squealed, ducking her head to beam at Mark, who occupied the passenger seat. "Did you see what I saw?"

"Yes, sweetie," he replied, smiling lovingly. "Looks like we'll have another wedding to attend soon."

She straightened and called out, "Congratulations!" Then she hurried up the path and hauled Avery into a hug. "I'm so happy for you," she said, kissing her friend's cheek. Nobody deserved a happily ever after more than Avery. She'd been Clarissa's life raft over the years. She shot Gareth a warning glance. "Take care of my girl."

If he hurt her again, so help her, she'd slap him into the next dimension. Gareth nodded to her. Then he and Avery exchanged murmurs and kisses. Clarissa backed away, not wanting to intrude. An arm came around her from behind and drew her into a strong male chest. She relaxed into Mark's embrace and tilted her chin up to kiss him.

"Oh. My. God."

Clarissa tried to pull away to say hi to Aria, who'd appeared in the doorway, but Mark followed her with his mouth, coaxing her into another kiss.

Aria shrieked. "You guys are so cute!"

Clarissa groaned, her cheeks heating. No doubt she was scarlet from her neck to her hairline. Aria laughed and backed away. "I'll give you some space. Come inside when you're ready. There's plenty of food."

Mark took Clarissa's hand and led her to the end of the porch, away from Gareth and Avery.

"We should go join them," she said.

"In a moment." Mark looked uncharacteristically nervous. "I love you, you know?"

"I know." She gripped his chin and drew him down to her level. "I *know*," she repeated, pressing her lips to his.

"You're perfect," he said, tucking a curl behind her ear with an expression of such utter tenderness that her heart zoomed into hyperdrive. "You're my dream come true." He pressed something into her hand. A gift-wrapped package with a red bow, no larger than a lipstick box. "Here's my Christmas present. I want you to open it before we follow them in."

"All right." She untied the bow and peeled the tape off, taking care not to rip the paper. It fell away, and she found herself looking at a small silver key. "What is it?"

"The key to my heart."

She rolled her eyes. "No, really?"

"It's a key to my apartment," he said, watching for her reaction. "Move in with me, Riss. I know you liked that storefront we looked at the other day. Buy it and come be with me. I'll make it worth your while. How do naked Sundays sound? I'll cook you brunch and give you orgasms."

She flushed, and her insides turned to goo at the prospect of spending idyllic weekends lolling about in bed with him. She'd never dared to hope for anything so wonderful before he came along. Shifting cities wouldn't be easy, but she'd already discussed a partnership arrangement with Leo, and he was on board.

"Yes," she said, loving the smile that quirked his lips and told her he was as blissfully happy as she. "On one condition."

"I can do naked Tuesdays too, but only at home. If I started at work, Sterling would have my head."

She giggled. "I'm not sharing you with everyone at the office. My condition is, I want everything with you. I want to meet your other friends, spend my free time with you, maybe marry you one day and have that family we talked about."

He seemed to think about it. Her stomach dropped to her shoes. But then he grinned. "The only problem I have with that is the 'maybe' you put in front of marrying and having kids. I definitely want that with you, however we're able to get it."

Relief rushed through her, followed closely by a wave of affection. God, she loved this playful man. She told him as much.

"And you make my heart beat, love," he replied, nuzzling her ear. "You give me hope again. Come on, there's a party happening. Let's go find the cake." Twining her hand with his, he led her toward the sound of Christmas carols and laughter.

More than that, he led her toward their future. Together.

THE END

THEN THERE WAS YOU – EXCERPT

Proposed conditions of sale:

1. Purchase of land is to the value of two million dollars.

2. The existing lodge cannot be demolished within ten years of sale.

3. No more than twenty people may be accommodated on the property at any time.

4. The waterfall trail must be maintained for visitor access.

5. The cabin may continue to be tenanted by Tione Kingi and his dogs (Trevor, Zee, Bella, and Pixie) for as long as they wish to stay.

6. The purchaser accepts responsibility for the care and feeding of the cat who lives beneath the lodge for the remainder of its natural life.

7. Any attractive male guest may be required, upon invitation from the Bridge Club, to attend one of their weekly gatherings (shirt optional, but not recommended).

Sterling Knight scanned the ridiculous list of demands he'd received from Katarina Hopa, who owned the beachfront lodge his company wanted to acquire, and returned to item seven, raising a brow. He wondered who was responsible for determining whether a man met the criteria for being "attractive"—and also what drug Mrs. Hopa had been under the influence of when she'd penned this letter.

If he agreed to her conditions of sale, the property would be rendered useless. His boss wouldn't be able to develop it, and Sterling wouldn't be able to prove how worthy he was of the great responsibility bestowed upon him. He shifted in the seat of his car, took a pen from his shirt pocket, and tapped each item in turn. Were there any he could accept?

For starters, the market value of the land was only a quarter of what she'd requested. He'd stopped by the place on the way to the cafe where he was scheduled to meet her in five minutes, and the building wasn't in great condition. He couldn't leave it standing because it would be an eyesore to the wealthy clientele he intended to attract.

Number three, he could work with. Keeping a resort on the smaller side would add to its perceived exclusivity. Number four was also a possibility, although he hadn't seen the trail, so he didn't know what he'd be working with. Still, having private access to a waterfall would be another draw-card for guests. Demand number five was impossible, as was six. If they demolished the lodge, the cat would be homeless. He'd do the right thing, though, and have someone catch the creature and take it to a shelter. Maybe this Tione guy. He sounded like he'd know how to deal with a cat.

He eyed the seventh request, rapping the pen against the paper as he thought. Who were the Bridge Club, and why did they want access to handsome guests? The whole thing sounded shady to him. Quite possibly illegal. He put a strike through the words, then tucked the paper into his pocket, adjusted his suit, grabbed his briefcase, and climbed out of the company car, locking it behind him. Haven Bay seemed like a safe little town, but hundreds of tourists passed through each day, and he wasn't taking any chances.

He made his way into the town square, a cobblestoned

area speckled with old-fashioned streetlamps like something out of a quaint English village, and searched for Cafe Oasis, where Mrs. Hopa had asked to meet him. Spotting it on the opposite side of the square, he made his way past a bronze statue of a man with a surfboard and pushed his way in.

A doorbell chimed as he entered, and he only just managed not to flinch in surprise—it had been a long time since he'd heard anything of the kind since they weren't popular in busier Auckland stores. The café's interior was charming, he supposed, if you liked wooden floors and patterned wallpaper. He didn't see anyone who looked like he believed Mrs. Hopa would, and he was debating whether to order coffee when the table nearest him fell silent, six gray-haired ladies turning to stare with expressions ranging from curious to hostile.

One of them, a cherub-cheeked biddy in a pink tracksuit, slowly rose and shuffled over. She was less than five feet tall, but her piercing blue eyes skewered him, threatening all kinds of harm that should have made him laugh, but oddly sent a cold shiver down his spine.

"Good afternoon, Mr. Knight," she said in a tone that wouldn't have been out of place in a face-off from an old western movie. He half expected a tumbleweed to blow by.

"Mrs. Hopa?" he asked, surprised. With a name like Katarina Hopa, he'd expected someone a little younger and a little more Maori.

"No." The old woman's voice was steely, her apricot lips pursed together. "I'm Betty. I represent Mrs. Hopa."

"Oh." He glanced back over at the table she'd come from. "Is she here?"

"I'm afraid not." Betty crossed her arms, scowling up at him. "You'll be dealing with us today."

"No offense, ma'am, but I prefer to deal directly with my business contacts rather than an intermediary."

"Too bad." Her eyes narrowed. "If I've learned anything in

all my years, it's that we don't always get what we want. As far as you're concerned, today we *are* Mrs. Hopa. We have her best interests at heart, and to be blunt, she doesn't want or need to speak to you." Then she took him by the arm, led him to her cronies, and claimed the last proper chair, leaving him with a stool that had no back and was half a foot shorter than the others.

He suppressed a laugh. The wily woman was trying Psychology 101 tricks to put him at a disadvantage. "Nice to meet you all," he said, nodding to each person in turn. "I'm Sterling Knight, and I represent Lockwood Holdings."

"We know who you are," one of them snapped, leaning across to glare at him. The set of her jaw and folds of her face reminded him of a bull terrier. "Tell us what you want."

He sat back. "Aren't you going to introduce yourselves to me?"

"No," the old bulldog growled. "That's not pertinent to this conversation. Tell us why you want Kat's property."

Judging from the determined expressions around the table, he wouldn't be making any ground until he gave them something to work with. That was fine by him. All negotiations required a bit of give on both sides.

"My employer would like to purchase Mrs. Hopa's property for a competitive price to redevelop the site into a five-star resort."

There was a collective gasp, then something thumped him in the chest, knocking the air from his lungs. He folded, clutching his ribs and hauling in oxygen to replenish what he'd lost. Once he'd recovered enough to straighten, he searched for whatever it was that had struck him.

A purple purse sat on his lap. Someone had thrown it at him with enough force to wind him. He rubbed his chest, wincing. Damn, these women were stronger than they appeared.

"Who did that?" No one so much as fidgeted in their seat.

244

He held the purse up. "I'll ask again. Who does this belong to?"

Betty snatched the purse from him and passed it to the woman on her other side, staring at him as though he were a rattlesnake. "Dear god," she said, appalled. "First you say you want to tear down Sanctuary, then you hold poor Nell's purse hostage. What sort of monster are you?"

"I wouldn't have damaged anything," he said in his own defense, not that any of them believed him. No matter. He knew the truth. He may be ruthless when the situation called for it, but he'd never harmed a senior citizen, and he wasn't about to start now.

"You actually want to demolish our beautiful Sanctuary?" another lady asked, her lower lip quivering.

Sanctuary, he'd learned, was what Mrs. Hopa had named her partially renovated lodge. It was obscure and strange, in his opinion. Not at all a good marketing tactic. He kept his mouth shut, knowing it wouldn't be wise to voice his thoughts.

"Not necessarily. The building could be relocated to another site, but we'd construct the new resort from scratch."

"Move Sanctuary?" the bulldog demanded. "Just how do you expect anyone to do that?"

"It's quite straightforward these days." He ran a finger along the edge of his tie and adjusted his collar. The conversation was veering dangerously off topic. "I'd really prefer to speak to Katarina about this directly."

Betty puffed up like an angry poodle. "There's no need for you to bother her with your crazy plans. Darling Kat has enough on her plate, and luckily she has us to keep the likes of you away from her."

He tried a different tack. "Let's be reasonable. I can see that Sanctuary means a lot to you, but it must be a drain on Katarina's resources. With the money she'd get from selling the property, she'd be able to start over elsewhere, and my company can help Haven Bay the way I'd like to."

"*Help* us?" a plump lady with a silver buzz cut demanded. "How on earth would you be doing that? We're overrun with tourists as it is. At least the ones we have are friendly. If you bring snobs into town, you'll ruin what makes the bay special."

Would he?

He dismissed the thought. Of course not. Things would change, but change meant progress, and progress was a good thing, even if it took people a while to realize it. Just look at what had happened with Eli's development in Itirangi. Everybody had hated the idea at first, but now it was a stunning success.

"I think you're being shortsight—ouch!" A heavy coin purse bounced off his shoulder onto the floor.

Betty scrambled to return it to the bulldog across the table before Sterling could get his hands on it. "Nice shot, Mavis," she said, lobbing it back.

Sterling stood, and kicked his stool away. He battled the urge to yell at them, or throw something. They were frail and more than twice his age—it wouldn't be fair to retaliate. That didn't stop his body from heating with frustration. He picked up his suitcase and gripped the handle tightly enough to cut into his palm. He couldn't believe he'd driven all the way from Auckland only to be treated like scum by these abominable ladies.

"You're all being incredibly rude," he huffed, shoving his free hand in his pocket so he didn't strangle someone with it. As the chief operating officer of a multi-million-dollar corporation, he didn't have the luxury of wasting hours on fools' errands. His heart sank at the thought of the mountain of work waiting back in his office, and his throat constricted. He closed his eyes until he'd regained his composure. "You should know better than to behave so poorly at your age." Then he swung on his heel and made for the door.

Something hit him in the back. He stopped, and turned around ever so slowly, scanning the floor until his gaze fell on a pink purse.

"It's rude to mention a woman's age!" one of the she-devils yelled.

He wanted to stomp the purse into the ground. To scoop up the remains and set fire to them. It would serve them right. But he prided himself on taking the high road, so he gritted his teeth, nudged the purse with his foot, and stomped out.

The old ladies had won this round, but he'd be back, and next time he wouldn't be leaving without Katarina Hopa's signature on a dotted line.

ALSO BY ALEXA RIVERS

Little Sky Romance

Accidentally Yours

From Now Until Forever

It Was Always You

Dreaming of You

Little Sky Romance Novellas

Midnight Kisses

Second Chance Christmas

Haven Bay

Then There Was You

Two of a Kind

Safe in his Arms

If Only You Knew

Pretend to Be Yours

ACKNOWLEDGMENTS

This book only came to fruition with the aid of a number of wonderful people. My early beta readers, who helped me complete a one-eighty to improve the storyline and characterization. My editors and proofreaders, Kate S and Hot Tree Editing. The crew at Deranged Doctor Design, who made me a beautiful cover. Finally, a massive thank you to my husband, for helping me nail down Mark's personality, and to my family and friends for their ongoing support. I love you all!

ABOUT THE AUTHOR

Alexa Rivers is the author of sexy, heartwarming contemporary romances set in gorgeous New Zealand. She lives in a small town, complete with nosy neighbors, and shares a house with a neurotic dog and a husband who thinks he's hilarious. When she's not writing, Alexa enjoys travelling, baking cakes, eating said cakes, cuddling fluffy animals, drinking copious amounts of tea, and absorbing herself in fictional worlds.

Made in the USA
Coppell, TX
12 January 2022